*No woman can resist unveiling the secrets
and dark passions that lie in wait . . .*

BENEATH THE RAVEN'S MOON

Acclaim for the award-nominated novel from
EMILY LaFORGE

"An intriguing modern-day gothic romance with an eerie *Twilight Zone* twist that will shock. . . . Emily LaForge knits a delightful tale that gothic fans will savor."
— thebestreviews.com

"Thrilling and chilling. . . . *Beneath the Raven's Moon* excites and thrills the reader. Fraught with twists. . . . Intricate and interesting, this romantic suspense is perfect reading material for a dark, windswept night."
— *Old Book Barn Gazette*

"The suspense . . . certainly keeps the reader going."
— theromancereader.com

"LaForge is especially adept at creating tense plots and authentic characters."
— *Publishers Weekly*

Also by Emily LaForge

Beneath the Raven's Moon

Published by Pocket Books

SHADOW
HAVEN

Emily LaForge

POCKET BOOKS

NEW YORK   LONDON   TORONTO   SYDNEY

This book is a work of fiction. Names, characters, places and incidents are products of the author's imagination or are used fictitiously. Any resemblance to actual events or locales or persons, living or dead, is entirely coincidental.

An *Original* Publication of POCKET BOOKS

 POCKET BOOKS, a division of Simon & Schuster, Inc.
1230 Avenue of the Americas, New York, NY 10020

ISBN: 0-7434-5614-9

First Pocket Books printing April 2005

10 9 8 7 6 5 4 3 2 1

POCKET and colophon are registered trademarks of Simon & Schuster, Inc.

Cover art by Franco Accornero

Manufactured in the United States of America

For information regarding special discounts for bulk purchases, please contact Simon & Schuster Special Sales at 1-800-456-6798 or business@simonandschuster.com.

ACKNOWLEDGMENTS

Some of the ideas included in the reading of the tarot in this story were gleaned from *Tarot Made Easy*, Nancy Garen, Fireside, Simon & Schuster, 1989.

For Liz Pace,
a good friend, with heartfelt thanks
for your wonderful support

The night comes on:
You wait and listen . . .
To all these ghosts of change.
They are you.

—Conrad Aiken, from "The Cloisters"

CHAPTER

One

LONG AGO, A STRANGER WARNED ME NOT TO MARRY Charles Colquitt. The spirits as well cautioned me against the marriage. They, like the stranger, feared that Charles would destroy me.

I wish I'd listened to them then; if I had, I wouldn't be running now.

There are many ways one can destroy the life of another; it doesn't always take a pickax or a gun. My husband's weapons were his words. They could be sharper, more deadly, than any sword or knife. They could slash and tear and bite, humble and browbeat. They could attack with great thunder, or sneak up quietly and strike when least expected.

If I'd let them, my husband's words could have sliced away my soul. As it is, I am missing great chunks.

But I am a Deveaux woman, and I endured through the years by calling upon the deep inner spirit of my people to give me strength. It was what he hated the most and tried hardest to kill—that part of me that managed to remain independent of him.

It all started, I guess, when I refused to take his name when we married. It's a Deveaux tradition; the strong-willed, spirited women of my family never adopted their husbands' names, and the land was always handed down to the women.

It was difficult at times to remember I possessed that Deveaux spirit. When Charles was particularly abusive, I had to consciously remind myself of who I was and where I'd come from, or he would have crushed my soul altogether.

This is another of those times.

I am Gabriella Deveaux, I silently remind myself as I enter the manic stream of traffic on the highway leaving the New Orleans airport. *I am the daughter of Juliette Deveaux, granddaughter of Ariella, and many generations descended from the legendary Angelique Deveaux, who first came to Louisiana from the Caribbean as a bride.*

The humid May air is thick and cloying, and I find it difficult to breathe.

I am Gabriella Deveaux, I repeat silently, *favored by the spirits, beloved by the spirits, empowered by the spirits.*

Where are those spirits now, when I need them most?

When I was younger, I used my Deveaux power, my special gift, to speak to my ancestors and draw from them the wisdom and strength that later saw me through my troubled times.

But I am also Gabriella Deveaux, the first woman in my family ever to abandon the legacy that has nurtured and protected our people since Angelique's day, our plantation, Shadow Haven. I broke our tradition and left our land to live in a place far away, among strangers. It displeased the spirits greatly.

When I married Charles, I turned my back on many things, seeking adventure and experience in a wider world. I was young then, too young to realize the enormity of my mistake. I left my place of power, my heritage, my ancestors, and now, when I'm desperate to reclaim my legacy, I wonder if the spirits will allow it.

The midday sun glares through the windshield, teasing a headache that already throbs behind my eyes. I turn the air conditioner a notch higher, but the sultry heat sucks the cool, wet mist from its teeth before it has a chance to circulate farther into the car. Sweat trickles down my back.

I am returning to Shadow Haven now, running for the protective grace of its shadowy bayou land. But will it receive me? And can it protect me and mine from the forces that threaten to destroy us? I have been gone many years. Is my power, my gift, gone as well?

Were those warnings true—has Charles destroyed me?

I keep glancing into the rearview mirror, fearing that I've been followed, although I don't think it's possible. Charles is dead, and I told no one of my plans to flee New York. It's just my persistent paranoia, one consequence of my eight-year marriage to Charles Colquitt.

Buckled in beside me is the only good thing to

come from that disastrous union, my daughter
Michaela, who fidgets in her own six-year-old
discomfort. Her mouth is an unhappy line, and she
rubs sleepy eyes. She doesn't understand what is
happening. I've promised her ice cream as soon as we
clear the heavy traffic, but she nods off before we
even cross the Huey P. Long Bridge.

The highway dwindles in width and quality the
deeper I drive into the lowlands of south Louisiana.
Steam rises from the asphalt, and the road reminds me
of a wet, black snake as it curves through the countryside. Small farms and weathered houses pass in a blur.
Cotton fields and pastures bake in the sun. The landscape is achingly familiar; I recognize the neighboring
farms, the little country church that stands at the bend
in the road on the way home. Nothing seems to have
changed much, except perhaps me.

A Dairy Queen appears on the right when I reach
the small town of Tibonne, and I slow the car. I haven't
had the soft ice cream from a DQ in years. Memories
of my childhood begin to surface. I went to school in
this tiny dot of a town, had friends I left behind without
batting an eye. I wonder if any of them are still around?

Michaela is sleeping soundly, so I pass up the DQ
even though my throat is parched. I'm anxious to
reach our destination and put this difficult journey
behind us.

But when I approach Shadow Haven and look for
the twin stone pillars that mark the entrance to the

plantation, I nearly miss my turn because they are so densely overgrown with weeds and vines. I'm filled with a sudden foreboding. For years, we've paid my neighbor, Conrad Armand, to care for the property, but from the looks of things, he hasn't been doing a very good job of keeping it up.

I stop the car between the two crumbling pillars and kill the engine, my heart beating wildly. Rolling down the window, I deeply inhale the rich, moist air, and it calms me almost immediately. I have always loved the smell of Shadow Haven—a blend of earth and sky, seasoned with the indescribable scent of the nearby bayou.

Primordial. Dank. Mystical.

Home.

Hopefully, the shaggy appearance of the seldom-used entrance is just an oversight on Conrad's part, and I'll find the stately old plantation house in better shape.

Whatever condition it's in, I think, drawing my long, dark hair away from the sweat on my forehead, it's the only option for us at the moment. It's my hope that here I can gather the remnants of my shattered soul, restore my power, and find the strength to face the coming events. I am hopeful, too, that Shadow Haven will be too far away, the legal system of Louisiana too difficult to penetrate, that my pursuers will in the end give up their hateful and unjust quest.

"Are we there yet?" Michaela stirs and sits up, her large, deep brown eyes still heavy with sleep.

"*Oui, chérie.*"

Michaela wrinkles her nose and frowns at me. "What'd you say?"

The language of my childhood, that languid, Creole French, feels good as it trips easily off my tongue, but it's unfamiliar to my daughter.

I smile at her, but it's a sad, poignant smile. Charles forbade me to teach Creole to our daughter; he'd considered it a bastardized pastiche of a language. Early in our relationship he'd seemed to find it charming enough, but being imperfect French, it didn't fit in his world. We argued fiercely about it at first, but as I did about so many things during our marriage, eventually I gave in. I simply found it easier to accede to his wishes than try to fight his indomitable will.

"Yes, baby, we're here."

I turn my gaze to the tree-lined lane in front of us and see that nature has taken over here as well. Grass and weeds choke the once manicured avenue, and vines entwine the heavy live oak branches overhead, creating an ominous dark canopy above the road. It looks—and feels—as if no one has cared for the place in a while. But I force myself to look beyond the overgrowth to the inherent decadent beauty of the land.

"Well, what do you think, *chérie?* It's beautiful, *mais non?*"

Michaela stares down the lane. "Looks kinda creepy to me."

CHAPTER
Two

CREEPY? SHADOW HAVEN ISN'T CREEPY. EVEN WHEN
Grandnana regaled me with scary stories about the
loup-garou, that wicked werewolf of the swamps, or
the ghostly lights that moved mysteriously through
the bayous, I didn't find this land creepy.

But I have to remember, Michaela has been raised
in a Northern suburban environment. Her outings
have been mostly to manicured parks and
playgrounds. She's never seen the mystical, twisted
branches of live oak trees or played in the ghostly
shadows cast by the gray Spanish moss that dangles
from most every limb. Grudgingly, I admit that to this
child of the Long Island suburbs, this scene must look
very creepy indeed.

I run my fingers through my hair and let out a long,
slow breath. "Don't worry, *chérie*. It's a wonderful
place. I grew up here. You're going to love it."

Michaela looks up at me anxiously. "This *is* just a
vacation, right?"

I can't tell her of the darkness of our plight, but I

won't lie. "I never said that, Michaela," I remind her. "I said we were going to come here and see how we like it."

"I don't like it. I want to go home."

I hold my tongue. I understand that Michaela's recent aloofness and insolence are part of the grief and anger she's holding inside. She hasn't accepted her father's death, and her whole little life has been turned upside down. Still, it's hard to hear her talk like this.

Patience.

As I have so often in the past ten years, I call upon this, my grandnana's mantra. Patience was her remedy for most everything that seemed wrong. *Have patience, child. Things'll all work out.*

Patience had indeed allowed some things to work out in my difficult marriage, but I have serious doubts if anything—patience, time, or distance—can save us from Charles's final perversion.

"This *is* our home, Michaela," I tell her, squeezing her shoulder gently. "Give it a chance, *chérie*. You'll discover Shadow Haven is a magical place, if you'll just give it a try."

"Magical? Like Harry Potter?"

I grasp the thin thread of her momentary interest. "Use your imagination. Look around. You might see fairies and angels and all sorts of magical playmates around here."

She shakes her head. "There're no such things."

I know better. I know just how magical Shadow Haven is, but this is a subject that I must address slowly and carefully with Michaela. In time, I will share with her the secret of her heritage, the gift of the unusual powers held by the Deveaux women, the gift she will one day likely develop. But not now. For us right now, it is a dangerous secret.

Without further argument, I start the car again and head down the lane, thinking about the Deveaux powers. Once I used them to further my career as a sculptor, communicating with the deceased loved ones of my clients and learning their hearts' secrets, which I transformed into unusual memorial statuary. But it's been almost a year since I last worked on such a memorial. I quit after one particularly violent encounter with Charles concerning the matter, and I haven't carved since.

It's also been years since I communicated with my grandnana's spirit. I haven't tried to contact her since leaving Shadow Haven. I concentrated on creating a bright new future with Charles rather than holding on to things from my past. That future is in shambles now, and I fear I've neglected my soul so long that I've lost the ability to reach those on the other side. Can such a gift atrophy from disuse?

A flicker of reflected light in the distance catches my eye, and I smile, recognizing its source. It is sunlight glinting off white polished marble in the nearby family cemetery. It's as if in answer to my question, the spirit of my beloved grandnana is beckoning from the memorial I carved for her, and my heart skips a beat. Perhaps her spirit has heard the longing in my soul and will reach out to me.

"You say there are no such things as angels, but I know where there's at least one," I tell Michaela.

She doesn't answer.

"Want to see her?"

She only shrugs, and I fight my fear and frustration. How can I reach her? Every day she seems to grow more distant.

Whether she wants to see the angel or not, I do. I steer the car down an even smaller, more overgrown lane to the Deveaux family burial plot. Grandnana always called it "the enchanted garden."

The angel is smaller than I remember, but I recognize in an instant its incongruous, impish grin. I carved this, my first memorial sculpture, at the request of Grandnana's spirit a few months after she died. She was with me every day as I worked on the marble, guiding my hand. When the grin emerged, I knew it was exactly how she wanted to be remembered—feisty, peppery, unconventional.

People who saw this angel indeed remembered Grandnana that way and remarked that it was the perfect memorial for her. I began to receive requests from others to create funerary monuments for their loved ones. I never told any of them, of course, where I got the ideas for the images I carved, which they claimed were compelling representations of the personalities of the deceased. The Deveaux gift had always been kept secret to those outside the family, and I never wanted anyone to know that I was able to call upon the spirits of those who had passed over and learn the essence of their beings.

My ability to commune with the dead was the secret to the success of my career—until I made the mistake of sharing that secret with Charles. He was family, after all. But telling him had been a huge mistake. It was on that horrible night that my already tenuous relationship with him finally fell apart.

I blink my eyes furiously, forcing these gloomy thoughts away and bringing me back to the moment.

"You see, *chérie*," I whisper, taking my daughter's hand and leading her toward the small cemetery. "There's a beautiful angel."

Michaela looks up dubiously. "It's not a real angel."

I wonder if Grandnana can hear us. What advice might she give me to help Michaela accept her father's death? She is so brooding and withdrawn, she won't let anyone hug her, not even me.

"No, she's not a real angel," I answer her, "but I carved her long ago to help me remember my grandmother. Sometimes when I come here, I can almost hear Grandnana speak to me."

Careful. Patience.

"It's spooky," Michaela insists. "I don't want to go in there."

We stand at the gate to the wrought-iron fence that encloses the sacred ground. I've always found the enchanted garden a friendly place, a place of peace and tranquillity where I was enveloped in the love of my people who had passed before.

But today I feel nothing but emptiness. There is no touch of Grandnana's spirit here now, as I'd hoped. In fact, I sense no spirit presence at all. Perhaps they have departed for good, since I have stayed away so long. Or else they're just not speaking to me.

The cemetery is as neglected as the road we came down, with headstones listing as the soil gives way slowly beneath them. A cloud shadows the sun, and an involuntary shiver runs through me.

"I don't want to go in there either," I agree with Michaela, "at least not now. Let's go on to the house. I'm tired, and there's still lots to do today."

It's late in the afternoon, and I'm exhausted, both physically and emotionally. I brought linens and a few items for the kitchen and bath in my suitcase for our first night at Shadow Haven. Tomorrow, we'll go to town and stock up on what we need. At the moment I want nothing more than to lie in the bed of my childhood and try to reclaim my lost spirit.

From the seedy condition of the lane and the cemetery, I expect the house to be likewise in poor shape, but I am not prepared for the disaster that meets my eyes when we emerge from the tree-lined lane onto the circular drive in front of the once-elegant old home.

I bring the car to a slow stop and cover my mouth with the back of my hand to stifle a cry of pain. *"Mon Dieu!"*

Triste is the impression that comes to me. Sad. The old house is incredibly sad. The windows are dark; most of the panes are broken. The porch sags unhappily, and thick vines choke the columns. The siding is weathered to a dull gray, with only patches of its former white showing here and there, like bandages.

I cannot speak. I can only stare at the house in horror.

Eventually, I manage to get out of the car, but my legs are shaky. "Stay here," I tell Michaela, sensing danger. I step onto the verandah and approach the front door with caution. A spider's web enshrouds the portal, its intricate architecture laden with moisture and the remains of some poor creatures ensnared in its layered labyrinth. The fabric of it hangs heavy, like a veil, as if attempting to conceal the corruption that lies beyond.

The late afternoon air is hot and so still that I have to remember to breathe. Blood pounds in my ears. I can't believe what I am seeing. Near tears, I brush the web aside and step through the half-open door, now bereft of the ornate stained glass that once graced its hand-carved face. My stomach lurches as I enter the massive foyer.

The place is in ruins.

Above my head, an angry gash in the ceiling is all that is left of the huge, ornate crystal chandelier that had hung there for generations. The cypress spindles that once supported the banister appear to have fallen victim to a chainsaw. Obscenities have been spray-painted on the silk wall coverings along the central hallway. Most of the furniture is missing, and what remains has been destroyed. There is a sense of evil in the very air, as if the *loup-garou* has visited here and left his ugly mark.

It takes every ounce of my will not to collapse in tears on the debris-strewn floor. What has happened here? Where is Conrad?

"Are we going to live *here*, Mother?" Michaela asks incredulously from somewhere behind me. I turn to my daughter, who is looking at the place in open dismay.

It is I who need the comfort of a hug at the moment, but I know Michaela won't allow me to touch her. Instead, I tousle her hair.

"Don't worry, *chérie*. I told you this was a magical place. You just watch. We'll make this old house beautiful again."

But even as I say the words, I wonder if it's possible. It will take a lot more than magic to fix what's wrong at Shadow Haven, and in our lives. . . .

CHAPTER
Three

MAGIC, I AM LEARNING, IS MUCH EASIER WHEN YOU have money. Although Charles was wealthy, he left none of his millions to me. Michaela is his sole heir. I could, as her guardian, use some of the money on her behalf, but considering my history with the Colquitts, Charles's wealthy parents, I want no part of that money. It will soon likely be tied up in court anyway.

Fortunately, I have some savings from my own earnings, as well as funds from a life insurance policy Charles took out early in our marriage and, I'm certain, forgot to cancel once he'd decided to shed himself of me. I also liquidated all of our household items, which included some expensive paintings, antique furniture, and Charles's collection of guns and other assorted items he valued. Antioch House, the estate liquidators and auction company he worked for, wrote me a check on the spot, saying they'd have no trouble reselling them. It was kind of them to help me out like that.

So, if I'm frugal, I can work some magic with the resources available to me.

I've hired a competent local handyman who is willing to work extra hours to make the old house habitable. In less than a week, Willie Johnson and his two helpers have cleared away most of the debris, replaced the front door, installed new windows, and made sure the electricity is safe and the plumbing operational. Michaela and I have been staying in a local motel in the meantime. We're both anxious to move in to Shadow Haven.

The upstairs flooring of the big house is damaged beyond cosmetic repair; leaks in the roof have rendered it unsafe, so Michaela and I will be living in first-floor rooms once occupied by servants at the back of the house. The work is, of course, far from completed, but this is sufficient for us temporarily.

We're on the front porch swing, awaiting delivery of new furniture. I let Michaela pick out her bedroom set and linens, hoping that once she's settled into a room of her own, she'll lose her resolve to return to New York. I suspect it's not New York she longs for so much as for a return to the life she's always known.

That life is gone forever, *chérie*, I think sadly, gazing at her beautiful little face. I am at a loss as to how to help her access the grief she so badly needs to express. If only she would break down and cry.

In the past week, I have tried repeatedly to contact Grandnana's spirit in the enchanted garden. I desperately need her advice, not to mention the comfort of knowing she is still here for me. But so far, she has remained beyond my reach. Each time I try, my fear and frustration mount. Will I ever be able to communicate with her again?

I hear the sound of a vehicle approaching and raise my head, gazing down the lane.

"Here comes the truck," Michaela says as she jumps from the swing and runs to the edge of the verandah. It's good to see the eager smile on her face. This is the first time since Charles died that she's shown much interest in anything.

I stand up and follow her to the porch railing, but frown when I see that the approaching vehicle isn't a furniture delivery van, but a sleek, black BMW convertible. The top is up, so I can't tell who is inside. Michaela darts toward the car before I can stop her. I have a bad feeling about this. I scarcely dare to breathe as I watch from the verandah.

A tall man slowly unfolds himself from the low-slung vehicle. He is dressed in a dark suit, white shirt, red tie. He carries a briefcase.

Everything about him screams "lawyer."

I bite my lip. So much for finding refuge at Shadow Haven.

"Michaela! Come back here," I call, but she stands her ground and eyes the stranger with open curiosity. I see him lower his large body until he is at eye level with my daughter. I don't want her talking to him. "Michaela! Come here right now."

She obeys at last, and the man stands again and

heads my way. He looks familiar, but I don't recognize him immediately.

"Good morning, Gabriella," he says. His voice is low and mellow, one that no doubt can easily sway a jury. "Remember me?"

And suddenly I know who he is. Jarrod Landry. He's the man who'd been a virtual stranger to me, supposedly a friend of Charles, who'd come here the night before our wedding and urged me not to marry Charles.

It was a bizarre incident, and I don't understand to this day why he did it. I didn't know him well; Jarrod had commissioned me by phone to create a monument for his recently deceased aunt, but I never met him until the unveiling of the piece. A friend of his from college, Charles Colquitt, had been at the ceremony, and Jarrod introduced us.

The rest, as they say, is history. We saw little of Jarrod during our whirlwind courtship, so I was shocked when he unexpectedly showed up at my doorstep and accused his friend of having some rather nasty character traits in an effort to dissuade me from the marriage.

After that terrible night, which ended in my asking him to leave, he disappeared from our lives. I was just as glad. It would have been awkward to be in his presence after that.

Especially after his warnings had proven true.

"What are you doing here?" I ask icily. His visit bodes no good.

He places his briefcase on the dry earth at the foot of the front steps. I do not invite him onto the verandah despite the heat of the day.

"I heard what happened to Charles. I came to see if you were . . . all right."

"How did you know I was here?"

He glances away momentarily, but long enough that I can see he's uncomfortable. "I . . . got a phone call from Elizabeth Colquitt. She told me you had left New York—"

"And she sent you here to find me." It was foolish of me to think I could hide from them at Shadow Haven. They knew my background; it wouldn't take much for them to figure out where I had likely gone. "I didn't know you and Elizabeth were so tight."

He doesn't reply right away, but rather gazes at me steadily, as if trying to decide what approach to take. He is a powerfully attractive man, ruggedly—and hugely—handsome. Tall, very tall, and broad-shouldered, built like an athlete. His hair is dark, black almost, although silver has threaded itself at his temples since last I saw him.

His eyes are dark as well, although his complexion is fair. His beard is a faint shadow beneath his skin. He looks as if he could have been descended from some long-ago French trapper. To my dismay, my heart skips a little beat as I look at him.

"I'm not here on Elizabeth's behalf, although she told me about the codicil to Charles's will," he says at last.

Heat flares in my cheeks. "That sorry son of a bitch," I growl, not caring about my low language. In my book, that's exactly what he'd turned out to be. "He had no right or reason to do what he did."

"As you know, Charles never cared about rights or reasons," Jarrod points out, although he stops short of saying I told you so. "He only cared about himself. But I'm curious why he did this. What could possibly have been in it for him?"

"He did it to hurt me. He hated me in the end." It hurts me now to admit this to him. "Did Elizabeth tell you he claimed I was 'mentally unstable'?"

He nods. "She said that shortly before he died, Charles told her that you were delusional, that you thought you could talk to the dead."

The blood drains from my face. "She told you that?"

"It's ridiculous, of course, and it'll sound silly in a court of law."

My voice falters. "Ridiculous. Of course." It takes me a moment to compose myself. "So, what are the Colquitts going to do about the codicil? Are they going to try to enforce it?"

I'm not stupid. I know the codicil is not about my sanity; it's about their money. As long as I have custody of Michaela and remain her guardian, I have access to the Colquitt millions until Michaela comes of age, a fact that must distress them thoroughly.

"They intend to take the issue to court," Jarrod tells me. "And . . . they've asked me to represent them, Gabriella." Jarrod sounds almost apologetic.

The anger that I live with, anger that has seethed for years, flares. He *ought* to be apologetic. He should be downright ashamed to be representing those awful people. But at least I know where we stand.

"I see." I put my hand protectively on one of Michaela's shoulders. "I hope they're paying you well," I add bitterly. How can this man, who warned me so adamantly against Charles all those years ago, who in retrospect seemed to be on my side, now in good conscience step across the line and represent the Colquitts?

"They're not paying me at all," he says.

"Yeah, right."

"I didn't say I was representing them. I said they want me to."

For a moment, hope flickers inside me, but still I don't trust him. "So, why are you here? Are you or aren't you their attorney?"

"I came here to see if Charles's claims were true."

I stare at him, not believing he could think such a thing even for a moment. "Thanks for the vote of confidence."

"Gabriella, I doubted they were true, but . . . I've known Charles for a long time, and it occurred to me that he could have . . . well, literally driven you crazy."

I toss my head defiantly. "Well, he didn't. He drove me to distraction sometimes. Hurt my feelings. Made me hugely angry. Disappointed me almost always. But I'm as sane as you or the next person. And I resent like the dickens that you could believe otherwise. If anyone was insane, it was Charles. Before he died, he was so obsessive and controlling, he was really quite sick."

I'm sorry my daughter is hearing this conversation. Her father was good to her, and she'd loved him. Hopefully, she's too young to understand.

"I'm an attorney, Gabriella. It's my job to get to the truth of matters." The edge of Jarrod's mouth quirks into a small grin, rendering him even more handsome. "I can see that you are quite sane. Looks to me like the Colquitts will have a good fight on their hands."

I relax slightly. "They can't have Michaela, Jarrod. She's my daughter, my baby. I'll do whatever it takes to stand up to them." Then my shoulders slump. "The problem is, I'm not sure what that is."

"It'll take money, for one thing, if it goes to court," Jarrod says. "A lot of money."

I wonder suddenly if he's come to offer his services to me for a price. "How much?"

"Depends on how long the case drags out. Some lawyers like that sort of thing. Makes for a good living. I like money as well as the next guy, but I hate domestic cases. The emotional pain can be incredible, and I've seen the process destroy lives. Both parties usually suffer; sometimes no one really wins in the end. That's why I rarely take on something like this."

I hate to admit it, but I find I like Jarrod Landry. He seems like a straight-shooter, something I'm not used to. But can I trust him? I have some rather large trust issues these days.

"So, are you or aren't you going to represent the Colquitts?" I ask again, since he never directly answered my question.

"I've known the Colquitts a long time. I told Elizabeth I would look into it."

His answer extinguishes my earlier flicker of hope. "I see."

Jarrod runs his fingers through his thick, dark hair. "Look, Gabriella, don't get me wrong. I don't want to do this. Maybe I can find a way to talk them out of it. But if I don't work with them, they'll find some other lawyer in New Orleans to represent them." His expression darkens. "There are plenty of attorneys who would jump at the money they're offering."

My stomach tightens. "So it's an enemy I know, or one I don't know."

Jarrod looks grim. "I admit I came here to check you out, based on Mrs. Colquitt's accusations, but I also came to see if somehow I could help you, Gabriella. The Colquitts are formidable enemies."

"Tell me about it. But you can't serve two masters, Jarrod. It's either me or the Colquitts."

"Let's hope it doesn't get that far. I'd like to try to head them off before anybody has to hire a lawyer."

"Head them off? Elizabeth Colquitt is probably the most determined person I ever met, except perhaps Charles. She isn't one to be 'headed off.'"

Jarrod crosses his arms over his chest. A furrow nestles between his brows. "Sometimes there are ways. . . ."

CHAPTER

Four

THE ARRIVAL OF THE DELIVERY TRUCK INTERRUPTS our distressing conversation. I would like to think he could do what he says, but I hold little hope that Jarrod can resolve things so easily. I can't imagine anyone talking the Colquitts out of the custody suit, not with so much money at stake. Either he knows them better than I do, or he's a naive fool.

Neither am I at all sure I can trust anything Jarrod Landry says. He appears to have integrity, but he's an attorney, a breed known for accomplished role-playing. He could be toying with my sympathies to get information that could be used against me.

Mon Dieu, I hate it that I'm so distrustful! But I dare not be otherwise. If I'd been more cautious when Charles was courting me, when he insisted that we marry only a few weeks after we'd met, I might have saved myself a lot of grief. I learned from that bitter mistake, and I'm not going to make another. A good dose of distrust now might save me from long-term disaster.

I also hate it that I seem to be so drawn to Jarrod Landry. The feelings he stirs inside me remind me of how very lonely I've been in my loveless marriage. I recognize that I'm probably very emotionally needy, and that makes me once again extremely vulnerable. I dare not trust my feelings any more than I dare trust Jarrod.

"Here, over here," Michaela says, her excited little voice echoing into the hallway. She is showing the movers where to place her bed.

Jarrod is helping the men bring the furniture into the house. He carries the kitchen table as if it weighs nothing. He may be a lawyer out to deceive an opponent, but he's certainly working hard at gaining my respect.

"Where do you want this?" he asks, shouldering the table, awaiting my decision.

I have purchased a piece that reminds me of the large old cypress table that once graced the kitchen. In times past, Shadow Haven was home to large families who ate in this room as often as they were served in the grand dining room. When my parents were alive, when I was very young, I remember happy times in this kitchen, with family and friends gathered around that table, singing songs and telling tales. With a tightening of my throat, I recall the scent of spicy jambalaya and gumbo, the delicious coating of butter on boiled crawfish, food I haven't prepared in years.

"You can put it there, by the window. Thanks." Jarrod settles the table in place, then goes to retrieve the chairs. Gazing around the huge kitchen, I think it too large for just the two of us. In fact, the entire house is too large. What are we going to do with all those rooms? Maybe I should sell Shadow Haven, or turn it over to the historic preservation people. On second thought, it's in such bad shape, I doubt if they would want it.

And besides, I want it, empty rooms and all. I walked out on my heritage once. I'm not going to do it again.

I feel as if I should invite Jarrod to stay for lunch as a thanks for helping with the furniture, but the truth is, I have little food in the house. The refrigerator and stove came on the same truck as the other furniture. I'd planned on going out later, taking Michaela to lunch at a restaurant, then making a foray to the local grocery store to stock the fridge.

It seems that Jarrod Landry has caught me unprepared on a number of levels.

At last the truck is empty, and our quarters in the back of the rambling house look less desolate. I decided not to furnish the parlor or the dining room just yet. I may want to try to find antiques appropriate to the period of the house. I did, however, buy two wonderful overstuffed chairs with an ottoman and an occasional table to place on either side of the kitchen fireplace, turning one corner of that room into a living area.

I tip the movers generously, and Michaela runs out to wave good-bye. "Mother, can we make up my bed now?" she asks, breathless. "Mandy needs a nap."

Mandy is her favorite doll, dressed in full bridal

regalia. Blue-eyed and blond-haired, Mandy was a gift from her grandmother, Elizabeth Colquitt. It was never said, but I knew Mandy was the image of the granddaughter Elizabeth always wanted. She never bargained for olive skin or Creole eyes.

"Get the new sheets and I'll help you make up your bed," I tell Michaela. She darts past Jarrod, who is standing awkwardly in the doorway, as if unsure what to do next. I go to him and take his hands. They feel huge and strong, as if they could protect the world.

"Thanks for helping us get settled," I say, but I find the touch of his hands most unsettling. "I . . . I don't know what to do right now, about the custody thing, I mean. I need some time to think. Do you have a card? Can I call you?"

He hands me an unostentatious white business card. "I'll try to work on getting Elizabeth to change her mind, but if she's determined to press the case, I can hold her at bay only for so long before she'll start looking for other representation. I'm sure you know how impatient she is."

I sit on the porch swing and watch Jarrod's car disappear down the dusty lane, my emotions in a turmoil. Why had he really come today? Was it out of mere curiosity, to see if the bayou girl had lost her mind in New York? Was it because he's going to represent the Colquitts and was checking out the opposition? Or do I dare to believe it was because he sincerely wants to help me, as he claimed?

No one has sincerely wanted to help me in so many years, I find that option difficult to believe. Maybe Jarrod doesn't like the Colquitts but knows I'll need an attorney and simply sees this as an opportunity to make a buck. Maybe he thinks I have money. I give a bitter, silent laugh at the thought. Of course he would think that. Most people did. After all, I was married to one of the richest men in New York.

I turn Jarrod's card over and over between my fingers. Maybe I'll call him—in a few days. I need time to think and consider my situation. I can't afford to make any more mistakes. I stand up and go into the house to help Michaela make up her bed. After that, there is an errand I must do, one I've been putting off all week.

CHAPTER

Five

I'VE KNOWN CONRAD ARMAND ALL MY LIFE. HE'S AN honest, hard-working farmer who has talent as a handyman as well. Before I agreed to move to New York with Charles, I extracted a promise from him that he would always maintain Shadow Haven. Money was no object for Charles, and I had my own inheritance to help support it. So we set up a special account at a local bank, and I hired Conrad to care for the property in my absence. Conrad is the salt of the earth; I've trusted that Shadow Haven has been in good hands all these years in spite of my own neglect of it.

I believed Conrad was caring for Shadow Haven in my absence, but obviously that wasn't the case. He took the money but allowed Shadow Haven to fall into a serious state of disrepair. At first, I was angry about that. Now I just want to know why he let me down. Surely there must be a reasonable explanation.

The Armand property is adjacent to Shadow Haven and runs in a narrow strip from the highway to where solid ground ends in the swampland of the bayou. The Armands raised several children here and managed to eke out a living from the land. Conrad had been too young to serve in World War II, but he fought in Korea and sustained a wound that won him a Purple Heart.

As I turn down the lane to his house, I have a moment's hesitation. What if there isn't a good reason why he let my property go to ruin? What if he just spent the money to improve his own life, thinking I'd never come back? What will I do if that's the case, sue him? It's a depressing thought, so I dismiss it. I hope he has a good reason, but no matter what, this is going to be awkward.

A tail-wagging mutt comes to the car to greet us, but no one appears on the front porch when the car pulls up. I take Michaela's hand. "Come along, *chérie*," I say overbrightly. "I want you to meet our neighbors."

Michaela doesn't answer but follows me up the steps and onto the porch. I knock at the door. "Anyone home?"

After a long moment, a woman comes to the door. She appears to be in her late sixties, with gray hair cut bluntly just above her shoulders, framing a leathered face. She peers at us from behind thick glasses. "Yes?"

I recognize Jeannette Armand immediately, but the woman obviously finds me to be a stranger.

"Jeannette? Do you remember me? I'm Gabriella Deveaux."

Tiny muscles in the woman's face twitch slightly as she works to remember. Then her eyebrows shoot up, and she covers her mouth with her hands.

"Gabriella! Oh, my, I'm sorry I didn't recognize you. You've been gone a long time. I . . . I wasn't expecting you." She reaches for my hand and draws me inside her house. "Please come in, *chérie*. Oh . . . oh, dear . . ." She grows flustered suddenly.

"Is this a bad time for a visit?" I ask. Glancing around, I see that the neat Acadian house I remember hasn't changed at all. Hardwood pine floors shine in the sunlight, and the entry hall is immaculate. Mrs. Armand has always been a great housekeeper and had in fact helped Grandnana maintain the house at Shadow Haven. Another reason I entrusted them with its stewardship.

"No, it's just that . . . well, Conrad isn't doing so well. He had a stroke a few years back, but came out of it pretty well, until another one hit him last year. He's . . . well, wait right here, and I'll see if he feels good enough to see you." She looks at Michaela. "This is your daughter, isn't it?" she says. "Looks just like you." Then she turns and hurries toward the back of the house.

I feel badly for Conrad and Jeannette. Two strokes. No wonder he hasn't been able to keep up the plantation. But why didn't they call me?

Moments later, Jeannette returns. "Please, come with me," she says, beckoning with her hand. "He very much wants to see you."

Conrad Armand's figure is skeletal against the pillows that support him in the low bed where he lies. His eyes are sunken, and one side of his face sags, giving him a grotesque expression. I feel Michaela's hand tighten around mine. I'm shocked as well. Conrad Armand had been a tall, robust man, tanned by the sun and muscled from hard work. This isn't him. This is but his ghost. My lips tremble, and I fear I might cry.

"*Bonjour, mi vieux ami,*" I murmur, stepping closer and taking his lank hand in my free one.

"So you've come home." His voice is surprisingly strong.

"Yes," I manage. "I . . . think I have. I want to—"

"I'm sorry about your house," he says. "I tried hard to keep up with it, but after this . . . happened, I couldn't do it anymore."

"Shhh. Don't worry. It's okay. But I wish you'd called me. I had no idea you were sick."

Jeannette's voice comes from behind me. "We did call you, *chérie*, right after the first stroke."

Stunned, I turn to face her. "You did? I never got any messages."

"Your husband said you were busy with your work, and he didn't want to disturb you. He told us he would take care of things and for us not to worry. He didn't tell you?"

My skin grows cold. Charles. He'd known what had happened and hadn't told me? Woodenly, I shake my head. "No."

"Well, shortly after that, the working account was closed, so we figured you'd made other arrangements to keep the place up. It was hard on us to lose that income right when all those bills from the doctor piled up, but we got through."

Charles.

"And that was five years ago?" I'm sick with shock and disbelief. Charles never said a word to me about Conrad's illness. Nor did he hire someone else to take care of the place. He just closed the account and let Shadow Haven go to ruin. It seems his betrayal of me began long before I ever suspected it.

I sink onto the side of the bed next to Conrad Armand's long, thin legs. I can't seem to stop shaking my head. "I . . . I can't believe this. I had no idea . . ."

"I kept an eye on the place as best I could," the old man continues, "but then those vagrants moved in, and it was more than I could handle."

"Vagrants?"

"Scum," Jeannette clucks. "Derelicts moved right into the house like a bunch of gypsies. We called the sheriff, and he kept trying to run them off, but with the place being vacant and all, he was fighting a losing cause. They just kept coming back."

I'm mortified. I had wondered who was responsible for all the damage. "Have . . . have you seen what they did to the place?"

Jeannette's face turns ashen. "God forbid such a thing could happen to that lovely old house. Yes, I saw—"

"It's a huge mess," Michaela pipes up unexpectedly. "We're living there now, but we might be going back to New York soon."

Jeannette frowns. "But I thought you said you were coming home."

"We are home. Michaela is just having a little trouble adjusting to the idea. Her father . . . died earlier this year, and, well, it's been tough on all of us."

"Oh, I'm so sorry. And to come back and find Shadow Haven like that . . ." Jeannette moans.

I hear Conrad swear darkly under his breath. I turn and clearly read the agony in his face, the guilt.

"Look," I tell him, "this is not your fault. I had no idea all this had happened. It's going to take some time, but we'll get it fixed up again." I hesitate, then add, "Those bums—do you think they're gone for good?"

Jeannette snorts. "Maybe so. The sheriff's pretty sharp. After several unsuccessful attempts at routing them, he became suspicious. Drifters generally don't stay in one place long. He began to suspect they were up to no good and called in the state narcs. They raided the place and found all kinds of drug stuff. Seems they were using the little airstrip out there on Grant's pasture to bring cocaine into the country. They apparently hid it at Shadow Haven until they could move it along the bayou and into New Orleans. That drug bust was big news around here for a long time." She eyes me shrewdly. "I'm surprised you never heard anything about it."

I'm devastated, not only to think how my home has been misused but also that I knew nothing of what had happened. Had Charles known?

"The sheriff told me he thought a couple of the dealers got away. Hightailed it into the bayou," Conrad adds. "But that was a couple of years ago. Nobody's seen them around these parts since. I'm surprised the sheriff didn't contact you when all that was going on."

Maybe he tried, I think grimly, and like Conrad, had been intercepted by Charles. Anger floods through me. Anger at Charles, and at my own stupidity in letting him get away with this. Charles had insisted on handling the business side of our lives, and knowing little about business myself, I had been just as glad to let him. It freed me up to do my art. As difficult as Charles could be, he was a lawyer and a successful and respected businessman. I had no reason not to trust him on that score.

"Did the drug dealers harm you? Or anybody else out here?" I ask the Armands.

"No. Kept to themselves. Guess they didn't want any of us snooping on them."

I wonder suddenly if it's safe for us to live alone at Shadow Haven these days. South Louisiana hasn't changed so much, but times have.

CHAPTER

Six

IT'S NEARLY FOUR O'CLOCK WHEN MICHAELA AND I return to Shadow Haven. After having a late lunch at the Dairy Queen, we made an extended shopping trip to the local market to stock the pantry and our new refrigerator. When I come in the door, I reflexively want to check the phone for messages, as I did back in New York. Then I remember—I don't have a phone.

I've purposely avoided getting a phone, another attempt at holding the outside world at bay. My thinking was, if I don't have a phone, I won't have to talk to Elizabeth Colquitt. I laugh silently at my folly. It's as futile a notion as imagining the Colquitts wouldn't find us at Shadow Haven. Seems I can run, but I can't hide. And I'm going to have to deal with the Colquitts, with or without a phone. I make a mental note to arrange for phone service tomorrow. It's a safety issue as much as anything. What if those drug dealers showed up again? I'd have no way of calling for help.

Scolding myself for being so illogical, I put the groceries away and wonder what I can do to fill up the early evening hours. I should be tired, but I'm not. I wish I'd stopped by the library. I need something to occupy my mind, something besides the worry of the looming lawsuit.

I hear Michaela in her room talking to her dolls. "Don't worry," she's telling them, "we'll be going home soon and you can sleep in your own room again."

Her words tear my heart out. Although I've tried to get her to understand what has happened, she's not willing to accept the events that so brutally sent her young world spinning out of control. The day I learned of Charles's death in the crash of his company plane, I took her onto my lap in the rocking chair where I'd held her since she was a baby. I tried to explain to her that there'd been a bad accident and that her daddy wasn't coming home again. She said nothing but squirmed off my lap and out of my arms, as if it were my fault her daddy was gone.

I kept a careful eye on her for the next few days, and I could tell she was watching for him to come home. She sat on the stairs by the front door for hours the day of Charles's memorial service, as if waiting for him to come and take her to the church. When Mrs. Bolton, that old dragon-faced nanny Charles had hired, tried to forcibly remove her from the stairs, Michaela had screamed in outrage. It was the only time I ever saw her disobey the stern nursemaid.

I sent Mrs. Bolton on her way that day. Then I sat down next to Michaela and tried to put my arms around her, but she shook me off. So we just sat there side by side, saying nothing.

Neither of us attended the service.

And neither of us cried.

Later, in the privacy of my bedroom suite, I sat up late and contemplated this turn of events. In all honesty, I wasn't sorry that Charles had died. His early demise solved a lot of problems for me, although I didn't know then how many other problems it would cause. But despite our emotional distance, in spite of his manipulation and attempts to dominate my life, a part of me loved a part of him. And I allowed myself a few moments to grieve that loss.

Michaela, on the other hand, to my knowledge has never once cried. Instead, she has denied reality and moved into a fantasy world where any minute her father will come through the door. I've tried to talk to her from time to time, but whenever I broach the subject, she becomes immediately distant and withdrawn. I've finally given up, hoping time will heal her sorrow.

So far it hasn't. And I'm getting really worried about her. Funny, I've spent my entire career creating memorials to help the living cope with the loss of their loved ones, but I can't seem to help my daughter with her own loss.

It occurs to me that perhaps I could carve a

memorial for Charles to help Michaela accept the reality of his death, but I put the idea out of my mind almost immediately. I'm afraid of what might emerge beneath my hammer and chisel. I'm so angry with him, I'd probably carve a demon.

If only I could get Michaela to talk about her feelings, to open up. . . .

I have a sudden inspiration. If ever there was a place to attempt a conversation about the dead, the enchanted garden would be it. Michaela didn't want to go into the family grave site upon our arrival, but we've been here a while now, and she's getting used to her new surroundings. Maybe I can convince her to go there with me.

I go to her room and lean against the door, watching her silently for a moment, think her the most beautiful child in the world. If only I could get her to smile more.

"*Chérie*, thanks for being such a big helper today," I say, going into the newly-furnished bedroom. "Your room looks really pretty. I like the bedspread you chose."

"Thank you." Michaela has her dolls lined up on the bed. "My children like it, too, sort of."

Before she can tell me that her "children" wish they could go home to New York, I say, "Well, you did such a great job with your room, are you up to helping me with another project?"

Michaela looks up. "What project?"

"Remember when we first came here, and I took

you to the enchanted garden to see my grandnana's angel?"

She nods unenthusiastically.

"Well, that garden is a special place for me, and I hate to see it all run down. Would you help me clean it up and make it nice, like you did with your room?"

"Can I take Mandy with me?" she asks, holding up the doll. Its bridal gown, made of silk and tulle, is not exactly an outfit suited for pruning and weeding, but if it makes Michaela happy to bring her along, what does a little dirt matter?

"Sure, baby. We'll find a safe place for her to sit and watch us."

I spray our arms and legs with insect repellent and dig out the gardening gloves and tools I purchased earlier at the market. I've been eager to get to work in the cemetery, thinking that perhaps if I restore its beauty, the spirits will be more welcoming.

It's early evening by the time we approach the plot of land armed with hoe, shovel, snippers, and loppers. The heat of the day has gone, and the late sunlight casts slanting shadows on the ground. We probably won't be able to stay long before it gets too dark to work, but it doesn't matter. The real work at hand is not to clear the cemetery; it's to get Michaela to open up and talk about her father's death.

She places Mandy on a clean stone at the edge of the plot where the doll can watch without getting dirty. "You be a good girl and stay right there," Michaela admonishes her toy.

"Let's clean around the angel first," I suggest.

Michaela looks up at the grinning statue. "Does she look like your grandnana?"

"No. She isn't supposed to. She's an angel who guards over Grandnana."

"Why's she smiling like that? I didn't know angels smiled."

"That's because my grandnana had a playful way about her. When I see the angel's grin, it makes me think about how Grandnana used to laugh and joke with me."

"But your grandnana can't laugh anymore. She's dead."

A small, sad pain shoots through me. "Yes, her body died, but I still remember her, and seeing the angel reminds me of her wonderful spirit."

"What's a spirit?"

I try to think back to when Grandnana had first explained to me about the spirits. It was after my mother and father were killed in a car wreck, when I was very young. "The spirit is the real person inside the skin," she'd told me. "We all are spirits, living inside a shell, kind of like an oyster or a crawfish. When we die, we shed our shell, but we still live in our spirit form."

I try this on Michaela, who frowns, trying to comprehend such an alien concept. "How can your grandnana live if she's buried under there?" Michaela points to the slab of stone topping the above-ground crypt, typical of burial places in the low-lying swamplands.

"Well, she doesn't exactly. It's just that here where she's buried I sort of get the feeling that she's nearby, like when she was alive."

"Can you see her?"

"No."

"Can you talk to her?"

Careful.

"Yes, I talk to her, kind of like you just talked to your doll."

"Does she talk back?"

She used to. "No, not the way we're talking. But sometimes when I come here and talk to her, I feel like she answers me, you know, in my head."

"Mandy doesn't talk to me."

"Mandy's just a doll." I go to the doll and pick her up. "But she's a very pretty bride." I pause, seeing an opening. "I was a bride once, but I wore a different kind of dress than this."

Michaela's head snaps up. "You did? What kind of dress?"

"It was a very pretty dress, but it wasn't white; I wore a dress the color of a sunset when I married your daddy."

The word "daddy" seems to hang on the air between us. I press on with guarded hope. "You know, *chérie*, your daddy loved you very much."

Her face falls and her bottom lip edges out. I'm afraid she's going to close me out. "I know he does," she says.

It doesn't escape me that she's still using the

present tense. But at least she answered me. "You know, your daddy is a spirit now," I say gently, kneeling beside her. "Just like my grandnana."

Michaela looks up at the angel and her face brightens perceptibly. "Can I talk to him, like you talk to your grandnana?"

Her question gives me pause. Michaela probably means "talking" like she talks to her doll, but if she has the gift, might she actually summon the spirit of her father? It's a troubling notion. First of all, it would probably frighten her, since she doesn't know about the gift or have any idea she might actually communicate with the dead. And secondly, what might Charles's spirit tell her? That she's to go live with her grandparents?

I hope sincerely she's too young to invoke her powers.

"I don't know, *chérie*," I answer at last. "You can try, I suppose, like you talk to Mandy."

But Michaela shakes her head. "It won't work, not unless he has an angel." She looks up at me, eyes wide. "Will you make me an angel for my daddy?"

CHAPTER
Seven

I DIDN'T AGREE TO MICHAELA'S REQUEST, NOR DID I turn her down. I told her I'd think about it. It's the best I can do at the moment. I have seriously mixed emotions about trying to create a memorial for Charles. I want desperately for my daughter to find a way to open up to her grief, but I fear the consequences if she's actually able to touch into Charles's spirit.

Now more than at any time in my life, I need the counsel of my grandmother.

Yesterday when I tried to communicate with Grandnana, I remembered a ritual I saw her perform when I was a child, a special incantation that she used to summon particularly stubborn spirits. A ceremony involving incense, candles, and chanting. I purchased the appropriate supplies today at the store, and now, under cover of darkness, I intend to return to the enchanted garden. I want no witnesses to what I'm about to do. To those not accustomed to speaking with spirit beings, it would look for all the world like I *am* crazy.

Michaela is sound asleep, and it's not far from the house to the cemetery. I think I can hear her if she awakens and calls for me. At any rate, I doubt that I'll be gone long, even if Grandnana's spirit comes forth. It's been my experience that spirit communication is very short and rapid. They haven't the energy to engage in lengthy dialogue, nor do they use words. Spirits "speak" to me in images that flash through my mind. They are most efficient communicators.

I take the small bag of candles and incense out of a kitchen drawer, pick up my new flashlight and am ready to make my way back to the cemetery when I remember Conrad's remarks about the drug dealers. He seems certain they're long gone, but I'm aware of how alone I am out here, how vulnerable. What would I do to protect myself if someone were to step out of the woods and come after me?

Don't be afraid of shadows, I scold myself. There's no *loup-garou*, no bogeyman, out there in the bushes who's going to come and snatch me away.

Still, I feel the need for something with which I can stave away my fears.

I go into my bedroom and retrieve a small overnight bag from beneath the bed. Opening the small padlock, I reach inside for the handgun and box of ammunition I know are safely stowed inside. Charles gave me the gun years ago and insisted that I take shooting lessons, even though our home had been protected by an expensive security system. I thought it was unnecessary, but in the end, I did as he wanted. To my surprise, I actually enjoyed the lessons and discovered that I was quite a good shot. I even won some medals for my marksmanship.

As I reach for the gun, my hand brushes against another object in the bag, and I recoil as if I've been burned. It's a torc, a wide golden necklace given to me by Charles last Christmas in a rare display of affection. But the moment he'd placed it around my neck, I felt a violent vibration that stung my skin. Without thinking, I tore it away before it burned me, an action that had so infuriated Charles that he'd jerked it from my hands and called me ignorant and ungrateful.

I stare at the torc in the moonlight. I'd forgotten I'd brought it with me. I came across it at the back of Charles's closet just before we were ready to leave and threw it into the bag. I don't want it, but it was too valuable to leave behind. There is something evil about it, though. I must get rid of it soon, just as I got rid of the rest of Charles's strange collections.

The gun is one gift I'm glad Charles gave me. I load it carefully, then tuck the rest of the ammunition away in the bag, relock it and shove it back under the bed.

I check on Michaela once again to make sure she is safe and sound, then hurry the short distance to the enchanted garden. Brilliant moonlight pierces the veil of live oak and cypress leaves and dapples the gravestones. The night is warm but not unpleasant. The mosquitoes have given up as they generally do after dusk. A light breeze has picked up, bringing with it the sound of the night creatures in the bayou. Bullfrogs and tree frogs. The eerie call of an owl. These are familiar sounds, nothing to fear, and yet I can't control a shiver.

Get on with it, I urge myself. Get to the ritual. Hastily, I place a stick of incense in a holder and set it on a flat gravestone near Grandnana's angel. The ceremony seemed strange and a little frightening to me when I was a child, because while performing it, Grandnana seemed to lose her senses for a time.

But it had worked, and I'm willing to try anything to break through to Grandnana. Perhaps the ritual will bring her spirit forth for me tonight.

I place a candle in each of the four corners of the cemetery, which I know to be at the four points of the compass, and then I form a circle between the points with more candles as I recall Grandnana had done. I light the incense and the candles, the glow of which dispels the darkness, but I keep glancing into the shadows, imagining that someone is out there watching. Get a grip, I tell myself, but I lay the gun on a gravestone close at hand.

I inhale deeply and close my eyes, then invoke the protection of the archangels who guard the heavens and the earth. Not having done this before, I wonder where that came from. Someone in spirit is here with me, guiding me. The notion fills me with peace and hope and an odd sense of power I haven't felt in years.

I remember that sense of power now. The Deveaux power. That feeling that I belong here at

Shadow Haven, that I am at home among my people, that I am loved, and that I can do anything I set my mind to. The Deveaux power. When had I let it slip away?

"I call upon the spirit of Angelique Deveaux," I summon in a loud voice. "Angelique, first mother of my family, send forth the spirit of your daughter, Ariella, my grandmother, that I may beg her forgiveness."

Even as I say the word "forgiveness," I realize that it is the one thing I've failed to do in my endeavor to return home. I have not asked for the forgiveness of my ancestors for leaving and for forsaking my heritage. Nor have I asked it of myself.

Something stirs nearby, a light breeze perhaps. Or could it be a sign that the spirits hear me?

Encouraged, I begin to tone, a technique Grandnana taught me that brings the voice in a low vibration from the belly to the throat. Toning is like humming a chant. I haven't toned since Grandnana died. Again, I get the sense that someone in spirit is guiding this ritual.

I begin to turn in a circle, slowly at first. I extend my arms straight out and turn faster. My long white cotton shift whirls around my body as I spin. The toning morphs into a chant, the words of which come from some nether reaches of my memory. It is a plea, spoken in the old language, to those who sleep beneath my feet, a petition for them to forgive me and allow me to return into their company.

I want to come home.

Consciousness ebbs, and my mind fills with brilliant splashes of color, reminiscent of the colorful clothing my grandmother often wore. I cling to the images, hungry for the presence of the woman who raised me and loved me and taught me the old ways. "Grandnana, *s'il vous plait*, show yourself now!" I continue to whirl in circles, arms skimming on the air, calling and calling for Grandnana. "Ariella! Ariella! Ariella!"

At last, dizzy and breathless, I fall to my knees and begin to return to a hazy consciousness. I haven't reached Grandnana, but I sense that the spirits have heard my plea. There is hope.

I'm still in a daze when suddenly the skin on my arm prickles. I become aware that the night is quiet now. Too quiet. The croaking and peeping and hooting have ceased. I struggle to my feet and reach for the gun. Has my chanting disturbed the night creatures, or is there someone else out there?

I hear something behind me and turn toward it. A footstep sounds on the path nearby. Blood hums in my ears, and my heart hammers. The figure of a man becomes silhouetted in the moonlight. He is large, square of shoulder, and comes to an abrupt halt when he sees the pistol.

"Gabriella," he says. "Lower the gun."

The voice is familiar, although in my semi-daze, I can't quite place it. The newfound sense of power that I had savored earlier vanishes, and I begin to tremble as I let the gun slip to the ground. I've summoned a spirit, after all.

"Charles?"

The figure moves closer, and my wits return. This isn't the spirit of my dead husband. The man on the path is very much alive.

CHAPTER

Eight

❧

"UH, TAKEN UP BALLET?" HE LOOKS BEWILDERED AND embarrassed.

I curse silently. Obviously, he witnessed my aberrant little ritual. I rake my fingers through my hair and take a step backward. "Jarrod, you scared the bejeesus out of me. What are you doing here?" After the toning and chanting, my voice is just above a rasp.

"I . . . had some business in Tibonne after I left you, then I had to make a run down to Napoleana. I tried to get your phone number from information when I started back to New Orleans, but I guess you haven't had time to have a phone installed. Since I had to come back through Tibonne anyway, I decided to stop by and see how you and Michaela were getting along." His speech is rapid; he sounds like a schoolboy making up an excuse for his behavior. He's obviously ill at ease, and I imagine he wishes he hadn't dropped by.

I wish that as well. I'd find the whole situation

amusing if it weren't so serious. It occurs to me if Jarrod is on the Colquitts' side, I've just given him some dandy evidence of my mental instability. "Bet you never expected to find me dancing in the cemetery," I say, trying to make light of it.

His gaze travels from me to take in the circle of candles flickering in the enchanted garden. "Not exactly. What . . . *were* you doing just now?"

Trying to talk to my dead grandmother, of course.

I think fast. "Umm . . . Michaela and I cleaned the graveyard today, and I . . . wanted to consecrate it with a special blessing ceremony." I put my hands on my hips. "Do you have a problem with that? Do you think it's a crazy thing to do?"

He gives me that crook of a grin that makes my heart do a little flip. "Good Catholic that I am?" he replies. "We're big into incense and candles and consecrations."

He, too, is making light of it, but I know he must find my behavior a little whacked. I would, if I were him.

"Look, I have to get back to the house," I tell him. "I left Michaela sleeping there a little while ago, and I need to go check on her."

"Gabriella, is everything . . . okay out here?"

His question is dead serious. He thinks I'm nuts. Maybe I am. Only a nutcase would move into a ruin of a house like Shadow Haven, isolated and incommunicado. Only a lunatic would whirl and chant in a cemetery by the light of the moon.

But there's more to his question. It has a protective

overtone, as if he wants me to ask him for help. I don't want his help, at least not at the moment.

"Everything's fine, Jarrod. Thank you."

Now go away.

His presence unnerves me, as does the way he's looking at me. If I didn't know better, I would swear there's a sexual longing in his eyes. But then, I am wearing nothing but a light cotton shift, and I'm standing between him and the candlelight. I might as well be naked. I find the thought disconcertingly arousing, and I cross my arms over my breasts.

He seems to get the message and averts his gaze. "Okay, then, well . . . I guess I'll be on my way." I think he's embarrassed that he's been caught looking. "If you're sure you're okay . . . ?"

I'm not sure I'm okay, or not okay. I'm not sure of anything at the moment, except that I want him gone. "Good-bye, Jarrod. I'll call you if I need you."

He returns his gaze to mine and holds it for a long moment, then at last he turns down the path and disappears into the night.

Jarrod's sudden and unexpected appearance twice in one day, especially his dropping by after dark, has me worried; I can't help but suspect he's spying on me. I wish to God he hadn't witnessed my ritual in the cemetery. I don't know where I stand with him, professionally as a lawyer, and . . . personally as well. As much as I'd like to, I can't deny my attraction to him.

I return to the house and tuck the gun safely away

in the overnight bag. Michaela is sleeping peacefully, as if she has no troubles in her life. I only wish that were the case.

I take a quick shower and fall into bed, exhausted at last. But sleep eludes me. I can't get my mind off Jarrod and the way he looked at me in the candlelit graveyard. I'm alarmed at the erotic sensations conjured just by thinking about him.

Good grief, I don't need this. I can't allow myself such feelings. I know nothing about Jarrod Landry except that he's a lawyer. He could be married, have a family. He wears no wedding band, but these days that means nothing. Still, as I lie on my bed in the darkness, I see that hungry look in his eye, and I feel the undeniably sexual response in my belly.

I toss on the bed, distraught, trying to analyze my attraction to him. It's been a long time since I've seen that look on a man, and I acknowledge that it turned me on. Am I really that emotionally needy? Am I genuinely attracted to Jarrod, or have I been so sexually forsaken that I'm ready to fall into the arms of any man who will pay some attention to me? God, that's pathetic.

At last I fall into a fitful sleep, and an alarming dream.

It's dark in the dream. I feel as if I'm in a hot, wet, eerie cavern. I hear the whine of mosquitoes and the scrabbling of some creature of the night. It's hard to get my breath, and my heart is pounding heavily in my chest.

Suddenly, something flashes silver in the darkness—the mane of a horse, or perhaps its tail.

No, it's a woman's hair, falling to her waist and glimmering as she turns to face me. Her strange eyes are a piercing indigo, and they seem to glow in the dark. Her expression is fierce.

"Why have you come?" she demands. "What do you want?"

The only reply is the lonely cry of an owl in the distance. And then there is silence. I shrink back against a clammy rock wall, wanting to disappear into the darkness, to run and hide from those haunting eyes. Then I see that she's not looking at me. She's looking past me, into the dark, seeking someone or something I'm unable to perceive.

"Spirit, reveal yourself or be gone!" she calls out in an impatient voice.

An icy wind whispers past my cheek, and I shiver. I believe I'm in a tomb. I can feel a presence now, although I see no one but the strange silver-haired woman. Then a foul odor assails me, the reek of rotten flesh and singed hair. My stomach turns in fear and disgust, and I try to run, but something is holding me back. Something rough and hateful and evil. I want to scream, but can't. I want to call for help, but there is no one to help me but the woman with the silver hair.

The evil is so powerful it pricks my skin, and I gag in revulsion. Something shoves me roughly in the middle of my back, and I'm propelled toward the woman at high speed. I slam into her, but pass right through her body into a chamber of light. Here there is no evil, no threat, no stench. Here I am safe. I turn and look behind me. The woman has followed me to this place. Her expression is still unhappy, but now it seems resigned rather than angry.

"Who . . . who are you?" I ask. Slowly, she raises her head and looks directly into my eyes.

"My name is Marie Françoise," she says, her voice low and hoarse. "I have a message for you from a spirit. Things are not what they seem. Great evil is coming, and you are in grave danger. Heed . . ." Even as she says the words, the image begins to dissolve. As I stare dumbstruck, the figure wavers and melts into a blue mist, leaving me alone in darkness once again.

CHAPTER

Nine

I AWAKEN FROM THE DREAM DRENCHED IN A COLD sweat. What was that all about? I've always been sensitive to my dreams, because often they've proven to be portents. I've felt uneasy since returning to Shadow Haven, but not as if I were in danger. What spirit would have such a message for me—*you are in grave danger . . . ?*

I get out of bed and draw a shawl over my shoulders to try to stop shivering. The dream images are still very real, although, as is the nature of dreams, they are beginning to fade. I'm left, however, with a residue of fear. It was only a dream, I try to tell myself.

Heed . . .

Or a message from a spirit I must not ignore . . .

I'm unsure if the woman in the dream was friend or foe. She delivered a message, but her attitude and demeanor were unfriendly and threatening, even in the chamber of light.

With shaking hands, I grope beneath the bed for

the travel bag that holds the gun. It may have been only a dream, but until I can sort it out, I'm taking it as a legitimate warning. Careful not to touch the torc, I wrap my fingers around the firearm. The idea of using it to actually shoot someone chills me, but it's my only defense right now. It feels cold and deadly in my hand.

I wander into the hallway, and my chill deepens. Maybe I'm just spooked by the dream, but I swear I feel that same sense of evil lurking nearby that I felt in the nightmare, although I hear nothing. Outside, the moonlight is bright and shines onto the verandah, mocking my fear.

I consider the other part of the spirit message— *Things are not what they seem. . . .*

What did that mean? I'm reminded of the legend of the *loup-garou*, a notorious shape-shifter—man by day, murderous werewolf by night. The *loup-garou* isn't real, of course, but rather a metaphor for appearances that deceive. Things aren't what they seem, and I mustn't trust my eyes, or my ears.

Or my desires.

Jarrod could be my *loup-garou*, pretending to be my friend by day, but working in the shadows behind my back to destroy me. It seems unlikely he's the one I'm being warned against, and yet he's the only person who has approached me with any kind of a threat—that of the Colquitts' lawsuit.

I pour a glass of milk and warm it in the microwave. I don't want to think about Jarrod like this, but now that the possibility has entered my mind, I can't seem to shake it. I can't imagine who else it could be.

The milk warms me at last, and I return to my bed. I place the gun on my nightstand and pull the covers tightly around my body, like a shield, as if the fabric could protect me. I feel alone and vulnerable in this big, dark house. It would be easy for someone to break in and commit whatever crimes they wanted.

Maybe I ought to reconsider living here, I think as I feel myself growing drowsy. Or maybe in the morning the dream will have faded, and the dire warnings will seem not so menacing.

Will you make me an angel for my daddy?

Michaela's request kept echoing in my mind, so yesterday I visited the quarry where I have purchased raw stone in the past. With Michaela's help, I selected several pieces of marble that have been delivered and which are now lined up against a wall in the big, almost empty parlor. The only thing remaining in here is a large mirror that was broken by the vandals, but which Willie and I haven't managed to take down yet.

The parlor will be my studio for the time being, if and when I decide to recommence my work. I kneel by one of the pieces of stone and run my hand over the cool surface.

Can I do this? Can I make an angel, or some appropriate image, for Charles? More to the point, can I do it without contacting his spirit? There are spirits better left alone, and I believe his is one of them.

My throat feels suddenly dry. I suppose I should at least try to carve a stone for Michaela's sake, even if it means having to encounter him in the Otherworld. Who knows? Maybe it would help me as well. Perhaps if I communicated with Charles's spirit, I might better understand who he really was, and why he treated me the way he did. Perhaps then I could find it in my heart to forgive him and at last put closure on our unhappy relationship.

I study each stone carefully and at last pick one that beckons me most. It is black marble, veined in white. It won't make a very good angel, but I have a feeling that whatever emerges from my hammer and chisel won't be angelic. It will, however, represent the real Charles Colquitt. I'm suddenly curious as to what it will be.

I lift the stone and place it on the small table that I've set up in the middle of the room. My heart is pounding as I pick up my tools and feel their familiar weight in my hands. I decide not to try to make spiritual contact with Charles; I'm still too angry at him. Rather, I'll seek inspiration from my memories.

I close my eyes and wait, but no inspiration comes. I concentrate my thoughts on Charles, try to visualize his image in my mind, but I can't even conjure up the familiar shape of his face. It's as if he is mocking me from the grave, hovering just beyond my reach, the same as he did in life.

My anger flares, and the thought suddenly strikes me that perhaps this, my constant and abiding anger against Charles, is blocking me and keeping me from reaching the spirits of my family. Perhaps this is why I've been unable to work at my profession for so long. I lay the tools down again, feeling desolate. If this is the case, then Charles continues to control me.

I can't carve anything for Charles, now or maybe ever. But I must find a way to help Michaela. I hurry from the parlor and go to the front porch to check on her. She's sitting on the porch swing with Mandy tucked into the crook of one arm. But she isn't playing with the toy. Instead, she's staring with an intense, rather glazed look into the nearby woods. I take a seat next to her on the swing.

"Hello, *chérie*. What're you thinking about so hard?"

Michaela's reverie is broken, and she turns her head toward me. "Who is that old woman out there?"

CHAPTER
Ten

MY HEART NEARLY STOPS BEATING, AND I TASTE SOUR fear in my mouth. "What old woman? Out where?"

The image of the silver-haired woman from my dream springs immediately to my mind. Could she be real? Was it her evil I felt so strongly in the night?

I silently reproach myself for not having made arrangements yet for a telephone. I keep forgetting about it, until moments when I'm feeling particularly vulnerable. Like now.

"There. In the trees." Michaela points into the woods.

I scan the thick Southern forest but see nothing. "It's just a trick of the light," I attempt to assure Michaela, needing the assurance myself. "There's no one out there."

"But I saw her," Michaela insists. "She was wearing a purple dress with yellow on it. And she talked to me."

Instantly, Michaela has my full attention. It's not the silver-haired woman she's seen. But could it be what I'm thinking? Grandnana's favorite dress had been purple and yellow.

"Where was she?" I ask her again, standing up suddenly, sending the swing out behind me. It returns, crashing against the back of my knees, but I hardly notice. Michaela hops down and goes to the edge of the porch.

"Over there," she says, pointing again. "But she's gone now."

My pulse pounds. "You said you were talking to her. How could you talk to her from the porch?"

Michaela looks up at me anxiously. "You're mad at me. I shouldn't talk to strangers."

I kneel down and put my hands on her thin arms. "No, I'm not mad at you. I just want to know what she said to you."

"She said she loved me and that she hoped everything would be all right soon."

"She said that to you . . . out loud?"

Michaela shakes her head. "No. I just sort of heard her—in my head."

So Michaela has indeed inherited the gift, and Grandnana's spirit is still around. I'm thrilled and terrified at the same time. What if Elizabeth Colquitt gets wind of this? She'd stop at nothing to convince a jury that I've somehow transferred my madness to my child.

"What else did she say to you?"

"She said to tell you to take me and go to find Mary Frances, or something like that."

My heart lurches. "Did she say who Mary Frances is?"

Michaela shakes her head. "All she said was that Mary Frances would keep us safe. What was she talking about, Mother?"

"I don't know. We're safe right where we are."

But are we? Jarrod has come upon us without any warning—twice. This apparition, if it was that, had come suddenly out of the woods. It wasn't a vagrant or a criminal this time, but someone like that could still come along and try to hurt us.

I suspect that it truly is Grandnana's spirit that Michaela has seen, but I feel compelled to make sure. I can't take the risk that there's someone lurking in the forest.

"Can you tell me again what the old woman looked like?"

"She had on this ziggy-zaggy dress, like it had lightning on it or something. Her hair was gray, well, kind of gray and black, and it was hanging down long. She had something around her neck, like a cross or something."

I need no further proof. Grandnana had loved that dress; in fact, she'd been buried in it, with her cross in her hand. I'm filled with joy—Grandnana is still here and making herself known, even if she can't reach me directly. Dare I hope that hers was the spirit bringing me the message in my dream?

"Do you know who that was?" I murmur before thinking about it. I can't take my eyes off the woods now. How I long to see that spritely spirit.

"No."

"That . . . was my Grandnana."

Michaela looks at me in open skepticism. "But she's dead. You told me she was buried in the graveyard, under the angel."

Heat rushes to my cheeks, and red-hot panic sets in. I shouldn't have let that slip to Michaela. And yet, it's her destiny, and she must know the truth sooner or later. She has the gift, and it's likely to manifest again. I don't want anything to frighten her. I clear my throat, resolved to handle this right.

"Remember we talked about spirits when we cleaned up the enchanted garden?"

"Yes, but you said you couldn't see the spirits."

I have to admit I've never seen a physical manifestation of any of the spirits with whom I've communed. Michaela's gift must be powerful indeed. "I've never seen one. But there are some people who can. You must be one of them."

Michaela's face brightens. "Then maybe I can see daddy and talk to him and tell him to take us back home."

I feel as if I've been punched in the stomach. Oh, dear God, what if that actually happened? "I . . . I don't think you'll be able to, *chérie*," I say quickly, trying to dislodge that thought from Michaela's mind.

"Why not?"

"Well, not all spirits come back to us. Sometimes they go into their new world and don't come back to this one." *Especially if they die a violent death.* That's what had happened to my own *maman* and *papa*. Perhaps that had happened to Charles as well.

It may be true, but it's exactly the wrong thing to say to Michaela. She dashes away from me and runs down the front steps. "No! My daddy wouldn't leave me. My daddy loves me. His spirit will come back and take me home."

"Michaela! Where are you going?" I start to go after her but stop when I see that she's gone only as far as a gnarled old tree at the edge of the forest. She's been told not to go farther into the woods without me, so I decide to let her work through this small bit of grief on her own.

Dejected, I sit on the verandah steps and let my eyes roam the woods looking for Grandnana. *Well, you've stirred up a pretty mess,* I say to her in my mind, not knowing if she can hear me. *Why don't you come back and help me straighten it out?*

A breeze rustles the still, hot air, then calms again, and for the first time since my return, I sense my grandmother's presence. It's faint but recognizable, and it's enough to summon long-overdue tears. "Help me, Grandnana," I whisper. "Help me help her to understand about her father. And tell me, please tell me, what danger are we in?"

I sit still for a long while, hoping, praying for an answer, longing for my grandmother's wisdom to show me the way, but there is no sound except the slight shimmer of leaves in the breeze, and I no longer feel the presence of a spirit being.

I get up at last and return to the studio, thinking of Charles and his relationship with Michaela. He had loved his daughter, as much as he was capable of loving anyone. Surely, if somehow Michaela summoned his spirit, he would do nothing to harm her. I eye the rock that seems to mock me from the carving table. "Okay," I say out loud, "let's give it another try."

Glancing out the window, I see Michaela now sitting at the base of the tree, talking to Mandy. I wonder what she's telling the toy so earnestly. That she hates this place? That she wants her father? That she's going to run away back to New York?

I let go of those disturbing thoughts and turn to the stone. Inhaling deeply, I work at consciously letting go of my anger and entering the peaceful, familiar trancelike state in which I do my best work. After a few long breaths, I begin to feel light-headed, and I wait, hoping for direction, a nudge from a spirit that tells me what to do. But nothing comes.

Patience.

It takes patience for these things to happen. Ten minutes pass. Twenty minutes, and still nothing.

Patience.

Patience, my ass, I think grumpily after half an hour has passed and no one in the spirit world has stirred. I have to do something about Michaela's unhappiness, and I have to do it now. I pick up one of my chisels and glare at the marble. "Charles, you son of a bitch, if you're in there, show yourself."

I give the rock an angry swipe with the chisel,

accomplishing nothing. My rage blazes out of control. I reach for my hammer and begin to attack the marble in earnest. It feels good to vent my frustrations and fury. Maybe something will come of it, maybe not. At the moment, I don't give a damn. Hammering away at the stone, I hammer at Charles as well. Hammer at Elizabeth and Rupert. Hammer at my fear and all that besets me.

Chips of marble fly, and one hits my cheek, slicing my skin. It's as if Charles has struck back. Shaken, I let the tools clatter to the floor. I brush my hand over the stinging cut and feel a tear that has slipped down my cheek. Blood mingles with the tear, staining my finger pink. I start for the medicine chest in the bathroom, but freeze in my steps when I hear Michaela scream.

CHAPTER

Eleven

I DASH OUT OF THE FRONT DOOR TO SEE MICHAELA still beneath the big tree. She's screaming and swatting at her body, doing a frenzied dance as if she's trying to rid herself of something.

"Fire ants," I swear under my breath and run to Michaela. She is covered with the vicious insects that sting without mercy and leave angry, red welts in their wake. Quickly, I pull off her sundress and skim her out of her panties, all the while brushing at the mean little creatures that crawl over her soft olive skin.

"Come on, let's get you into the shower," I say, picking her up and running toward the house. She continues to wail, and I have to fight to keep from joining her. I kiss her flushed cheek and let her down gently just outside the shower stall in the small bath beneath the stairs.

I turn on the faucets and adjust the temperature until the water is just above tepid. Then I lift Michaela and, fully clothed myself, step into the stall with her. I don't thrust her directly under the spray, but rather fill my palm with water and brush it gently over her tender skin.

"It . . . iiit's cold," Michaela sobs, drawing away.

"It'll help cool the stinging," I tell her, applying another handful of water to her back, then softly wiping my wet hand across her cheeks and brow. I check for ants, but see none, and Michaela's earlier screams have subsided to deep, racking sobs, so I don't think she is still being bitten. I kiss her again and continue to apply the cool water. "There, is that better?"

Michaela sobs and nods and then throws her arms around my neck and clings to me as if for dear life. I'm overcome with emotion; this is the first time since Charles's death that she has allowed me to hold her. And hold her I do, as tightly to me as I can. I wish it hadn't taken a fire ant attack to get us here, but I savor the moment. Rocking my baby back and forth in the shower, I hum an old tune Grandnana sang to me when I was a child in need of soothing:

Hush little baby, don't say a word,
Mama's going to buy you a mockingbird,
And if that mockingbird don't sing,
Mama's going to buy you a diamond ring . . .

After a few moments, Michaela is calm, and I reluctantly release her enough to turn off the water. "Let's get you dried off and see what we can do about those bad old ant bites."

"I . . . I didn't mean to get into them, Mother," Michaela says.

"It's not your fault," I assure her, toweling her gently. I wish Mrs. Bolton hadn't implanted such guilt in my daughter. Michaela frequently apologizes for doing something bad, whether she has or not.

"Sometimes you can't see an ant bed," I tell her. "I've stepped in plenty during my life."

"We don't have ants in New York."

"Not this kind," I agree. "Now, let me see where they bit you."

Michaela allows me to examine her body. Most of the bites are on her feet and legs, but unfortunately, a few are on her arms, and there's one on her left cheek. "Oh, my poor baby," I cry when I see the swollen red lump on her face. "Here." I hand the towel to Michaela. "Hold this while I get some ointment."

Grandnana taught me the healing power of herbs and other plants that grow wild on the plantation, and since my return here, I have concocted several simple recipes and put together a basic first aid kit. I hadn't known I would need it so soon.

Fetching a small round jar from the medicine chest, I open the lid and smell the scent of the lavender oil that I've blended with witch hazel and aloe vera in the salve. This ointment is supposed to ease the pain of insect stings. I hope it works on ant bites.

"Smell," I say with a small smile and hold the jar to Michaela's nose.

"Smells good," Michaela agrees.

"Put a little on your finger and rub it where it hurts," I tell her, taking some on my finger as well and touching it to her red cheek.

"Ouch," she says, squirming. But she allows me to apply enough to do some good. Then she digs her finger into the jar again and reaches up to my face and dabs some on the wound caused by the flying marble chip. "You hurt yourself, too," she says.

It's my turn to wince. I'd forgotton all about my injury. "It's just a little scratch, but thanks. Now we'll both be good as new."

When we've tended to the rest of Michaela's bites to the satisfaction of both, I take the softest sundress and underpants I can find from Michaela's dresser. "You were a very brave girl just now," I say. "Can you put these on while I make you something special for lunch?"

"Peanut butter and jelly?"

I'd intended to make some crepes or maybe boil some of the crawfish we bought at the nearby fish market. To my surprise, Michaela has taken a liking to crawfish dipped in melted butter. But all she wants after this trauma is a peanut butter and jelly sandwich. "If that's what you want, that's what you'll have. Grape or strawberry jelly?" I'll save the crawfish for supper.

Michaela thinks for a long moment, as if the decision were earthshaking. "Grape," she decides at last. "Can I have Kool-Aid, too?"

After lunch, I switch the ceiling fan in Michaela's room to high speed even though there is a small window air conditioner in the room. It's midday, mid-June and "hot as the hinges of Hades," as Grandnana used to say. The time of day a person went down for a little nap. I'd forgotten about nap time, like I'd forgotten so many things about life here on the bayou. Fire ants included. But since returning to Shadow Haven, I've resumed the custom of an afternoon doze, and even Michaela seems to like this quiet time.

"Want me to read you a story?" I ask, brushing Michaela's dark hair away from her face.

"The one about the magic pony?"

I smile and nod. "That's a great story."

Michaela races to a set of shelves along one wall of her bedroom and selects the book. When she comes back to me, she says, "Mother," in a tone that sounds like a question.

"Yes, *chérie?*"

"Will you put your arm around me while you read?"

I MUST HAVE DOZED OFF ON MICHAELA'S BED AFTER
we finished reading the storybook, because I'm
awakened suddenly by the sound of a car
approaching. I slip my arm from around her and hurry
to the front door. I half expect to see Jarrod there,
since he is still unable to call me. Perhaps he has some
news about the Colquitts. But when I look out on the
driveway, I see a black-and-white police cruiser.

"Hello, Gabriella," the sheriff greets me as he steps
out of his car and into the late afternoon heat. It only
takes me a second to recognize this man. I went to
school with him back when his own daddy was the
law around here. I think he always had sort of a crush
on me.

"Danny Comeaux," I say, smiling but cautious as
my gaze darts beyond him to his official vehicle. "So
you're the sheriff now?"

"I am. Took over when Pa retired a few years back."

"Is this a friendly visit, Danny," I ask, "or an official
one?"

Danny hesitates a beat too long. "A little of both, I suppose."

I'm suddenly filled with dread. Behind me, I hear the screen door slam, and Michaela comes to my side.

"This is my daughter, Michaela," I introduce her to Danny. "Michaela, this is Mr. Comeaux. He's our sheriff." It sounds funny to introduce a childhood friend so formally, but Danny is the law now. I want him to know I respect that.

He comes a few steps closer. "Pleased to meet you," he says to Michaela, then gestures toward the ant bite on her face. "That looks like it hurts," he says. "What happened?"

"Fire ants," Michaela replies. "My mother put salve on them, and they don't hurt now."

"Well, that's a good thing." I see him release a long breath before he says anything further, and cold apprehension washes over me. Why has he come here?

Danny removes his western-style hat, wipes his forehead with the sleeve of his shirt, then replaces the hat. "I heard somebody was living out here," he says in a slow drawl, "but I didn't know you'd come home, Gabriella. You doing okay? Need anything?" he asks.

"We're fine, thank you."

He eyes me uncertainly and acts as if he has something else on his mind. "Ah, can I come in?" he asks politely. "There're a couple of things I need to talk to you about."

"What things?" There is nothing I want to talk to him about. Not as long as he's wearing a badge.

"Things maybe we should talk about in private," he replies with a nod toward Michaela.

The knot in my stomach tightens. Does his visit have something to do with the Colquitts' custody schemes? "Come onto the verandah," I invite stiffly. "Michaela can hear anything you have to say."

Danny raises one booted leg and places it on the first step, but he doesn't come any farther. "I . . . uh . . . think this is best said *entre nous*." His eyes are harder now, official.

I feel a chill in spite of the heat. I hold his gaze long enough to know he means business. *Entre nous*. Between us. Reluctantly, I turn to Michaela. "Can you be the hostess and pour some iced tea for Mr. Comeaux?"

Michaela gives me a disbelieving look, but then smiles broadly, as if proud to be given such a grown-up assignment. "Sure."

"You know where the tea is, in the pitcher in the fridge. There's those plastic cups in the cupboard, the red ones? Bring out three of them. And the sugar bowl."

When Michaela has gone back into the house, I turn to Danny Comeaux. "Talk fast."

The sheriff steps onto the verandah at last and takes a seat in one of the faux wicker chairs I bought at Kmart. They aren't the real thing, but plastic holds up better than wicker in the humid climate. He leans forward, arms resting on his thighs, and looks up at me with large, brown eyes. In them I read an apology even before he speaks.

"Social Services got a call this morning," he says in a low voice. "Somebody reported a case of child abuse out here."

My skin prickles and turns cold. "What? Who? . . ." I'm too shocked to think.

"It was an anonymous call. Amie Fontaine, she's the social worker, said it was a woman with a Northern accent. Amie asked me to come over here and check it out." He takes his hat off and balances it on his knee. "I'm sorry, Gabriella. I know it's nonsense, but . . ."

Outrage quickly replaces my shock. "It's a hateful ploy, and my mother-in-law's behind it," I tell him, bristling. "She's a mean, manipulating old biddy."

I pace the length of the porch and back, trying to calm down before addressing him again. I know I shouldn't be mad at Danny. Don't kill the messenger and all that. But to think that horrid woman would stoop to making an anonymous phone call to accuse me of child abuse! Obviously, Jarrod has called her and confirmed that Michaela and I are living here. I wonder if he knows about the phone call to Social Services?

"Mother-in-law?" the sheriff asks.

"Former mother-in-law," I correct myself. "My husband is dead, Danny. His parents have never liked me, and they're trying to get custody of Michaela.

They're going to try to prove that I'm mentally unstable and therefore an unfit mother. I guess they're going to throw in 'abusive' as well."

"Geez, nice folks." He squints at me, then asks with a wry look, "Whatever made you take up with a Yankee, Gabriella?" He says it as if all Northerners have horns and a tail.

His question, although serious, makes me smile. But my amusement is short-lived. What indeed made me take up with a Yankee? I'd been a bayou girl down to my toenails. I must have really been crazy back then.

I ignore his question. "I guess those ant bites don't do my case any good. Do you think I'm abusing Michaela?" I need to know whose side he's on.

"No," he replies without missing a beat. "This is horse-hockey, and we both know it. Kids get into ant beds all the time. I'll tell Amie to forget that call."

"There'll be more," I assure him, certain that Elizabeth will keep up the harassment until Jarrod or some other lawyer can manage to get the courts to hand Michaela over to them. "I knew she was cold and calculating, but I never dreamed how vicious she could be."

"Mother, can you open the door, please?" Michaela calls out, and our privacy is over. I'm glad Danny insisted on it, though. Never in my wildest imagination would I have guessed why he'd dropped by. I hold the door while Michaela comes out with a sweating pitcher of iced tea.

"Here, I'll take it now," I say, reaching for the heavy pitcher.

"I can get it," Michaela objects. "I'll put it on the table." I back off, smiling at my daughter's pride in accomplishing her mission without having spilled anything. Michaela returns to the house and brings out the three red cups and the sugar bowl and places them next to the pitcher on the table. "Can I pour, Mother?"

"If you want."

When Michaela hands the sheriff his glass of tea, he says, "You're quite a grown-up girl. What grade are you going to be in?"

Michaela lifts her head proudly. "I was a kindergarten baby last year, but this year, I'm in first grade."

"That's a big step," he says. "You're going to like Sister Carmen. She's still teaching first grade at St. Agnes." He turns to me. "You remember her, don't you?"

I accept a glass of tea from Michaela, then take a seat on the porch swing. "How could I forget?" I answer with a wry grin. "She was a wonderful teacher, but I was scared silly of her at first. I'd have thought she'd be retired by now."

"Next year, I think. She's not so bad," Danny says to Michaela. "You don't have to be afraid of her."

"Oh, I'm not going to go to school here," Michaela informs him. "My daddy's going to come for me, and his spirit's going to take me back to New York where we live."

Thirteen

I SEE THE STARTLED LOOK ON DANNY'S FACE, AND I'M filled with utter distress. I want to explain, but Michaela's unexpected statement has left me speechless.

The child sips her tea, then adds, "Mother is going to carve an angel so I can talk to my daddy," as if it made perfect sense. Danny eyes me and raises his brows, inviting an explanation.

The heat in my cheeks deepens. Will the sheriff think I've been telling Michaela inappropriate things? Does that constitute child abuse these days?

"I'm a sculptor," I explain to him, hoping to make sense out of Michaela's wild tale. "I'm trying to carve a memorial for Charles to put in our family cemetery. There were no . . . uh . . . remains found in the plane crash." This last is spoken over a tightness in my chest. Even though I feel very little grief over Charles's death, the violence of it still rocks me from time to time. "I thought it would give Michaela something to remember him by."

I see Danny visibly relax; he takes a long drink of the iced tea. "I see," he says after a moment. "Memorials are important. I remember the one you carved for your grandmother. It always made me smile. She was a spry old lady. I always liked her." Then his smile turns to a frown. "So, are you going back to New York?"

I shake my head. "Michaela is homesick, and she's having a hard time accepting her father's death. This is my home, our home now, what's left of it. I guess you know what happened here. Were you involved in that drug raid?" I ask, suddenly remembering Conrad Armand saying the sheriff had called in the state narcotics squad. But he hadn't mentioned that Danny was the sheriff.

"Yeah." Danny's tone is regretful. "I'm sorry it ever came to that. I thought they were just a bunch of drifters who'd taken over the place, and I tried to run them off several times. Then one day I saw some guys out here who didn't look like the other bums. They were dressed in dark suits, and their expensive cars were parked out front.

"It finally hit me what was going on. The supposed vagrants turned out to be drug mules for the mob. I felt like an idiot for not having investigated drugs sooner. But I called in the state narcotics team, and they made a huge raid on the place. Sent a lot of bad guys to prison." He looks down at his hat that he's turning nervously in his hands. "I'm real sorry for what they did to your house, Gabriella. It's partly my fault for not moving on them sooner."

The story shocks me all over again. "What happened to my house is no one's fault but my own, Danny. I didn't stay in touch—"

"I called you right after the drug raid," Danny interrupts, as if eager to defend himself. "Your lawyer called me back, told me he'd get you the message. I figured if nothing else, you'd want to file an insurance claim for the damage to the house."

"My lawyer? I didn't have a lawyer."

Danny frowns. "I swear that's who I talked to."

But I get it suddenly that I'd indeed had a lawyer. I'd been married to him. Charles strikes again.

"I . . . I'm sorry about the confusion, Danny," I stammer, too embarrassed to admit the truth to him. "I guess it's too late to do much about it now."

"You could try. File a claim anyway. Maybe you could get enough money to pay for some of the renovations. Looks like you've already started fixing this old place up."

I'm also too embarrassed to tell him I doubt there's been any insurance on the place since Conrad's stroke. If Charles was willing to let Shadow Haven go to ruin, it's doubtful he'd wasted any money on insurance.

"We've made some progress, haven't we, Michaela? Got some new furniture, painted a few walls—"

"Want to see my room?" Michaela asks eagerly. She's obviously taken a shine to Danny Comeaux. Maybe it's the hat.

He glances uneasily at me, but I just shrug. "It's okay. I want you to see we're not living in squalor or anything, even though we've only managed to fix up a few rooms at the back, and the kitchen."

"I'm not here to pry."

I cock my head to the side and smile weakly. "Yes, you are. It's your job. I want you to go back and report to Social Services that things are just fine here, and that my mother-in-law is only trying to stir up trouble. Please, check it out inside."

I wait on the porch while Michaela shows the sheriff around, taking the time to cool my jets. I'm incensed at what Elizabeth Colquitt has done.

"Things are looking good in there," Danny says coming back onto the porch. "It's going to be a big job, though, Gabriella."

"I know. I want to bring Shadow Haven back to its glory, but it's going to take time, which I have, and gobs of money, which I don't have," I say with a rueful grin.

Danny turns his hat in his hands and looks extraordinarily uncomfortable. I thought we were through, but I can tell he has more to say. More bad news?

"What?" I ask.

He goes over to the table, picks up his iced tea glass and takes a drink before answering. He glances at Michaela, who has dashed off in pursuit of a butterfly.

"There was a fellow from New Orleans came into

the courthouse the other day, snooping around the tax office," he says. "He asked for the file on Shadow Haven, and Rosalie Odette, our clerk, took a look at it after he was gone."

I feel a tremor begin to shake my already unstable world. "What was in it?"

"Looks like somebody's gotten pretty far behind on paying the taxes on the place, Gabriella," he replies uneasily. "Guess Conrad let it slip when he got sick."

I stare at him, completely speechless. The blood seems to have drained from my head, and I'm dizzy. I hope I don't faint. But I know the truth. It wasn't Conrad Armand who'd failed to pay the taxes. It was Charles. Now I begin to shake in earnest. Why did Charles do these things? This land had value. Why had he let it go to ruin and risk having it sold off for back taxes?

But the answer strikes me with a cold brutality.

Because Charles didn't own this land.

When we married, Charles insisted that we sign a prenuptial agreement that prevented the assets he owned prior to the marriage from belonging to me afterward. I hadn't minded, because I wasn't after his money; indeed, I had no idea how incredibly wealthy he was. But perhaps I'd had some subconscious inkling even then that things wouldn't work out, because almost in retaliation, I insisted that Shadow Haven remain mine alone after the marriage. Charles hadn't liked it, but there wasn't much he could say, since he'd protected his own assets from me.

But when Conrad became ill and Charles intercepted the call meant for me, and apparently Danny's call as well, it appears he took the opportunity to get back at me for that move. Charles, to whom possession was everything, retaliated by letting my beloved Shadow Haven fall into ruin, knowing eventually it would likely be sold on the courthouse steps for back taxes.

I feel so betrayed I can't breathe.

I'm also astounded that the situation has only now been discovered. Or perhaps the tax office has been trying to collect for years and Charles ignored them. Whatever the case, the lawyer from New Orleans who brought this to Danny's attention could only be Jarrod Landry.

"How . . . much do I owe?"

Danny looks miserable. "More than thirty thousand dollars."

"Thirty thousand dollars!"

"I'm sorry I'm the one to have to break this to you, but I thought you'd want a heads-up about it. Jake Elden, our tax collector, is likely to call on you in the near future."

"It's okay, Danny. I . . . had no idea the taxes hadn't been paid. I'll take care of it right away."

He drains his glass and places it on the table by the pitcher. "Thanks for the tea, Michaela," he calls to her where she's playing in the yard. "Sure hit the spot on this hot day."

Michaela looks up at him, smiling. "You're welcome. Can you come again?"

He grins first at her, then at me. "I'll stop by from time to time, see how you're doing."

"Really, there's no need—"

He tips his hat. "My pleasure. Besides, it's my job to make sure everybody in the parish is safe and sound. Call me if you need me."

I watch Danny stride toward his cruiser and consider his parting words. Does he think Michaela isn't safe?

Fourteen

AFTER DANNY LEAVES, I FEEL AS IF I'M GOING TO explode. Damn Charles! Damn, damn, damn him! And damn Jarrod Landry! He must have gone directly from here to the tax office the day he came to call. I remember him saying, when he so cunningly dropped by the night I was prancing in the graveyard, that he'd had "some other business" in Tibonne that day.

Well, my back taxes are none of his business! It's clear to me now who he's really working for. He did a good job for Elizabeth that day, really earned his pay. He found out where we were living, under what marginal conditions, he got evidence that I might be mentally unstable, and he found out I'm in a precarious financial condition concerning Shadow Haven.

Damn, damn, damn him!

So much for his wanting to help me. If he was on my side, he would have told me about the taxes.

I hug my arms tightly around my body, as if trying

to keep myself from falling off the planet. I feel hopeless and helpless, vulnerable in a world that's gone cockeyed. I know I must pull my head from the sand and deal with all this, but I don't know what to do, where to turn.

I fall into the cushions of the porch swing and begin to push it to and fro with a gentle motion. In time with each movement, in a low voice I begin to chant the words that help me remember who I am: "I am Gabriella Deveaux, daughter of Juliette Deveaux, granddaughter of Ariella, and many generations descended from Angelique Deveaux, who endowed the women in her family with strength and special powers. I am Gabriella Deveaux, I have the Deveaux power. I am strong and can do anything I set my mind to. . . ."

My mind veers off the chanting and I remember the spirit's warning that "great evil" is approaching. What is "evil" anyway? I wonder. Aren't people who lie to you evil? Is there such a thing as lying by withholding the truth? Jarrod hasn't exactly lied; he's just failed to tell me a rather major piece of information. Why? Because he's going to use that information against me, even as he claims he wants to help me?

Things aren't as they seem. . . .

No, they aren't. And Jarrod Landry is not what he seems either. I must remember who I am and hold on to what power I have in his presence. I'm strongly attracted to him, and therein lies great danger. Until I know whose side he is on, I must guard against feelings that could weaken my judgment and place my future, and that of my daughter, in jeopardy.

As if I've conjured up the devil, Jarrod shows up at our doorstep the following morning. I'm not surprised when I hear his car in the drive. I've had a feeling all morning that he was coming our way, and it's rendered me a nervous wreck. It's one of the downsides, I'm discovering, of exploring the extent of one's psychic powers. You begin to sense things, both good and bad. I have only been toying with stretching my psychic intuition, and already I can tell a difference.

To remain steady as I waited for Jarrod's arrival, I made up a batch of beignets, those sugary fried treats so famous in New Orleans. Michaela has helped and is covered with powdered sugar when she hears the car. Before I can stop her, she races to the front door to see who has come to call. I wipe my hands on a towel and try to compose myself. I must be very careful what I say to him, although I intend to give him a good piece of my mind for snooping into my business.

I reach the front door in time to hear Michaela say, "We're having ben-yays. Would you like one?"

"They're my favorite," Jarrod says, his gaze moving from Michaela's to mine as I approach. "I'd love one, if it's okay with your mother."

No, it's not okay. Since my troubling dream and Danny's visit, I'm wary of Jarrod Landry. I'd rather he not come here again. But Michaela is already dragging him through the front door. I remember how eagerly she welcomed Danny yesterday. Is it her father she misses, or a male presence in her life?

"What are you hiding?" Michaela asks, pointing to the hand Jarrod holds behind his back.

"Oh, just a little something I brought along for you." He hands her a brightly wrapped package. Michaela looks to me for permission to accept it, and I shrug. *Sure, why not bribe the little girl to gain her affection, Mr. Lawyer?*

Very carefully, Michaela eases the cellophane tape away from the gift wrap to make sure she doesn't tear it, and I see Jarrod frown. He probably can't believe Michaela shows so much restraint when her mother dances half-naked by candlelight in the cemetery.

"Look, Mother, an alligator," Michaela says, holding up a plush toy.

"It's wonderful, *chérie*," I reply unenthusiastically. "What do you say?"

Michaela turns to Jarrod. "Thank you, Mr. Jarrod."

"You're welcome. Just make sure that's the only 'gator you play with," he teases.

"Don't worry, I'm not going out there," Michaela assures him, looking out the front door into the sleepy, swampy landscape of her new home. "I saw real alligators on the Discovery Channel. They're dangerous." She looks up at him. "I can't watch the Discovery Channel anymore. We don't have a TV."

Jarrod glances at me and cocks a brow. I feel my hackles rise. "It's not because I can't afford it," I reply a little too defensively. "There's no cable out here and I haven't had time to get a satellite dish."

Michaela ushers him into the kitchen.

"I'm not sure it's a bad thing, not having TV," he says mildly. "Guess you haven't had time to get a phone, either."

His manner is irritating. I follow him into the kitchen, ready to let him have it when the opportunity presents itself. I don't want to blow up in front of Michaela, however, so I invoke the patience mantra and try to act as if everything is just peachy.

He takes a seat at the table by the window, and I set down a small plate, then push the beignets toward him. "Want coffee?"

"Yes, please."

"*Au lait?*"

"No, just black."

It could be my imagination, but he seems nervous. Or am I perceiving him like that because I'm a basket case myself? I turn my back to him to pour the coffee so he won't see my hands shake. Even so, the cup rattles in the saucer when I serve him.

Michaela sits at the table with us for a moment, then moves off with her new toy to one of the two large chairs in the corner of the kitchen by the old stone fireplace. If I keep my voice low, she'll be out of earshot. I turn to Jarrod.

"I take it you've talked to Elizabeth," I confront him at last.

"She called again yesterday morning," he admits.

"She wasn't happy that I hadn't called her right away after coming to see you."

"Why didn't you?" I'm not sure I believe he didn't.

"It bought us a couple of days."

"What difference does that make? Why not just go to court and get it over with?" I can't keep the bitterness from my voice.

He turns to me, frowning. "Is that what you want?"

I plop down in the chair opposite him and cross my arms on the table. "Of course that's not what I want. But that's what's going to happen, isn't it? So why not get it over with?"

"Gabriella, what's wrong? What's happened that you're so angry this morning?"

"Angry? Me angry? Whatever would give you that impression?"

"Body language. Tone of voice. The look in your eyes." He pauses, then adds with a hint of a smile, "bared teeth?"

"You are really something, you know that, Jarrod? You barge in here uninvited, sit at my table, drink my coffee, and act like this is some kind of joke."

The smile dies in an instant. "It's no joke," he says. "I'm sorry. But you weren't like this the other day. What's happened?"

"The sheriff dropped by yesterday with a couple of little bombshells, thanks to you."

"The sheriff?" He is clearly surprised, or an excellent actor.

"Seems like after Elizabeth found out from you

where we were, she called the parish Social Services department and reported a case of child abuse here. They sent the sheriff to check it out."

Jarrod's face turns a shade of red, and a frown furrows his brow, but he doesn't say anything. He probably already knew about this. Might have been his suggestion.

"Of course," I continue, my temper rising, "you know all about the unpaid taxes after your little visit to the courthouse. I'm sure Elizabeth was delighted to learn that tidbit, although the situation is her own son's doing, damn his hide."

At this, Jarrod bolts out of his chair and moves around the table, taking the seat next to me. He reaches for my hands, but I pull them away. He reaches for them again and this time holds them tightly. "Elizabeth knows nothing about the taxes. And I knew nothing of her phone call."

I hold his gaze steadily with my own and try to ignore the pulse I feel beating rapidly in his hands. I must hold steady and stand up to him.

"Yeah, right. Jarrod, why can't you just be honest and say you're representing them? Why all this pretense that you want to be my friend?" I bat my eyelids against the tears that threaten. I will not cry. I will not show weakness.

"I'm not exactly representing them," he says quietly. "But there are things you don't know, Gabriella. This is a much more complex situation than you can imagine. I didn't call Elizabeth back right away because I need some time to . . . work some things out."

"What things? And if the situation is so complex, why don't you explain it to me? Do you think I'm stupid?"

"Of course I don't think you're stupid. And maybe in time, I can explain," he says, and he looks oddly sad and troubled. "In the meantime, I'm doing everything I can to find a way to get them to drop all this so that it never goes to court."

I want to believe him. I want so badly to believe him. His hands are warm and strong around mine. His voice sounds sincere. And I desperately need a friend.

Still, I withdraw my hands and fold them in my lap. "How much time do you think it will take to, as you say, work those things out?"

He hesitates, as if trying to decide where to go next in this unhappy conversation. "I've hired a man in New York, Gabriella. A private investigator. He's looking into Charles's recent activities to see if he was involved in anything . . . shady or immoral. If he was, I believe I can use that information to get the Colquitts to back off. They deplore anything scandalous." He looks me in the eyes. "That's one reason I came back to see you today, to see if you know of any such thing we could use."

I'm stunned. Charles had been less than a wonderful husband to me, but I never suspected him of being involved in any kind of shady dealings. And yet, there is his deceit concerning Conrad Armand and the unpaid taxes. If that isn't shady, I don't know what is. Still, I find Jarrod's inquiry distasteful.

"Isn't this rather crass? I mean, coming to the grieving widow to get dirt on her dead husband?"

"Crass as it may seem, damn it, I've played hardball with the Colquitts before. I agree it's not a pretty approach, but it's the kind of thing that might stop them."

His straightforward and fervent answer startles me, and I settle back in my chair, considering his strategy. It's possible that it might work, if there's anything bad to be found out about Charles. I deplore the artifice, but then I see Michaela curled up in the chair in the corner, playing happily. I think about all the times Charles and his parents hurt me. I think about losing Michaela to them.

And suddenly I don't find Jarrod's approach so offensive after all. It's time I played hardball as well. "I guess I can go along with that, but there's a few matters I want cleared up between us first. Let's talk about your visit to the tax office in Tibonne."

Fifteen

"WHY DID YOU GO THERE, JARROD?" I DEMAND, "AND why didn't you tell me what you found? If you're really on my side, why didn't you come straight here and let me know I was in trouble?"

Jarrod eases back in his chair and takes a deep breath. "I told you the other day that it's my job to learn the truth about any situation in which I'm involved as a lawyer," he says, not boastfully but earnestly. "That means finding out where my clients might be vulnerable. I know you don't consider yourself my client, but if I'm going to resolve this out of court, I need every bit of information I can get to make that happen. I don't want any surprises. So, since I was in Tibonne, I decided to see what the legal status of your property is. It's public record."

He leans forward again and rests his arms on the table. "Why didn't I come tell you right away? Actually, that's why I came back here that night after my appointment in Napoleana. But you . . . uh . . .

were preoccupied with your ceremony, so I decided to wait until a more appropriate time. Like today."

A silence falls between us. That would explain his sudden appearance in the enchanted garden that night. He must have seen the candlelight on his way up the lane and stopped to investigate. His reason for going to the courthouse in the first place makes sense as well. "Well, okay, then," I mumble, not eager to let go of my anger. It helps me keep my distance.

"I'm sorry if I've stirred up trouble, Gabriella," he says. "But if Elizabeth and Rupert learn about the unpaid taxes, they could use that as an example, for instance, of your supposed . . . irresponsibility."

"My irresponsibility! It was Charles's job to pay those taxes. Charles assured me when we got married that we would always keep Shadow Haven in good condition."

"And you believed him?"

Four little words. How they sting.

I can't bring myself to answer that at the moment. I don't want to think what a fool I was to believe anything Charles Colquitt said. I stand and go to the window, shoving my hands deep into my jeans pockets, my back to Jarrod. Only then can I find the words to reply.

"I believed Charles for a long time, Jarrod." My voice is tight. "Our life together was . . . difficult, but he always took care of Michaela and me. We wanted for nothing, except his love. He was a respected businessman, involved in civic organizations. Cold and aloof to me, though Mr. Charming to the outside world. But I had no reason to believe he wasn't taking care of Shadow Haven." I explain to him the arrangements we'd made with Conrad Armand.

Jarrod considers what I've told him in silence for a few moments, then, as if he has me on the witness stand, asks, "Why would Charles accuse you of mental instability?"

His question catches me off guard, and I'm not prepared to answer it. So I hedge. "I . . . I'm not sure."

"Can you think of anything, an offhand comment or some kind of behavior that he found odd and disconcerting, that might have triggered it?"

Cold sweat prickles my face. I know exactly what had provoked Charles, but I'm not about to share it with anyone else, ever, except Michaela, when it's time for her to learn more about the gift of the Deveaux women. I remember clearly that horrible night when I dared to share with my husband the secret to my success—my ability to commune with the dead.

Celebrating the successful conclusion of one of my commissions, we'd enjoyed a lovely, quiet dinner, drank some wine, and I was feeling confident because Charles had been unusually complimentary about my work, probably because I had pleased one of his most important clients. His solicitude gave me false courage, and the wine muddied my judgment. I decided that the time had come for him to know the truth.

But when I told him, his face had turned white, and it contorted into a horrible expression. At first I thought I'd frightened him, but then suddenly he jerked me out of my chair and slapped me hard across the face.

"You crazy bitch!" he'd shouted. "You stupid, crazy bitch! What're you trying to do, ruin me? Don't you ever talk like that again. If my colleagues heard you, they'd never let me live it down."

Absently, I touch the cheek he had struck. "I . . . I can't," I stammer, meaning *I can't tell you*, but Jarrod thinks I can't think of anything.

"There's nothing, an incident, a specific argument, that comes to mind? Something must have happened to have to put such a notion in his head, even if he knew it was a lie."

I bite my lip. There were lots of things that could have caused Charles to make up that lie. He'd always told me I was different, and after the glamour of our elopement wore off, when I moved into his world, he'd realized just how different. A girl from the bayou, no matter how attractive, was a fish out of water in his New York society.

Standing here, looking back from a distance of time and space, I can see that even early in our marriage, Charles had been embarrassed by my peculiarity. Shortly after we returned to New York, he'd started criticizing the way I dressed, the way I cooked, even my language. He criticized many things about me over the years, except my art. Perhaps the clients to whom he introduced me saw me as an eccentric artist, not a bayou girl. At any rate, they praised me, commissioned me, and paid me well, and Charles didn't dare criticize that.

He was fine with my work until I told him that I talked to his clients' dead loved ones. I guess that sent him over the edge. I was just too different, therefore I must be crazy.

"Charles . . . hasn't loved me in a long time, Jarrod," I attempt to explain, a pain tightening my chest. I turn to him. "You were right when you told me that night I'd never fit in with his world."

Jarrod looks uncomfortable. "I should never have come here that night. I was way out of line."

"Why did you come, Jarrod?" I welcome the opportunity to deflect the conversation from myself and to get an answer to that eight-year-old question.

"When you and Charles started dating, I had no idea things would get so serious so fast. I was shocked when he told me you were getting married, and I guess I thought it was my duty, however misguided, to warn you about him." He presses his lips into a tight line, as if to cut off further explanation. But I'm not going to let him off the hook. I want to know more.

"You and Charles were friends then, or at least that's what I thought, until you told me all those things about him."

"Charles was my friend, once," Jarrod replies in a heavy tone. "He was a difficult friend, but I always cut him a lot of slack because I felt sorry for him; he was under incredible pressure from his parents. But he betrayed our friendship in a way that it could never be fully repaired."

His expression is sad, but he continues. "I'd contacted Antioch House in New York to help me liquidate the art and antiquities in my aunt's estate because she had many valuable pieces and frankly, they're the best in the business. I didn't know at the time Charles had gone to work for them, or that they'd assigned him to my project. I was shocked and upset when he stepped off the plane, but when I called the company to ask for someone else, they had no one available. That's the reason he was at Aunt Rebecca's memorial service, not because he was my friend."

I'm dying to know what Charles did to destroy the friendship, but the look on Jarrod's face stops me from pressing him further. Whatever it was, it's obviously still very painful for him.

"I'm sorry. I was just curious. . . ."

Jarrod clears his throat. "It's water under the bridge. I guess we'd better get back to the subject, why Charles accused you of being mentally unstable."

I fidget in discomfort. "There could be any number of things he held against me that he could have twisted into his wretched accusation." I tell Jarrod about Charles's constant criticism of my oddball ways. "He was never happy with me after we left Shadow Haven."

"Why did you stay with him, Gabriella?" His question is probing but gentle.

A lump forms in my throat. "I . . . I thought about leaving many times. But Michaela loved Charles, and in his own way, he loved her as well. She was happy, and that's what I wanted for her. I was afraid if I left Charles, she'd be the one who'd suffer the most."

We are silent for a long time before Jarrod resumes his line of questioning. His voice is quiet when he does.

"You say Charles hadn't loved you for a long time. Maybe he wanted a divorce, but for appearances didn't want to be the bad guy. So he made up the accusation of you being mentally unstable to give him an excuse to bail on you." Then he adds in an undertone, "He's pretty good at bailing on women in trouble."

"What are you talking about?"

"I'm talking about Charles wanting to walk out on his responsibility to you." His quiet tone is gone, replaced by a harshness, a sudden anger that I don't understand. "Did he ever threaten to have you committed or anything?"

His question takes me by surprise. "No. That would have been too big an embarrassment to him and his precious family. Besides, he knew I wasn't crazy. I'd never pass their tests proving I was mentally unstable. No, he just started staying away from me. In our last couple of years together, he was gone on business most of the time, which was fine with me, but it was hard on Michaela. He was on a business trip when he died."

"Elizabeth said he was killed in a plane crash?"

"Yes. It was his company plane. It crashed into a mountainside in Montana." I didn't mean to confide anything to Jarrod about the strange circumstances surrounding my husband's death, but my words tumble out.

"It was a total shock to me. He was supposed to be in a meeting in Toronto. Even his boss didn't know what he was doing flying over Montana."

"Was he having an affair?"

Another pain shoots through me. "I wouldn't be surprised. Charles was a virile man. . . ." I let the implication lie. I can't bring myself to tell Jarrod that I hadn't slept with Charles in more than two years. It made sense that he would seek sex in other places.

"That may give us something to work with," he says, his tone all business now. "I'll put my man on it, see if he can find out if Charles had another woman. Now, tell me about your work," he goes on with relentless determination. "Elizabeth mentioned that you were gone a lot and claimed that Michaela had been raised mostly by her nanny."

My temper flares again. "She would say that, wouldn't she, because it serves her case, but she has no idea how often I was gone. Mrs. Bolton had a great deal of influence on Michaela, unfortunately, but she certainly didn't raise her."

"Elizabeth told me she hired the nanny, at Charles's request. Didn't you have any say in the matter?"

"I didn't want a nanny." I'm seething again. "But

Charles was adamant. He insisted that I resume my work shortly after Michaela was born, and Mrs. Bolton came with top-notch references. I gave in to Charles; sometimes it was easier to do that than put up with his tantrums."

Jarrod glowers. "I understand. Been there, done that. But being the devil's advocate, it's not unreasonable for him to have offered you some help with child care."

"No," I reply, but I remember the violent argument that had erupted between us over the hiring of a nanny so early in Michaela's life. "I suppose it isn't. But he insisted that I take up my work again as soon as I could, when I . . . I just wanted time to be a mother."

Jarrod's eyes light up for a moment, and he smiles. "Tell that to a judge, and Elizabeth Colquitt will have a harder time than she expects."

CHAPTER

Sixteen

THE MORNING HAS FLOWN. THE REMAINING BEIGNETS lie cold and unappetizing on the plate. Our conversation lags. I'm emotionally drained from answering Jarrod's very personal questions about my relationship with Charles, and I'm glad he seems to have finished with them.

At the same time, my earlier distrust of him has dissipated. I don't know why he's working so hard to get the Colquitts to give up their quest, even paying a private investigator out of his own pocket, but it seems he means me no harm. Perhaps his motives have nothing to do with helping me, but rather stem from whatever happened that destroyed his friendship with Charles. Maybe he feels that by thwarting Charles's wishes as expressed in the codicil, he'll gain some kind of posthumous revenge.

Whatever his motive, I've seen another side of Jarrod this morning. Before, he seemed to exude an almost cocky confidence, but today, I caught a glimpse of pain from time to time reflected in his eyes when he spoke about his former friend. I guess we both carry some battle scars from having known Charles Colquitt.

Jarrod gets ready to take his leave, and Michaela and I walk him to his car. Before he gets in, he bends and picks her up in his large arms, and I'm astonished to see her give him a hug. It occurs to me that Michaela is as emotionally bereft as I am and equally as vulnerable. I hope Jarrod's overt attentions are sincere, and that she can trust him with her own fragile affections. I would happily kill him, or anyone, who hurt her with deceit.

"Call me," he says to me over her shoulder, "if you need anything at all."

There is a tiny lightning second when his gaze locks with mine, and I feel that undeniable sensual chemistry that exists between us whether I like it or not. I swallow, remembering the disconcerting sensations that swept over me the night he came upon me in the graveyard.

"I . . . okay . . ." I stammer, not knowing what to do with these feelings. They are dangerous, I know, and threaten to undermine my newfound determination to reclaim the soul of my Deveaux heritage.

I wonder what Jarrod would think if he knew the truth about my gift. Would he, like Charles, be afraid of it? That's a question that will never be answered, because I'll never share that secret again with anyone who is not a Deveaux. Still, I wonder if Jarrod has the capacity to accept what Charles could not. He sets

Michaela down, engages my gaze for a moment longer, and then is gone.

As I watch the BMW round the bend in the lane and disappear into the shadows beneath the canopy of trees, I have to admit I'm sorry to see him go. How odd and inconsisent of me. This morning, I never wanted Jarrod Landry on my property again. By noon, he's managed to maneuver his way back into my trust, and, it would seem, into my heart as well.

Nothing is as it seems. . . .

I nod to the warning that sounds crystal clear inside my head. "I know, I know," I whisper. It's good that something is reminding me of what I seem to so easily forget when I'm around Jarrod. My determination needs backup, and my head needs to stay firmly in control of my heart.

Jarrod's assessment of the damage the Colquitts could do if they learned about the unpaid taxes prompts me to take care of them immediately. No one, especially not the tax collector, is going to lay a hand on Shadow Haven now that I've returned. It may be too big for the two of us, but it's my home, and it will remain so until I pass it along to Michaela.

"Come on, *chérie*," I call to Michaela. "Get on your sandals, and I'll take you to town for lunch."

The tax office is in the old courthouse building that dominates the town square. Before the big discount store came to the outskirts of Tibonne, the square had been a thriving community center, with shops and a small movie theater, a place where neighbor greeted neighbor and shared a few minutes on a park bench.

But as I pull into a parking space in front of the courthouse, I see only a few people in the square. There are a couple of shops left, but there are also lots of empty storefronts. This change in Tibonne saddens me.

Our footsteps echo on the well-worn hardwood floors of the courthouse hall, and I locate the number of the tax collector's office on a faded menu board. The place smells dank and musty, and the outside heat follows us down the hallway.

The tax office itself, however, boasts an air conditioner, and although the furniture is worn and shabby, the desks are neat, the counter clean and polished. No one is present when we enter, so we sit in the small waiting area. Moments later, I hear a noise and look up to see the face of a little girl peering from behind the counter. Her eyes are large and brown and curious.

"You here to see my mama?" she asks.

I grin. "I don't think so. We're here to see Jake Elden."

The girl frowns. "Oh, Jake's not here. He doesn't come to work 'cept sometimes."

A part-time tax collector? Maybe that's all Tibonne can afford these days. Maybe that's why my unpaid taxes have gone unnoticed for so long.

"Who works here most of the time?"

"My mama."

"And her name is . . . ?"

"Rosalie Odette." The girl beams proudly. "She'll be right back."

Slowly, the imp edges around the corner and approaches Michaela. "My name's Kisha. What's yours?"

Michaela cocks her head slightly. "Michaela," she replies hesitantly.

"You from around here?"

"I, uh . . ." Michaela glances uneasily up at me, and I expect she's about to reply that she is from New York. But she surprises me.

"I'm living at my mama's plantation," Michaela says.

My eyes widen, and joy leaps through me. Michaela hadn't exactly said she lived at *her home*, but neither had she announced that she was from New York. And she'd used the term "mama" rather than "mother." Perhaps because that's what Kisha had called her own mother. Whatever the reason, I don't care. I'm thrilled.

A stout woman bustles through the door and stops when she sees the three of us in the waiting area. She places hands on hips and looks at Kisha. "Why, Kisha, what are you doing? I told you to stay behind the counter."

"This here's Mi-KAY-la," she says, pronouncing the name slowly, as if it were exotic to her ears. "She lives on her mama's plantation."

At that, Rosalie Odette's head jerks toward me, and in an instant, we recognize each another as former classmates in high school. I stand up. "Rosalie? Rosalie Simmons?"

Rosalie looks at me with shining eyes and a poignant smile. "I heard you were back, Gabriella."

I grimace. "I imagine you've heard more than that. I'm here about the taxes due on Shadow Haven."

Rosalie's bright smile fades. "I'm sorry about all that. Nobody'd have known if that man hadn't come snooping around." She gives a small laugh. "Guess I did my share of snooping too, after he left. That's when I found out your family's place was in trouble."

Out of the corner of my eye, I see Kisha beckon to Michaela to follow her behind the counter. Michaela looks to me for permission, and I look in turn to Rosalie.

"Oh, it's okay. I bring Kisha in when there's no school. She likes to play office. I set her up her own little desk, and she has a calculator. Figure it's good practical training for when she grows up. Wish they had computers here, but the parish is too poor for that."

The two little girls skitter away, and I'm happy that perhaps Michaela has found a playmate. Rosalie takes the seat vacated by Michaela, and to my surprise, takes both my hands in hers.

"How you doing, Gabriella? It's been a long time since I've seen you, and I heard from Danny that your husband died recently. Is there anything I can do to help?"

At this woman's compassionate offer, my throat tightens. What a long time it's been since I had a friend. Someone who wasn't also Charles's friend, someone who might see my side of things. Jarrod claims to be my friend, but the jury's still out on that one.

"I . . . I'm trying to get my life back in order," I admit, letting down my defenses just a little, "but it's difficult. I left so long ago, and coming back isn't as easy as I thought. The house was in really bad shape when we first got here, but I've managed to sort out and fix up some of it. We're living in a couple of back rooms until I can restore the rest of it. It's not so bad, but—"

"—it's not so good, either," Rosalie finishes for me. "I'm aware of what happened to the house," she says. "Damn shame about those druggies. And poor old Conrad. He was beside himself when all that happened. Said he'd tried to get in touch with you but never got to talk to you directly."

I straighten and take a deep breath. I'm not going where Rosalie's conversation is leading. "I'm here about the back taxes," I remind her. My cheeks grow warm with embarrassment. "I know this sounds lame, but I didn't know they hadn't been paid. . . ."

Rosalie pats my hand. "Maybe we can get Jake to let you pay it out over time," she suggests.

I shake my head. "No, I have some money from Charles's insurance, and I want to pay the bill in full right away." I take out my checkbook. "Can you get the records and tell me exactly what I owe?"

Rosalie's eyes widen slightly, and I imagine her curiosity is raging. The Gabriella she knew in high school certainly couldn't have written a check for such a large amount as I believe I owe. She goes to a filing cabinet in the inner office and produces the file on Shadow Haven. "Thirty-one thousand, two hundred and ninety-eight dollars. That'll catch you up until next January."

I swallow hard. Neither am I accustomed to writing checks that large. But I have the money to cover it—and more—although the need to resume my career suddenly becomes more urgent.

I hand the check to Rosalie, making sure she changes the mailing address on the tax records so I won't miss another notice when they come due again. I also get the name of a local insurance agent, with the intent of purchasing sufficient coverage on the house in case of another disaster.

We hear the girls giggling and turn to see them whispering little-girl secrets.

"Looks like they've hit it off," Rosalie says. "Tell you what. I'm taking the afternoon off to be with Kisha. Gonna take her to McDonald's for lunch and then to a movie. Would you like a little 'mother's-day-out'? I'd be happy to take Michaela, too, and bring her home this evening. We live on the road out to Shadow Haven."

I'm startled by the offer. I hadn't thought I needed time away from Michaela, but now that Rosalie mentions it, it occurs to me that I haven't been away from her one single day since I fired Mrs. Bolton. Am I so frightened of losing my daughter that I haven't let her out of my sight? Watching Michaela at play with another child makes me consider that perhaps she needs time away from me as well, and time with someone her own age. I turn to Rosalie.

"You know, I think that would be great. Michaela's been so lonely." I dig in my purse and draw out my wallet. "Let me treat."

But Rosalie raises her hands, palms toward me. "No way. You've been through some hard times lately. Let me take Michaela today. You can treat another time."

I'm deeply touched at her consideration. I guess I've forgotten the kindness of friendship. I summon my voice. "Thank you, Rosalie."

Seventeen

ROSALIE BRINGS MICHAELA HOME LATE IN THE afternoon. Although I missed my daughter and kept looking for her as I ran my errands, I also enjoyed the free time. I went to the library, had the car serviced, signed up for homeowners' insurance, and bought a present for Michaela and her new friend, a swing set for the side yard at Shadow Haven. I hope I can put it together by myself.

"Can you stay for a while?" I ask Rosalie. "I have some mint tea in the fridge."

She hesitates, then says, "Sure, why not? I don't exactly have a hot date waiting on me or anything."

While we sip our tea I learn that the last ten years haven't been easy for Rosalie either. Both her parents died, and her husband left her for another woman. Still, she's managed to keep her spirits up and get on with her life. I can learn a lesson from Rosalie Odette.

Even as she tells me her story, she doesn't pry for details about mine, and I'm grateful. I wonder if Danny told her about the anonymous phone call to

Social Services and that my ex in-laws are trying to take custody of my daughter. If she knows, she isn't saying anything.

She helps me assemble the swing set, and I discover that she's pretty handy with a screwdriver and pliers. "Living alone can have its benefits," she tells me as she tightens the last screw and we heave the frame into an upright position. "You learn to fend for yourself. 'Course, sometimes it gets mighty lonely."

I don't mention that one can get lonely in a marriage as well.

"What are you going to do with yourself out here all alone?" she asks, the first really personal question she's put to me.

"That's a good question. I expect I'll have to go back to work once we're settled." I explain to her what I do for a living, leaving out, of course, the part that concerns my gift.

"You carve cemetery statues?" Rosalie is incredulous, then breaks out in hearty laughter. "You always were the strange one, girl. I never thought about it, but I guess someone has to make those monuments to the dead."

I take her comments in good stride. It *is* a rather unusual occupation. My concern, which I do not share with Rosalie, is where I will get customers. In the past, Charles brought clients to me, contacts he'd made at the firm where he served as legal counsel, Antioch House, Liquidators of Fine Art and Antiquities. I have a few names I can use for reference, and, it occurs to me, once this custody business is behind us, maybe Jarrod could introduce me around in New Orleans.

"Being the parish clerk, I know who all's died around here," Rosalie says with another laugh. "I'll see if I can send some business your way."

After Rosalie and Kisha leave, I miss them. How good it was to have someone to talk to, someone I can trust without wondering about ulterior motives. Michaela, too, seems happier tonight for having been with Kisha.

Patience. Grandnana knew what she was talking about. It takes time to build a new life, make new friendships. Time, and the will to keep on going. Meeting Rosalie today has raised my spirits, and I go to bed with a lighter heart, even though I can't ignore the dark forces that beset me.

Another powerful dream assails my sleep tonight, a horrid, terrifying nightmare that even in my slumber I recognize as a portent of things to come.

In the dream, I'm running through the swamp, trying to escape somebody or *something* that is determined to destroy me. At first it's a vague threat, dreamlike marsh gas leading me ever deeper into the swampy bayou. I don't want to go there, but I'm unable to break away from its spell. I struggle to turn away, and at last plunge backward into the darkness.

And then I am running. Something is following, something with foul breath and yellow eyes. Tree branches brush against my face as I struggle through the wooded swampland, desperate to elude my pursuer. The hanging moss stings the skin of my cheek, skin already sensitive where Charles has slapped me.

Charles! It is Charles who is chasing me. Renewed terror sends my heart racing. I must get away from him. He'll kill me if he catches me. Looking over my shoulder, I can see his yellow eyes gleaming in the darkness. Yellow eyes, and savage white teeth.

This is Charles, and yet it isn't. What creature is it that's breathing heavily close behind me? Fear and panic threaten to overwhelm me. I know this creature. It's the *loup-garou!* By day a man, by night a wolf, the feared monster of the swamp. Cursed beast, who kills and maims without mercy. He's a shapeshifter, and in my dream, he's showing himself in the form of Charles.

Run! My breath tears painfully from my lungs as I pick my way through the dangerous terrain. On one side is a black water swamp, on the other a dense, tangled forest with cypress knees waiting to trip me up.

"You bitch!" I hear him call, and it's Charles's voice that echoes through the night. "You crazy bitch!"

I cover my ears with my hands and run on into the darkness. I run and run until I become suddenly aware he's no longer following me. I pause, listening, like a deer alert for a hunter. He's out there, but he isn't chasing me now. And then I hear diabolical laughter.

"You think you can run away from me, Gabriella? You think you've escaped? You'll never escape, because you're mine. I own you, and I'll never let you go." That's Charles's voice, I'd swear it.

Malicious laughter again, and suddenly Charles, not the *loup-garou*, is standing in front of me. His eyes reflect an evil yellow glow, and his lips are stretched back in a wicked, mocking smile. "You can't run from me, Gabriella," he says. "I want what's mine. You'll do as I say." And then he reaches out and places the evil golden torc around my neck. "You will wear this, bitch. You ungrateful bitch!"

My skin sears beneath it's weight. "No!" I scream, clutching my neck in agony as the torc burns a deep wound into my skin. "No-o-o-o!"

CHAPTER

Eighteen

THE DREAM SCREAM TRIES TO TEAR FROM MY THROAT, but it erupts as only a choked, gurgling sound. It awakens me nonetheless, and I sit up, soaked in a cold sweat, heart thundering. I rub my neck, half expecting to feel the burning torc there, but my skin is bare and cool.

I hug my knees to my body and try to stop shaking. It was only a dream, I tell myself, gulping in long breaths of air. A bad dream. But it was so *real*. I can almost smell the foul breath of the *loup-garou*.

But there's no such thing as the *loup-garou*; it's just a Cajun fable favored in the swamps. Whenever Grandnana had told me about the *loup-garou*, she'd always laughed afterward, assuring me there was no such creature.

After this dream, I'm not so sure.

It takes a few moments for me to calm down enough to get out of bed. I fumble in the dark for my woven cotton shawl that I keep on my bedside chair and sling it over my shoulders. I tiptoe into the large front room of the dark, empty house. It was only a dream, but I peer out into the night anyway, making sure the yellow-eyed monster isn't lurking outside.

I go to Michaela's room, needing to assure myself that she is safe from the dream-beast, and to my relief, I see that she lies in peaceful slumber, her dark hair splayed over the white pillowcase. One hand is above her head, the other near her cheek. I stroke my daughter's hair, and a pain sears through my heart. I'm sorry Michaela longs so for her father, but deep in my heart, I believe that she's safer in the world with Charles dead.

You're mine. I own you. You'll do as I say. . . .

The words from my dream illustrate exactly how Charles perceived our relationship. He was the possessor, I the possession. As was Michaela. As was everything in his life. Charles Colquitt could not be happy unless he owned and controlled everything around him. Suddenly, I get it why he'd freaked out when I told him about my gift. It wasn't because I was too different and peculiar. It wasn't even his fear that I would embarrass him with my mumbo jumbo, as he'd called it.

No. He came unglued because, like my name, my gift was a part of me he could never own.

I guess that was too much for his ego to bear, for from that moment, he began to disown me. He called me crazy. He added the codicil to his will. He told his mother that I was delusional. Charles, who rarely spoke to his mother.

Unsettled, I curl into a rocking chair to watch over my sleeping daughter. I begin to rock gently, thinking about this night's dream and going back to the one I had earlier in which a spirit had spoken through the silver-haired woman, warning me of impending danger. Were the dreams related?

The *loup-garou* who chased me through this dream could represent the evil of which the spirit warned. The *loup-garou*, the shape-shifting beast. *Nothing is as it seems.*

I think about the silver-haired woman. Who was she, that reluctant messenger? She'd given me a name in the dream, but it has faded in my memory.

As I rock, listening to the night sounds outside, I think about Grandnana's spirit's appearance to Michaela. I remember Michaela telling me that the old woman she saw wanted me to go and find somebody named Mary Frances.

Mary Frances. It sounds familiar. *Mary Frances. Mary Frances,* I think as I rock. The name isn't quite right, but with each tilt of the chair, it morphs ever so slightly until it becomes *Marie Françoise. Marie Françoise. Marie Françoise.* The name of the woman in my dream.

Then, from the shadows of my childhood, memory flickers faintly, bringing to mind an image of a woman around the same age as Grandnana, with silver hair and strange indigo eyes. With that image comes the sound of city traffic, and I see myself as a child, holding on to Grandnana's hand and entering a store or shop of some kind. I recall the acrid smell of incense and a heavy feel to the air.

I'm about to fully remember the incident when I suddenly become aware that a heavy silence now surrounds me. The tree frogs have grown still; the night sounds have ceased. I distinctly feel a dark energy, an evil in the air.

And then I hear voices, muffled but identifiably male, and the hair on the back of my neck stands on end.

I jump out of the rocker and dash to the front of the house where I think the voices are coming from. The moon is just beginning to rise, but there is light enough to outline the figures of two men who are stealthily approaching the house.

My skin turns icy. I've forgotten once again to get a cell phone, and there are prowlers on my land. Sickened with fear, I run into my bedroom to get the gun. I have no other choice if I wish to fend them off. I'm shaking so badly I can hardly manage to unlock the travel bag, but eventually I lay my hands on the gun and am able to load it.

As I emerge again into the hall, I hear a footstep on the verandah. What should I do? The men are going to break into the house, of that I have no doubt. Visions of the vandalism wreaked upon my house by the drug runners flash through my mind, and I wonder if these two intruders might be the ones Conrad Armand had mentioned who might have escaped the drug raid.

And then I think of Michaela. Dear God, I can't let them get to Michaela. Impulsively, I jerk the front door open and turn on the porch light. The two men are wearing ski masks, so I can't see their faces, but I can guess their surprise. They freeze like animals caught in headlights.

"Get off my property," I demand, praying that my voice doesn't crack. "Get off now, or I'll shoot."

Neither man says a word, but one laughs, shakes his head slowly and takes a step toward me. I raise the gun. "I'm warning you." As if he hasn't heard me, the man takes another step in my direction. If I don't stop him now, he'll reach me and take the gun, and no telling what might happen then. My heart in my throat, I aim for his leg, but my hand is shaking badly. Still, I pull the trigger, and the man falls to his knees.

"Jesus!" the other man swears. "Wait! Don't shoot! Let me get him, and we'll get out of here. Just don't shoot!" He speaks with a heavy Latino accent.

I'm quaking so hard I doubt I could shoot again, but I hold my ground. "I'll kill you if you ever set foot on my land again," I tell them, and mean it.

I hold the gun in both hands, still pointing it in the direction of the wounded man and watch as the able one lifts him over his shoulder and scuttles away into the night.

Only when they're gone does the enormity of what I've done hit me. I might have killed that man. Just because I aimed low doesn't mean I hit him in the leg. The way he fell forward, I didn't see the wound.

Dear Jesus, Mary, and Joseph! Bile rises in my throat, and my stomach roils. I barely make it to the porch rail before I retch violently over the side.

"Mama? Are you sick? What happened?" Michaela comes running onto the porch, and her eyes grow wide when she sees the gun. "What's that?"

I look down at the weapon. "That," I murmur, "is really dangerous in my hands at the moment."

That, also, I admit silently, is all that stood between us and bodily harm. I figure the men had come to rob the house, but I have little doubt they might have attempted to rape me as well. Perhaps they would have kidnapped Michaela. I don't like what I've just done, but I had to do it.

Shaking and sweaty, I put my hand on Michaela's shoulder. "Come on, let's go back to bed. I thought I heard an animal on the porch. I shot the gun to scare it away." It wasn't a total lie. Those men were animals, and I don't think they'll come back, at least not tonight.

I tuck Michaela beneath the covers, but I have no intention of going back to my own bed. I turn out the lights, make sure the doors and windows are all locked, and settle down again in the rocking chair, gun in my lap, this time to guard against more than nightmares.

Of one thing I am certain. My dream was precognitive. The creature who chased me through the swamp in my dream showed up on my doorstep only a short while later. Perhaps there is such a thing as the *loup-garou*. If so, I believe I've met him face-to-face.

My stomach has stopped churning, and I begin to think rationally about what I've done. I've committed a crime. I've injured another human being. I believe my actions were justified, but in the morning, I'll have to go to town and turn myself in to Danny Comeaux.

Nineteen

THE NEXT MORNING, MICHAELA AND I RETURN TO the old courthouse, this time seeking the sheriff's office. For a brief, delusional moment just before we left, I considered not coming after all, trying to pretend the incident never happened. But the bloodstains on the porch are vivid and incriminating. I decided it's better to confess up front and hope for the best.

Danny Comeaux is at his desk reading the local newspaper when we come in. His eyes brighten, and he grins and stands up when he sees us.

"Morning, Gabriella, Michaela. You all doin' all right?"

My hand tightens instinctively on Michaela's shoulder. "I need to talk to you, Danny. Can I leave Michaela with your dispatcher for a moment?" I ask, nodding my head in the direction of the woman who occupies the only other room in the cramped quarters. I know the woman is a dispatcher because the sign on her desk says so. I thought about letting her go down the hall to play with Kisha, but I don't want Rosalie to know that I've come to see the sheriff.

"Sure, she'll be fine with Maxine," the sheriff replies, coming around his desk and speaking briefly with the dispatcher. "You can sit right here," he says to Michaela, pointing to a large old wooden desk chair. "Want a soda?"

"No, thank you, sir," she answers stiffly. I know Michaela is not happy at being left out of the conversation, but I don't want my daughter to hear what I have to tell the sheriff. Michaela settles into the indicated chair and takes out her GameBoy, and I breathe a small sigh of relief. She's such an obedient child. I have to give Mrs. Bolton credit, at least in part, for that.

Behind closed doors, I turn to Danny. "I came to report a crime," I begin, uncertain of how to proceed. From Danny's demeanor, it appears no one has filed murder charges against me. Yet.

His dark brows draw together. "Crime?"

I produce the gun from my purse and lay it on his desk. "I shot a man last night."

Now the brows go straight up, and he stares at the weapon that lies between us. "Please, sit down," he says.

I take a seat, mainly because my knees are weak, and I'm afraid my legs will give way beneath me. I didn't sleep the rest of the night, and my whole body aches with fatigue.

"Tell me what happened," Danny says in an even voice.

I explain about the two men who'd approached the house in the night, and of my attempt to warn them away. "But one of them just kept coming, and I . . . I pulled the trigger." I look at him, feeling bloodless. "I didn't mean to hurt anyone, Danny. But he was so close . . . I'm not sure where the bullet struck. What if I . . . killed him?"

I'm more frightened than I've been in my life. If I murdered that man, I could go to prison, and there would be no hope for Michaela and me. Even if I wasn't convicted, just the fact that I shot someone could give the Colquitts more proof of my "instability."

"No one's reported anything to me," the sheriff says after a long silence. "I could check the hospitals around here, but my bet is those guys don't want the law on them. They probably won't seek professional medical help."

"But if I killed him?" I can't seem to leave this thought alone.

"If you did, he's probably at the bottom of the bayou by now."

"Danny! How can you be so calm about this?"

"Look, Gabriella, you and I both know that life back in those bayous is different than it is in town. There's a different code, a different law. They take care of their own. Those boys were up to no good. They're not about to get close enough to civilization that the law might snag them. If I get a missing persons report, or the guy turns up at a hospital, then I'll come for you. But right now, you're the only one who's claiming an attempted murder, even though it sounds like self-defense to me. If I were you, I'd shut my mouth, take my kid and my gun and go on home."

He pauses, then adds, "Gabriella, maybe it isn't safe for you to be living all alone out there. Why don't you move into town?"

"I looked for a place to live while we're fixing up Shadow Haven, Danny. There's just nothing decent available."

He gives me a measured look. "Why are you coming back to Tibonne at all? This is a dying little town. There's nothing here for you."

I swallow hard. "I'm not coming back to Tibonne, Danny. I'm coming home to Shadow Haven. It's my land, my heritage. With what I do, I can work anywhere."

"Aren't you worried those men might come back, or some other intruder might come prowling? Why didn't you call me last night and at least give me a chance to get out there and help you?"

I bite my lip. "I don't have a phone yet, Danny."

"RadioShack," he says grimly. "Make it your next stop."

I do. I purchase a cell phone and sign up for the service, then head back to Shadow Haven. My intention is to charge the phone's battery, then place a call to Jarrod. But there's no need . . . Jarrod's car is in the drive when we reach the house.

His car is there, but he's nowhere to be seen. "Jarrod!" I call out, and then I notice the front door is standing wide open. How did he get in?

We're almost on the porch when he comes charging down the central hallway toward us. "What the hell happened here?" he booms.

Startled at his thunderous outburst, I take a step backward onto the verandah. "You might explain what you're doing here," I demand in return. "How did you get into my house?"

Jarrod glances at Michaela and refrains from whatever he was going to say. For the moment. I take it it's not something he wants her to hear. "I see you have a new swing set," he says to her calmly.

"My mama got it for me, and she and Miss Rosalie put it together. Want to see it?"

"I . . . uh, need to talk to your mama for a bit, but I can watch you swing from here. How high can you go?"

"High as the sky. Watch, Mr. Jarrod."

She bounces off, unaware of the tension between Jarrod and me. When she's beyond hearing distance, Jarrod turns to me, anger and frustration written on his face.

"I came because I couldn't get you by phone," he says in a lower voice, "and I needed to warn you about something. But when I got here, nobody was home and there's blood on the porch. I broke into your house, which was way too easy, by the way, because I thought you or Michaela might be inside and hurt."

He pauses, then asks again, "Gabriella, what happened here?"

I look down and see dark stains on the old wood of the verandah. I look up again at Jarrod who is standing firm, wanting an explanation. I grow cold all over.

"Come into the house," I tell him, "and get off my case about the phone. I bought one just this morning."

"It's about damn time." He takes it from me without asking and begins to assemble it, ready for the battery to start charging.

"I'm perfectly capable of doing that," I snap.

He just glares his response and plugs in the phone. "Can I have the number? It's a long way to come out here every time I need to talk to you."

"Look, Jarrod, I'm sorry you're so upset that you had to drive all the way back out here. Yes, you can have the number, but remember, nobody's hired you to defend me. This is all your own doing."

I scribble the number on a sticky note and hand it to him. "Now, since you're here, why don't you tell me why you came?"

"What about the bloodstains?"

"We'll get to that. You said you came to warn me about something."

He eyes me for a long moment, then says, "It seems I've misjudged Elizabeth Colquitt somewhat. I thought she'd have a little patience with me, even though I've been dragging my feet on her demands.

But she faxed a letter to me yesterday informing me that her offer is withdrawn, and that she's hired other counsel."

"Is this good news or bad news?" Personally I'm relieved to know that Jarrod isn't going to be representing the Colquitts. But he's clearly troubled.

"It's not going to make a damn bit of difference as far as I'm concerned," he says. "I'm not calling off my dogs. I will find a way to keep her from doing this, whether you want me to represent you or not."

"But why? Why are you so determined to help me out?" This just doesn't make sense. I haven't paid him a penny, and yet here he is gnashing his teeth to stop the Colquitts from getting custody of Michaela.

The set of his jaw is firm. His gaze is level when it meets mine. "I told you, I have some history with the Colquitts. They think because they're rich they can do whatever they want, right or wrong. Let's just say I feel morally obligated to pursue your defense. And believe me, you're going to need somebody on your side. In her letter, Elizabeth told me who she's hired. His name is Ira Peabody, and he's the biggest sleazebag attorney in New Orleans."

Twenty

I HAVE TO CONSCIOUSLY SUMMON INNER STRENGTH to remain steady, but I feel as if I'm about to go over the edge. My nerves are shot, and I'm sure I have a rock in the pit of my stomach. First the bad dream, then the intruders, my trip to the sheriff, and now this. It's been a pretty bad day, and it's not yet noon.

"So what do you think Peabody will do?"

I remember sitting at the table just yesterday asking Jarrod to get on with things. It's as if my words were magic, and my wish, whether I meant it or not, has come true. Grandnana always used to warn me, "Be careful what you ask for." I wish I'd remembered that yesterday.

"First, he'll take the Colquitts' money to the bank so fast it'll make their heads swim," Jarrod replies. "Then he'll proceed to take your life apart. He'll have you served with papers, call you in for deposition, he'll make sure you're examined by Social Services . . . it's not going to be fun."

His words terrify me more than the men who tried

to break into my house last night, because I don't know how to defend myself. I can't just take out a gun and shoot Ira Peabody like I did the intruders. He sounds like the perfect henchman for Elizabeth and Rupert Colquitt. Jarrod is right; they are formidable opponents, and I'm at the bottom of the food chain as far as they're concerned. They'll stop at nothing to get what they want. All my brave thoughts about restoring my Deveaux power shimmer and dissolve beneath my growing fear.

"Jarrod," I squeak in a too-small voice. "What am I going to do?"

I must look pitiful, because his expression changes immediately. He comes to me and puts his hands on my shoulders. "I have my own reasons for taking on the Colquitts, and I'm actually glad Elizabeth tried to hire me, because otherwise I probably wouldn't have known what they're trying to do. I'll fight for your right to retain custody of Michaela, if not for you, then for . . . shall we call it . . . old time's sake. The underdog needs a champion when it comes to standing up to the Colquitt family. But," he lowers his voice and places a finger beneath my chin, "I wish you'd let me help you because you want me to."

My heart is thundering, and my skin burns where he is touching me. I need help, God knows, and here is Jarrod, ready to stand by me. What's wrong with this picture?

Nothing that I can see; it's just a niggling feeling that it's not quite that simple. Does he really want to help me, or does he see an opportunity to use me somehow to effect some sort of revenge against the Colquitts . . . for old time's sake?

I wish I knew more about Jarrod.

My other worry is that I'm so attracted to him that it would be easy just to turn this whole matter into his hands. But I mustn't ever let myself fall into that trap again. I will never turn the reins of my life over to another as long as I live. Jarrod is a powerful man, physically attractive and strong in character. It would be easy for him to take over, probably without either of us even realizing what was happening, as just took place with the telephone.

Still, I have no one else I can turn to.

"Okay," I say, tilting my head up slightly. "I give up. Yes, I need your help, Jarrod. But I'm not sure I can afford you. Paying the back taxes and spending money to refurbish Shadow Haven have seriously depleted my bank account."

"I don't want your money, Gabriella. This isn't about money. It's about justice. Doing what's right. The Colquitts aren't concerned about what's 'right.' All they care about is their money."

I know from experience that what he says is true. But he says it with such venom it scares me. What did the Colquitts ever do to him that he's reacting so strongly against them? Was it just Charles who betrayed him? Or did Elizabeth and Rupert have something to do with that betrayal? There is so much I want to know.

"I want to pay you, Jarrod," I say, drawing away from him and taking a seat in one of the overstuffed chairs by the kitchen fireplace. He sits in the other, and I'm glad for the space between us. It makes me nervous when he's too close. "I always pay my bills. It's just the way I am. I took care of the taxes yesterday, by the way."

"Good. That's one less thing they'll have in their bag of tricks. And I'll see if I can get a restraining order to keep Ira Peabody from harassing you." He leans forward, resting his arms on his thighs. "But first, I want to know how that blood got on your verandah. That big of a stain wasn't caused by a scratch."

I can avoid it no longer. I tell Jarrod about the two men who tried to break into the house last night, and how I dispatched them. He lets out a low whistle and rubs the bridge of his nose. "This isn't good."

"No, it isn't good. I might have killed that man for all I know. I was so frightened I hardly remember pulling the trigger. All I could think of was protecting Michaela." I tell him about my confession to Danny Comeaux, and of the sheriff's reaction.

"What do you think they were after?"

"Who knows? I have nothing of value in here." We grow silent for a moment, then I murmur, "I'm in trouble, aren't I, even if the sheriff is choosing to look the other way at the moment?"

Jarrod runs his fingers through his hair. "You could be, if Ira Peabody hears about it. He could use it as part of his evidence to prove that you're an unfit mother. It's not so much that you shot somebody, but that you'd bring your child to live in such a dangerous place to start with."

"Shadow Haven isn't dangerous," I object.

Jarrod is quiet again, then echoes Danny's earlier question. "Why is it so important to you to remain here? I know this is your home, but your people have all passed on, and this place is isolated and run down. Why don't you sell it and move to New Orleans or someplace where you'd be safer and more comfortable?"

I sniff at that. "You think New Orleans is safe?"

Jarrod grins. "Okay, point taken. But why not go someplace else? Baton Rouge, maybe. Or Jackson."

I shake my head. "I might as well go back to New York. I don't know anyone in Baton Rouge or Jackson. Why should I go someplace even more foreign? At least here, I'm at home. I have my people—" I break off before I say too much.

"What about Michaela?" he asks, apparently not hearing my slip. "What if those men had broken in here last night?"

"They didn't, did they?" I reply defensively. "Look, if you're here to put a guilt trip on me, you can leave now. I know the risks I'm taking, but this is my home. This is where I want to be. I want to raise my child on the land where I was born and raised. I want her to know life here at Shadow Haven. I want her to grow up differently than she would if she lived in New York."

"And what if those men come back, Gabriella? The sheriff's probably right that they won't press charges through the usual channels. But they could come back and take their own revenge."

Jarrod is scaring me again, and he's making me face things I'd rather not look at. Like the risk at which I might be placing Michaela. I've never felt so torn. Of course I'd never do anything to hurt Michaela, and yet by remaining at Shadow Haven, I might be doing just that.

I think of the dreams and of Grandnana's warnings. Were the intruders the evil of which she spoke? By shooting one of them, have I brought on even greater evil? Will they, like Jarrod is suggesting, come back and try to hurt us?

"Will you at least let me help you make this place more secure?" Jarrod asks, jarring me from my frightening thoughts. "I know you have new doors and windows, but a door without a deadbolt is easy pickings for burglars." He gets up and goes to the kitchen window and examines the lock mechanism on it. "This kind of window is easy to break into as well," he says. "All an intruder has to do is break the glass, reach in and turn the latch."

I'm ashamed at how little thought I've given to the security of Shadow Haven. I guess I thought that deadbolts and burglar alarms were for New York. Shadow Haven has always been just that, a haven, a safe place.

Nothing about it seems safe at the moment.

"What can I do? I can't afford more new windows."

"Well, if you're hellbent on staying here, then we should at least find some better locking devices for them."

He returns to where I am standing. "What about the gun? What'd you do with it?"

I flinch at the mention of the weapon. "I took it to town to give to Danny," I tell him, "but he didn't want it. Yet, anyway. Right now, it's in my purse."

"Loaded?"

I shake my head. "Don't want to do that again."

"I understand your feelings, but it likely saved your life last night. Do you have a license for it?"

"In New York."

"I'll help you get one here in Louisiana. In the meantime, keep it someplace safe but handy."

My stomach turns at the thought of ever touching that gun again. I hand him my purse. "You want the gun put away safely, you do it."

"Okay," he says. "Where do you usually keep it?"

I hesitate. "Uh, in the bedroom. In a bag under the bed."

Jarrod takes the gun and heads into my bedroom. I follow him, wishing I hadn't been so headstrong. I'm uneasy at his being in my personal space.

He sits on the bed and takes out the travel bag. But when he opens it and peers inside, he frowns. He reaches in and brings out the golden torc.

"What's this?"

I instinctively take a step backward. "It's . . . a torc.

A necklace. Charles gave it to me last year for Christmas. But I don't wear it. Can't. I'm allergic to gold." *And to whatever evil energy that thing carries.*

He frowns. "Do you know where Charles got it?"

That seems a strange question. "He bought it. I think it came in a box from Tiffany's. Why?"

Jarrod studies it for a moment, then places it back inside the bag. "Just curious," he says, then puts the pistol inside the bag. He zips the bag closed and snaps shut the small padlock that secures the case. "I assume you've taught Michaela not to touch guns."

Resentment flares that he should think me so careless. "She's never seen that gun before last night. But Charles taught her about gun safety." Even as I mention it, I wonder just how much Charles had impressed on Michaela not to touch his guns. He'd had quite a collection. His guns were among the first things I liquidated from our house. "I'll talk to her again at any rate," I add, less defensively.

"The gun should be safe from Michaela locked away in here." He stands and comes to me. Taking my hand, he turns it palm up and drops the small key into it. "Just make sure you know where this is, in case you need to get it in a hurry again."

CHAPTER

Twenty-one

I BECOME SUDDENLY AWARE THAT WE HAVEN'T HEARD from Michaela in the extended interlude we've spent inside the house. Sometimes she plays by herself very well, but often, especially when some kind of new toy is involved, she's eager to show it to me. And Jarrod had told her he'd watch her from the verandah before we went inside.

But there's been no "look, Mama, watch me," or "see how high I'm going." In fact, I haven't heard as much as a squeal of delight from the yard. A presentiment comes over me. Michaela's disappeared.

I dash out of my bedroom and toward the front porch. To my dismay, but not my surprise, she's not on the swing set. Nor do I see her anywhere in the yard. "Michaela," I call out, panic seizing me. "Michaela!"

Jarrod runs out of the house behind me. "What's wrong?"

I don't answer him, but return to the house and fly down the hall to her room. She's not there either.

"Michaela!" My cry echoes through the nearly empty house. Dear God, where can she be? What's happened to her?

Jarrod is briskly walking the perimeter of the house when I emerge again into the yard. "I don't see her," he says. He, too, calls out her name. The apprehension I see on his face raises my own.

I stand very still, my pulse pounding. I'm trying to think rationally, but my fear is that the intruder I didn't shoot last night has returned and kidnapped Michaela from right beneath my nose.

I wish I'd shot both of them dead.

"Jarrod, where is she?" My voice comes out in a near shriek.

"Kids are adventurers," he tells me, his tone calmer than I could ever manage at the moment. But then, it's not his child who's lost. "I remember once my little sister decided to crawl under the house and see how long it would take us to find her. We had all the neighbors and the police looking for her when she finally got hungry and came out."

Maybe Jarrod's right. Maybe Michaela got mad at us for leaving her to her swing set and was hiding just to scare us. "Michaela, come here this instant," I demand. Then I wheedle, "I've got Kool-Aid and cookies for you."

There's no reply except the slight rustle of the wind in the live oaks. I close my eyes and try to let my intuitive feelings tell me where to look for her. They don't, but they do give me the sense that she's physically okay and not too far away. Maybe the kidnapper hasn't gone far with her yet.

"Okay," Jarrod says, interrupting my reverie, "let's think about this logically. She was in the yard less than twenty minutes ago."

"We've been in the house longer than that, haven't we?"

He frowns. "Could be. Say half an hour. Where could she go in that time?"

Desolate, I stare into the woods. "In there. Or to the bayou. To the highway. None of them safe places." I grab his arm. "Jarrod, what if one of those guys from last night came back and has kidnapped her?"

"Let's not go there just yet." He heads to his car. "She's probably around here somewhere. I'll drive out to the main road. You check the house again. She could have gone upstairs to hide."

Reluctantly, I do as he suggests. Shadow Haven is a large old house with lots of hidey-holes. Maybe she was playing hide-and-seek with her dolls or some such. But my intuition tells me she's somewhere else. Somewhere outside.

The sagging stairs creak as I hurry to the second floor. It, too, has a long central hallway, with three bedrooms on each side. One by one I explore the rooms. Most are bare of furniture, but there are closets where she could be hiding. "Michaela?" I call softly. "Please, baby, come out."

The room darkens perceptibly as a cloud moves in

front of the sun. As I did last night, I sense a presence either in the house or close by—an evil presence, menacing and dark. The notion, as ridiculous as it is, that the *loup-garou* has seized my little girl, crosses my mind.

"Michaela!" I scream. "Michaela!" But I'm answered only by silence.

After quickly but carefully searching each room, upstairs and down, I'm convinced that Michaela isn't in the house. I go outside and peer beneath the verandah. She's a small girl; she could have burrowed into the very narrow crawl space there. But the clouds continue to play with the sun, creating patterns of light and shadow that make it nearly impossible for me to see into the darkness beneath the house.

I hear a car and turn to see Jarrod's Beamer coming up the lane. And I'm overjoyed to see that there's someone in the passenger seat. A short someone. I run to the car and grab Michaela in a huge hug when she pops out the door.

"Oh, baby, thank goodness you're safe. Where did you go?"

She lifts her head and says, as if it's her normal behavior, "To your Grandnana's enchanted garden." I see her turn to look at Jarrod. "He came and found me there, but I wasn't lost."

"She was in the cemetery," Jarrod confirms, "deep in conversation with somebody I couldn't see."

"It was that old woman," Michaela tells me before I can try to stop her. I don't want Jarrod hearing what

I know she's about to say, but she blurts out, "The one you said was your Grandnana. I heard her calling me when I was swinging, and I went to see what she wanted."

I look from Michaela to Jarrod. His brow is creased and his head cocked slightly to one side in silent query.

I don't even think about trying to explain. I kneel beside Michaela and wipe the sweat from her face. "You mustn't go wandering off like that, *chérie*. You scared us to death. There are things in those woods that can hurt you."

"Nothing hurt me. But your Grandnana told me to tell you to hurry up and find that friend of hers, Mary Frances. She said that the last time, too, remember?"

"I remember you telling me that. Listen, how about some Kool-Aid and cookies? You're hot. You need something to cool you down."

"Kool-Aid, yeah!" she says and runs into the house.

I turn to Jarrod. "You're sure there was no one in the cemetery?"

"Of course I'm sure. It's not a very big place, and the only sort of person I saw besides Michaela was the statue of the angel."

I raise my eyes to meet his gaze. "Thank you for finding her. I don't know what's gotten into her. She's usually so obedient."

"Does she often . . . uh . . . hear these things?"

"No. This is something new." So far I've managed

not to lie to Jarrod, nor to tell him the truth. Sort of a turnabout for us.

"Like an imaginary friend, I guess," he ventures, and I let him assume that.

"I guess. Want some Kool-Aid?"

"No, thanks. But I do need some more of your time. I need some more information from you. I want to be prepared to defend you, if things go that far."

Twenty-two

ꉫ

WE'RE IN THE KITCHEN, SEATED AGAIN AT THE TABLE, with mint tea and Jarrod's yellow legal pad between us. Michaela is napping, and Jarrod and I are discussing the possible scenarios that might play out in court, when we hear a car approaching.

"Who on earth could that be?" I wonder if Rosalie has decided to drop by. Shadow Haven is remote, but I've had so many visitors in the last few days, I'm beginning to feel like it's Grand Central Station. I go to the verandah to see who's coming.

It isn't Rosalie.

The car is a bronze-colored Cadillac, and the fat man who steps out frowns when he sees Jarrod. "Well, I'll be damned. If it ain't the do-gooder. Imagine meeting you here."

"Hello, Ira. I sort of expected you'd show up."

The man is a walking cliché for a Southern lawyer; he could have come straight from Central Casting. He has to weigh more than three hundred pounds, and his pale beige suit is stained with sweat. He wears a hat to match the suit, and shoes to go with the outfit. He approaches me with a waddled gait and holds out a card.

"Name's Peabody, ma'am," he says. "I'm with the law firm Peabody, Settle, and Peabody." He laughs. "I'm the second Peabody. My old man started the firm."

And was probaby the only reason this man had his name on the door, I surmise. I take his card, look at it, and return it, my hand feeling dirty.

"What can I do for you, Mr. Peabody?"

"I'm here at the request of my clients, Mr. and Mrs. Rupert Colquitt."

"And what is it that Mr. and Mrs. Colquitt have hired you to do, Mr. Peabody?" Of course, I know perfectly well why he's here, but I might as well make him earn some of that money.

The smarmy smile leaves his face, and he cocks his head toward Jarrod. "Let's not play games, Ms. Deveaux. I know they tried to hire old Landry here first, but he didn't move fast enough to suit them, so they hired me instead. Since he's standing on your porch, I guess you know exactly why I'm here."

I clench my fists. "Maybe Mr. Landry saw the injustice in what my former in-laws are trying to do and didn't want to be part of it."

"Or maybe he's got the hots for you," Peabody replies, giving me a lascivious wink.

Revolted, I take a step in his direction. For the second time in not too many hours, I order an intruder away. "Get off my property, Mr. Peabody. You're trespassing."

I am aware that Michaela has awakened and come out the front door. I wish she had been able to nap on through this nasty little encounter.

Jarrod comes down the steps. "You're making a big mistake, Peabody," he says in a low, menacing tone. "You have no idea what you're getting yourself into. If you're smart, you'll do what I did and tell those people to leave Ms. Deveaux and her daughter alone. There are no grounds for their case."

"Maybe no, maybe so," Peabody says, eyeballing the run-down condition of Shadow Haven. "Mrs. Colquitt told me to expect them to be living in squalor out here in the back of nowhere. Guess I could say she was right."

I feel as if I'm going to explode. "Leave now, Mr. Peabody, or I'll call the sheriff." I think about the gun. Good thing it's locked in the travel bag.

"I came here to talk to the little girl," he says, not budging. "Come here, honey." He wiggles his finger at Michaela, who huddles beside me.

I take my daughter firmly by the shoulder. "You leave her alone."

"I just want to ask her if she's doing all right. If she's happy here, or," at this point he raises his voice to make sure Michaela hears him, "if she'd like to go back to New York and live with her grandmother and grandfather."

I hold my breath. This is exactly what Michaela

has said she wanted ever since we came to Shadow Haven, at least the going back to New York part. Will she come out with it now?

But Michaela says nothing. She reaches for my hand and clenches it. She buries her face against the side of my leg, as if she doesn't want to look at Ira Peabody, much less speak with him.

Jarrod goes over to Peabody and takes him by the arm, turning him back toward his car. "Time to go, Ira. We'll see you in court if we have to. But don't come here again. I'll have a restraining order against you by morning." Then he lowers his head and says something I can't hear. I see the fat man's face turn red. He gives Jarrod a dirty look, then hurries away toward his car, turning back to glare.

"Have a good day." Jarrod waves and points his finger toward the lane. I hear him add under his breath, "Asshole."

When the Cadillac turns the corner, I begin to shake. "Dear God, how could they stoop so low as to hire someone like that?" I murmur.

"Mama, what did that man mean asking me if I wanted to go back to New York and live with Grandmother and Grandfather?" Michaela's voice sounds small and scared.

I close my eyes, summoning courage. Should I tell her what her grandparents are trying to do? I'm terrified that Michaela might jump at the offer.

Before I can answer her question, Jarrod goes to her and picks her up. "How about you and your mama going into town with me for dinner? It's getting late, and I'm hungry."

I appreciate him attempting to divert her attention, but I'm not the least bit hungry at the moment. Ira Peabody is enough to ruin anyone's appetite. "Jarrod, that's nice, but it's not necessary. It's only four o'clock. I have food in the house. You're welcome to stay for dinner here."

He puts Michaela back on the ground and looks at his watch. "Guess it's not as late as I thought, but I don't want to leave here until I know you two are more secure in this house. I'll go into Tibonne and get the deadbolts and window locks, and a little Chinese takeout, if they have it here, and we can eat later."

"Where don't they have Chinese takeout?" I ask wryly. The truth is, between last night's incident and the arrival of Ira Peabody, I desperately want more locks between us and the outside world. "What do you say, Michaela, want to eat Chinese tonight?" It had been one of her favorite treats in New York.

"I guess so." Her little face is troubled, and she's still gazing down the lane, as if she's afraid Ira Peabody will come back.

Jarrod departs for Tibonne, and I corner Michaela for a bath. We have some girl-talking to do before he gets back.

"So, you think you saw Grandnana again today?" I ask casually as I turn on the shower and test the water temperature.

"Uh-huh," Michaela says. "I wish we could use one of those bathtubs upstairs. This shower is icky."

There are several bathrooms on the second floor, added sometime in the 1950s to accommodate the many guests Grandnana and her husband used to entertain. It's a shame that we're crowded into this tiny cubicle beneath the stairs. I turn off the water and wrap a towel around Michaela's naked little body.

"Okay, squirt, let's go upstairs and see if we have any hot water there." The thought of a long soak in a perfumed tub has its appeal to me as well, but I don't know if the second floor plumbing is fully functional yet.

We're in luck. Although at first the water gurgles and spurts in rusty hesitation from the spout on the tub in one of the front bedrooms, eventually the color clears and hot water mixes into the cold. I've brought soap and baby shampoo, and we get to the job in earnest.

"Now, about Grandnana. How did you know she was calling you?"

"I heard her. She said she was waiting for me by the angel statue."

"And was she?"

"Uh-huh."

"And she told you to tell me to find her friend, what was her name?"

"Mary Francie or Frances or something. I can't say it right."

"Marie Françoise?"

"Yeah. Marie Francewoise." She draws out the last syllable and giggles.

"Did she happen to tell you just who this Marie Françoise is?" I don't recall knowing anyone by that name, but again I get a mental image of a little shop on some side street in the French Quarter.

"No. She just said we gotta go there so we'll be protected."

"Protected? From what?" I hope Grandnana hasn't said anything that might frighten Michaela. But I also wish she'd give us a clue as to who is posing a threat to us, and in what form.

Apparently her appearance to Michaela was mainly to admonish me again to find Marie Françoise. "Did she say anything else?" I ask Michaela.

She shrugs her small shoulders. "She told me she loves us and that you should keep on trying, but I don't know what she means."

I think I know. She means I'm to keep trying to reach her. Which means she believes I can do it. That part of the message gives me courage.

There is one other bit of business we must get to before Jarrod returns. "Michaela, when you see Grandnana or talk to her, it's . . . it's kind of important to keep it a secret just between you and me."

"A secret? Why?"

Because people will call you crazy, that's why.

"Well, think about it. Most people can't see spirits or talk to them the way you and I can."

"They can't?"

"No, darling, they can't. It's a special gift we have. All the girls in our family, the Deveaux women, have had it. My mother, Grandnana, her mother, clear back to one of our great-grandmothers named Angelique. But we can't tell other people about it because they sometimes don't believe us."

"But I saw her, I really, really saw her. . . ."

"I believe you. But . . . Mr. Jarrod might not. Maybe it's better not to talk about it in front of him."

"Okay." Michaela sounds both disappointed and resigned. "But I saw her and I talked to her."

"I know, baby. And I thank you for giving me her messages. Now, how about a little spray of my special perfume?"

Bathtime is behind us, and I hope Michaela remembers not to bring up the subject of her conversation with Grandnana in front of Jarrod. If he wants to believe she was talking to an imaginary friend, so much the better.

But I have to deal with the message Grandnana has gotten through to me three times now, once in a dream, twice through Michaela.

Find Marie Françoise.

CHAPTER
Twenty-three

JARROD RETURNS BEARING A LARGE SACK FROM THE
Ace Hardware store, square white boxes in a plastic
bag, and a couple of bottles in a brown paper sack.

"Nerve tonic," he says, grinning and holding up a
bottle of cabernet with a French label on it. "And I
brought this for you, young lady," he says, handing
Michaela a large plastic container of red soda. "I thought
the wine might help settle our stomachs," he explains
to me. "Ira's enough to make you want to puke."

I laugh. "My thoughts exactly."

"Before we get to this," he indicates the Chinese
food, "I want to install the deadbolts in the front and
back doors. Maybe your handyman can take care of
the window fixtures tomorrow."

Jarrod goes to work, and I transfer the Chinese
food into glass containers and set them in the oven
to keep warm. In less than an hour, he's finished,
and he produces a key for each lock. "Don't keep
these in the locks. Put them somewhere else close at
hand. If a burglar breaks the glass, he still can't open
the deadbolt unless he has a key."

Moments later, Jarrod pours the wine into a couple of my new wineglasses, and I feel better after just one sip. I don't know whether it's the wine, or having Jarrod around. I want to be self-sufficient, like Rosalie, but I have to admit it's nice to have a man to help with things like deadbolts. I know nothing about hardware. Neither did Charles. He always just called someone to do that kind of thing.

"Want to sit on the verandah until the mosquitoes run us back inside?" I suggest. In spite of Louisiana's heat, I enjoy the climate, especially in the early evening when it begins to cool.

Michaela brings a large plastic glass filled with the red soda outside with her and successfully maneuvers onto one of the faux wicker chairs without spilling it. Jarrod and I sit side by side in the porch swing with our wine. We must appear for all the world like a happy little family, gathered to relax a bit before supper.

Little would anyone suspect that Jarrod's not the daddy; he's just a lawyer who's trying to keep the little family from being torn apart.

He raises his glass and clinks it against mine. "Here's to better days."

"I can drink to that."

Then he grins across at Michaela. "So, now tell me about this imaginary friend of yours."

I nearly choke on my wine. I'd hoped he would forget about that.

Michaela scrunches her little face into a confused frown. "Excuse me?"

I try to catch her eye and give my head a little shake, but I don't know if she sees me or understands my meaning.

"You know, the old lady you said you were talking to in the graveyard."

Astonishingly, Michaela doesn't miss a beat. "Oh, there wasn't anybody there. You didn't see anybody, did you, Mr. Jarrod?"

"No, but I thought I heard you talking to someone."

"I was talking to the angel, you know, the one that flies over Grandnana's grave. My mama carved it. She's got a funny smile."

"What did you say to the angel?"

"Oh, it was just general angel-talk."

I chuckle. This little one is good. I'm going to have to watch out for her as she grows up, and make sure she knows the difference between lying and keeping a secret.

Jarrod, too, smiles. "I guess I wouldn't understand. I've never talked to an angel."

"Me either. They don't talk in New York."

After a long silence, Jarrod asks her, "Do you miss New York, Michaela? Do you want to go back there?"

What is he trying to do? I think in a panic. Why is he opening that barrel of worms that Ira Peabody brought to our door? I'd hoped we had successfully evaded that subject.

I hold my breath. What if Michaela says yes? Would she really choose the senior Colquitts over her own mother? And if that's what she really wants, can I stand in her way?

Michaela doesn't answer right away. The silence is so deep I can hear the buzz of a bumblebee foraging in the honeysuckle at the far end of the verandah. Sweat gathers on my brow.

"I did," she replies at last, "but now I don't know."

I manage to take a breath again. I dare not look at Jarrod. I suspect he's wearing his lawyer's hat, trying to find out the wishes of the child whose custody is being decided. Maybe it's good he's broached the issue now, out of the hearing of anyone but us. At least we'll know where Michaela stands on the matter when Ira Peabody raises his ugly head again.

"Do you like living here?" Jarrod asks gently.

Michaela shrugs. "I didn't. But now it's not so bad."

"What about your Grandmother and Grandfather Colquitt? Would you rather go live with them?"

Michaela's head jerks toward me, and I see a frightened and bewildered look in her eyes. Suddenly, she drops her drink, and red soda splashes everywhere. With a cry, she jumps off the chair and dashes for her bedroom.

I hear Jarrod swear softly. "I'm sorry," he says as he removes a dripping cushion from the chair where Michaela had been sitting. "I didn't mean to—"

"I'll get some towels." I hurry into the house, annoyed at Jarrod. He may not have meant to upset Michaela, but his questions were too harsh, too direct. The child wasn't on a witness stand, for God's sake.

I peek into Michaela's room. She's lying facedown on her bed, sobbing, one thumb in her mouth. I remember the wars Mrs. Bolton fought in getting her to quit sucking her thumb. I haven't seen Michaela do that since she was three.

"It's okay, baby," I say, sitting beside her and stroking her hair. "Mr. Jarrod was only trying to find out what you want."

"I don't want to go with that fat man," Michaela whimpers.

Is it Ira Peabody that Michaela's afraid of? "Oh, *chérie*, no one would ever make you go with him." I shudder in disgust. No wonder she's so upset. "No, baby, no." I draw Michaela into my lap and rock her. "Nobody is going to make you do anything you don't want."

Including staying here?

I have to face it. I will do anything to keep Michaela with me, except make her miserable. I had hoped she would grow to love Shadow Haven, but I don't believe there's been enough time. I wonder if there will be now, with the Colquitts breathing down our necks.

"What I want," Michaela says, a sob escaping her small throat, "is my daddy."

CHAPTER

Twenty-four

JARROD IS GONE NOW AND A STORMY NIGHT IS UPON us. Lightning flashes and thunder shakes the very beams of Shadow Haven. The tempest reflects my mood. I think about what happened just before Jarrod left.

"I'm sorry," Jarrod apologized again when I returned to the verandah after Michaela fell asleep. He was sitting on the railing, and behind him, the trees shivered in the rising wind. "I'm not very good with kids."

I leapt at the opportunity to learn something about him. "Do you have any children, Jarrod?"

"No."

"Are you married?" I didn't mean for the question to come out so bluntly, but with my feelings for Jarrod in a muddle, I wanted—needed—to know the answer.

"No."

My mind eased. "Have you ever been married?" I ventured, feeling in a perverse way that it was my turn to punch at him with questions like he had Michaela.

Maybe it was my way of getting back at him for sending her into such a tailspin.

"No," he replied again, then stood to leave. "Guess I'd better go."

Oddly, although I was annoyed at him, I didn't want him to leave. "You haven't had dinner."

"I'm not hungry. Promise me you'll lock the deadbolts tonight, and tomorrow get Willie over here to install those extra locks on the windows. I bought enough for the downstairs. You're probably okay on the second floor. Your phone won't be charged until morning, so I'm going to leave mine here for you. There's a storm coming; I doubt anyone'll be snooping around tonight, but if you hear anything suspicious, please, call 911."

Then to my utter astonishment, he bent and kissed me lightly on the cheek. He said nothing further, just got in his car and drove off, leaving me shaken and confounded. What kind of lawyer kisses his clients good-bye?

I have the doors locked securely, but I'm nervous about the windows being vulnerable. I take the gun from its hiding place and load it, move the rocking chair from Michaela's room into the center hallway, set Jarrod's cell phone on the floor next to the chair, and prepare to keep an all-night vigil. Jarrod doesn't think the prowlers will return, but I've heard the *loup-garou* loves a good storm.

I don't know how much later, but I'm awakened from my dozing by an unfamiliar small ringing sound.

It rings three times before I realize it's Jarrod's cell phone. I grope for it and try to see what button to press to answer it. My eyes feel grainy, and they're not focusing well. When I finally succeed, it's my voice that doesn't want to work so well. "Hullo," I rasp into the phone.

The male voice that comes through isn't Jarrod's, and it sounds as if it's being deliberately muffled. "You stay out of this business, Landry," it warns. "Stay away from Gabriella."

My blood turns cold, and I can find no words to answer him.

"You hear me, Landry?" the voice says again, sounding impatient. "You're poking into things that don't concern you. Stay away from her or you'll be sorry."

With that, he hangs up. Adrenaline screams through me, and I tighten my grip on the gun. Who was that, and how did he know Jarrod was involved, even tangentially, with me? The name Ira Peabody comes to mind. Jarrod said he was a sleazebag. But could there be someone else?

The storm has subsided to an occasional flare of distant lightning and a light rain that strikes the windowpanes. I go into the kitchen. The red digits on the clock radio read 1:15. I don't want to turn on any lights and make myself an easy target in case someone is outside, watching, waiting. I would feel like a fool calling 911 because of this phone call, but I must call Jarrod. Someone's threatening him now, because of me.

I fumble for the flashlight I keep inside a cabinet,

then search for Jarrod's card where I laid it on the counter. I dial the number listed as residential, but I get no answer. That's odd. It's the middle of the night. He should have been home hours ago. I call his office. Again no answer. And no answering machine at either place. There are two other numbers on the card, his cell phone, and a pager.

I dial the pager and leave his cell number for a response. I'm worried now. What if he had a car accident in the storm?

I return to my rocking chair, Jarrod's cell phone in one hand, the gun in the other, and await a return call. I begin to rock rhythmically, back and forth, back and forth, to stem my rising apprehension. Where is he?

Suddenly, a car's headlights streak through the glass panes of the front door, and I bolt out of the chair, thinking maybe I should call 911 after all. The lights go out, and I edge to the front window. I peer into the night and see Jarrod's convertible in front of my house.

What on earth? How could he have gotten here with such lightning speed? How did he even know to come here? I don't have those answers, but I'm decidedly glad to see him.

He gets out of the car and runs to the house, and I open the door before he can even knock.

"Gabriella," he calls my name, and before I know what's happening, he takes me into his arms. "What's wrong? What's happened?"

I can't answer because suddenly his lips take mine in a breathless kiss. He holds me tightly, as if I might vanish if he were to let me go. In his embrace, my terror and apprehension melt into a liquid warmth in my belly. I have no idea how my rescuer got here so fast, but I don't ask questions.

Instead, I open my lips to his fervent kiss. He runs his fingers through my hair and draws me against the hardness of his body. We are heat and steam and need against each other.

At last he moves his kisses from my lips to my cheeks and along my neck. "Are you all right?"

I'm not sure, but I think I'm feeling more all right than I have in the last eight years. I touch the stubble of his beard, inhale the man-scent of him. "I'm okay, Jarrod, I just got frightened."

"How? Who frightened you?" The way he says it, it sounds like he's ready to kill whoever it was.

But I don't answer right away. Instead I ask, "Where were you? How did you get here so fast? I . . . I only paged you a minute ago."

"I never left," he admits. He rests his forehead on mine. "I wasn't about to leave you alone after all you've been through last night and today. So I parked down the lane, out of your sight, but where I could watch the house, just in case those guys came back."

I'm so stunned I don't know what to think. Jarrod, my protector. Why has he taken it upon himself to do this? And what are we doing here in this intimate embrace? I thought he was just my lawyer, but . . . things seem to have shifted.

We take a moment to catch our breath, but our fingers entwine. "Okay, now tell me what happened," he says.

"I got this weird phone call. Or I should say, you got this phone call. Some guy whose voice sounded muffled said for you to stay out of this business and to leave me alone."

His fingers grow still. "What?"

"I can't remember his words exactly. The call woke me up, and I was taken by such surprise, I couldn't believe what I was hearing. But he said something like, 'Stay out of this business, Landry. Stay away from Gabriella. You're nosing into things that don't concern you.' Then he said something like 'Stay away or you'll be sorry.' And then he hung up."

"Peabody. That disgusting pig."

"That's what I thought, too."

"Probably hired some poor flunky to do it. Where's the phone? The number should be on the caller ID."

We go into the kitchen and turn on the lights. I hand him his phone, and he pulls up the digital display of the number of the incoming call. As I watch, he dials that number and waits to see who answers.

The phone rings and rings, but there's no answer. "I'll trace the number in the morning," Jarrod says, disconnecting the call. "It'll probably turn out to be a pay phone on the interstate or some other public place."

"Jarrod, you're taking this so lightly. Doesn't it bother you that someone called in the middle of the night and threatened you?"

"Think about who it could be," he says, taking my hand again. "The only people who know that I have had any recent contact with you are Elizabeth and Rupert Colquitt, and their slimy attorney, Peabody. Now, I can't exactly see the Colquitts dirtying themselves with such a melodramatic little deed, but Peabody would probably get off on it. He watches too much TV."

"Elizabeth made that anonymous phone call to the parish Social Services," I remind him.

"Elizabeth, or someone she hired. Although she might have done it herself. She has a theatrical streak in her."

"How do you know so much about the Colquitts, Jarrod?"

I regret asking the question the moment the words are out of my mouth. His expression shutters immediately, and he drops my hand. "It's too long a story to go into right now," he says. "Maybe sometime I'll tell you. Right now, I'm starving. You got any ice cream in this house?"

"I have ice cream, but how about Chinese food? Some nice guy brought a bunch over earlier, but we didn't eat it."

CHAPTER
Twenty-five

OUR EARLIER INTIMACY SEEMS TO HAVE VANISHED when we turned on the lights, and our relationship has returned to the business at hand once again. Still, something has changed between us. There is no denying that powerful kiss. Or that we both wanted it. My skin is still heated from being in his arms.

I warm the food in the microwave and in a few minutes we're devouring King Pao chicken and spicy shrimp with veggies. Jarrod pours the remaining wine for us. Neither of us says a word.

"Gabriella," he speaks at last, breaking the awkward silence. "I, uh, don't know what came over me. . . ."

"I hope you're not going to apologize for kissing me," I tell him. "I didn't seem to mind, in case you didn't notice." I grin at him, and he grins back. He is so good-looking, especially when he smiles. I wonder why I didn't take more notice of him that day when he introduced me to Charles. I guess because Charles began his pursuit of me from the first moment we met, and Jarrod was pretty much out of the picture.

I can't help but wonder fleetingly what my life might have been like if things had taken a different turn, and I'd been courted by Jarrod instead. Of course, it's a waste of time to even think things like that. I can't rewind my life and do it over again. I have to look forward now, and make the best of the consequences of my decision to marry Charles years ago.

"It's unethical for a lawyer to romance his client," Jarrod breaks into my thoughts, taking my hand. His touch sends delicious shivers through me. "At least while he's on the job."

My emotions are in a turmoil. I think I could become kind of crazy about Jarrod, but he's right, getting involved romantically, at least until the custody suit is settled, is probably not a good idea. "I never hired you," I remind him, "but I think I need you as my lawyer."

"I think you do, too." A frown darkens his expression. "I'm not being egotistical. It's just that I know Ira Peabody and the forces that you're up against. I don't think he'll come here again, but he's an aggressive S.O.B., and I'm sure we'll hear from him again soon."

"What about the investigator you hired? Has he come up with anything on Charles?" My anxiety begins to creep in again.

"I haven't heard from him in a couple of days. So the answer is—not yet. Dobbs is one of the best in the business, though. If there's something to be uncovered, he'll find it." He hesitates, then adds, "I've been thinking about that gold torc you have in the bag with the gun."

A little chill runs through me. "What about it?"

"I don't think it came from Tiffany's. If I were a betting man, I'd say it's an antiquity. And likely quite valuable."

"An antiquity?" I don't know why I'm so surprised. Charles traded in fine art and antiquities. "But why didn't he just tell me that?"

"That's what I'd like to know," Jarrod replies. "Why lie and say it came from a jeweler, unless . . . it was stolen."

"Stolen! You can't be serious. Why would Charles steal something? He had all the money in the world."

"Charles would do anything that served his purpose, whatever it might be. I don't know that he ever stole anything, and I agree, it doesn't make sense that he would. But . . . I knew Charles well. He did a lot of things that didn't make particular sense. At any rate, I called Dobbs and left a message for him to check the antiquities grapevine and see if there's any rumor about a missing golden torc."

This gets stranger and stranger. I don't know what to think.

"Did Charles collect artifacts and art and things like that?" Jarrod asks.

I think about all of Charles's treasures that he kept under lock and key, some even in a vault in the house. "He had a lot of pieces in various collections.

I told you Charles traveled a lot. When he'd come home, he'd often bring expensive, exotic gifts for everyone in the household."

"Exotic?"

"Once he gave Mrs. Bolton, our nanny, some intricate little sculptures that he said he'd bought in a bazaar in Morocco. He brought Michaela strange primitive dolls from time to time, then wouldn't let her play with them. They went into a locked curio cabinet."

"Guilt gifts for being gone?"

"That's pretty much what I always took them for. But Charles liked to collect things. In retrospect, I don't really think they were gifts, I think that was his excuse for buying what he wanted to own. He had cabinets full of odd things when he died."

"What did you do with them?"

"I took them to Antioch House, where he worked, and asked them to liquidate them for me. I got rid of his gun collection, some paintings, antique furniture. In fact, they brought their truck to the house and loaded up everything they thought they could sell. I was glad to get rid of it. I hated all that stuff."

Jarrod grows quiet. We've finished the meal, so I remove the plates and leave him to his musings. I can't imagine that he's on the right track, suspecting Charles of thievery. But I give him credit for trying every possibility. If he could prove that Charles stole valuable antiquities, the threat of a scandal might be enough that the Colquitts would drop their suit. I'm not sure how ethical this all is, but Charles is dead; he can't be brought to trial for criminal behavior. Perhaps his punishment will be that his parents will disclaim the codicil and leave us alone.

It's now nearly three A.M., and I'm overcome by a heavy fatigue. But there sits Jarrod at my table. What am I going to do about him?

As if he reads my mind, he stands up and stretches. "Guess I'll get back to bed," he says with a small smile. "But I won't bother parking down the lane now that you know I'm here."

"You're not going to sleep in the car. I don't know how you sit in that little thing, much less try to sleep there."

"It's too late to get a hotel. Besides, I've assigned myself to be your bodyguard, I guess. I need to be close by."

"I don't need a bodyguard, Jarrod, but it's true that it's too late for you to find another place to stay. You take my bed, and I'll sleep with Michaela."

"I can't do that."

"You can and will. It's the least I can do. You'd think with all those bedrooms upstairs, I could find better quarters for a guest, but this will have to do for now."

He argues awhile longer, but at last I win and send him off to sleep in my room. The idea of Jarrod Landry in my bed is a turn-on that I try to ignore; I try to focus instead on the fact that he cares enough about Michaela and me that he became our secret bodyguard. I don't know where this is all headed, but for the rest of the night, I can sleep in peace.

CHAPTER

Twenty-six

"WHAT'S MR. JARROD DOING IN YOUR BED, MAMA?"
Michaela is up at dawn, exploring the new sleeping
arrangements, but I've had barely three hours of
shuteye and am not ready to greet the day.

"Sleeping, I hope," I groan and roll over. "Come
back to bed. It's too early to get up." But she runs
around the bed and pokes her face close to mine.

"Why is he here?" she asks excitedly. "Is he going
to come live with us?"

I open one eye and see a gleam of hope in her big
brown ones. "No. He had to come back here on
business kind of late last night, and I didn't want him
out on the highway in that storm." I give up on sleep
and ease onto one elbow. "Did you sleep well,
chérie?"

She ignores me. "Is he your new boyfriend,
Mama?"

Her question catches me totally by surprise. I roll
over again and put my feet on the floor, trying to
think quickly how to answer her. The truth is, I don't

know. I deflect her question with one of my own. "What makes you ask that, *chérie?*"

Michaela grins. "He seems to like you a lot."

"He's trying to help us, Michaela."

"Help us do what?"

"Keep the fat man away," is the only way I know to answer her. "There are some business things that he's helping me to take care of."

"I like Mr. Jarrod."

"I like him, too, but he's not my boyfriend." I decide that's the truth, and get out of bed. Michaela's up, bright-eyed and ready to go, and obviously she's not going to let me go back to sleep. "Want some breakfast?"

We go into the kitchen, where I pour cereal and milk into a bowl for Michaela. I peel a banana for myself, and wander to the window where I look out on the already hot Louisiana morning.

Is he your new boyfriend, Mama?

I told her no, because I think that's the way we left it last night. But I can't lie to my own heart. I want him to be my new boyfriend. And I think he wants to be. Maybe when this is all behind us, we can see where we stand on the matter. In the meantime, there's a lawsuit facing us, and we have to take first things first.

I go back to the sink and begin to straighten up the kitchen, when I spy Jarrod's briefcase sitting on the low table next to the overstuffed chairs. He'd brought it into the house last night after acquiescing to my insistent invitation.

On the floor near the case lies a small black book, its leaves open. It looks like an appointment book. He must have placed it on top of the briefcase, but sometime during the night, it fell to the floor. I go to pick it up and see that it's turned to the current month. I'm not one to snoop, but I'm so curious about Jarrod that I can't help but take a peek.

My attention is drawn immediately to the notations made on the squares for each Saturday: "Dinner with Valerie."

My fantasy of a romance with Jarrod dissolves in a heartbeat. Valerie. Who's Valerie? He told me he wasn't married, but that didn't mean he didn't have a steady girlfriend.

What kind of game is he playing with me? How could he kiss me like that last night if there's another woman in his life?

I slam the book shut and toss it onto the table next to the briefcase. My pulse begins to pound heavily behind my eyes. I feel like a fool for having fallen so eagerly into his arms. For having those erotic thoughts about him as he slept in my bed.

For having trusted that he kissed me because he cared for me in a special way.

That's the bottom line, I guess. Trust. Valerie, whoever she is, obviously can't trust him to be faithful, although she doesn't know about that passionate kiss. If she can't trust Jarrod, how can I?

That thought rocks my entire boat. If I can't trust him on a personal level, I can't trust him on any level.

He obviously wants to work on this case, but I'm certain now, because of his reticence to tell me his history with the Colquitts, that it has more to do with wanting them to lose rather than me to win.

I'm so tired and angry and frustrated I could chew nails. I go back to the kitchen sink and wash up Michaela's cereal bowl and spoon, trying to decide what to do next. I'm wearing the nightshirt and soft knit pants I slept in, and I feel a little exposed in my nightclothes. I want to get dressed, but Jarrod is still asleep in my room.

I decide to risk it and tiptoe into the bedroom to get something to wear. I ease the door open without a squeak, but I have to work at not letting out a squeak myself when I see him lying half-naked beneath my sheets. He's sleeping on his back, and his square shoulders take up the full width of one pillow. His arms are at his side, long and muscular, sprinkled with black hair like his chest. I can't see more of his torso, but he doesn't need to be uncovered for me to be aware of his obvious erection.

My face flushes, and I turn away. I have got to stop fantasizing about this man.

Quickly, I rummage in my bureau for clean clothes, and I'm about to leave the room when I hear him say, "Good morning, Gabriella." I think I'm going to melt at the sound of his voice.

Instead, my body freezes to the spot. I don't turn to look at him. "Good morning, Jarrod. Sleep well?"

"Better than I would have in the car."

"That's good. I was just getting some clothes. Sorry I woke you up."

My voice is tight and cold, and I guess he hears my distress because he asks, "Is something wrong?"

I'm amazed at his audacity. The man kissed me thoroughly last night, spent the night in my bed where he lies mostly naked with a hard-on, and yet has a steady Saturday date with another woman. Today is Saturday. He'll be with Valerie tonight. Has he no shame?

"I . . . I just want to shower and get ready for the day," I stammer, glancing over my shoulder at him. "I didn't mean to bother you."

To my consternation, Jarrod sits up, and the bedclothes fall to his waist. "I'm glad you woke me up. I've got to be going, too. Thanks for putting me up."

Before he can get out of bed and tempt me further, I hastily leave the bedroom and hurry into the small shower cubicle, where I wash and shampoo quickly, towel off and step into clean jeans and a knit shirt.

I'm glad Jarrod is going to be leaving. Somehow, I have to make it clear to him that he doesn't need to return to Shadow Haven. We can do our business mostly by phone, or I'll come to his office if I have to. But I don't want him physically close to me.

I guess I'll let him continue to represent me, despite my doubts, because if nothing else, his determination to defeat the Colquitts is in my best interest.

But my interest stops there. It has to.

When I come back into the kitchen, I find that Jarrod has made coffee and is engaged in an animated conversation with Michaela. She is showing him her GameBoy, and he's complimenting her on her skills.

Mr. Nice Guy. Ha.

I pour myself a cup of coffee, load it with milk and sugar, and try to quell my irritation.

"So, you're off now?" I say, holding a verbal, invisible door open for him.

He leaves Michaela and the GameBoy and comes to me. He's fully dressed once again, wearing the white shirt and slacks he had on when he arrived yesterday. They look just as good on him now as they did then, even if they're a little rumpled. "I've got to go back to New Orleans," he tells me, running his fingers along one of my arms.

I step back. "Yes, I imagine you do."

"Gabriella?"

"What?"

"What's the matter?"

I turn to look at him, trying to hide my disdain. "Nothing's the matter. Why?"

"It's just that . . . well, last night . . ." He lets the inference hang in the air. Last night I was nice to him, today I'm not.

"Last night was a mistake, Jarrod. You said so yourself. Unethical, I think you called it. Well, you're right. It was unethical, and it can't happen again.

You're my attorney. And from now on, we can do our business by phone, or if you need me to, I can come to your office. But you're excused as my bodyguard. There's no need for you to come back to Shadow Haven again."

The mix of pain and confusion on his face nearly cuts my heart out, but I think about Valerie. Maybe there's a logical explanation for Valerie. Maybe she's not his girlfriend. Maybe she's his mother, or a favorite aunt.

But probably not. A man like Jarrod wouldn't have a steady date with his mother.

I trusted Charles, and he broke my heart. I believed him, and he nearly destroyed me. It won't happen to me again.

I walk to the front door and open it. "Call me and let me know what's going on with the case," I tell him as he goes out.

He pauses at the door and gives me an unhappy, troubled look. "You call me when you're ready to explain what's going on here."

Twenty-seven

THE MORNING IS HOT AND HEAVY WITH SUMMER humidity, and by eleven o'clock, I'm dripping with perspiration. I've finished painting the hallway, and I stand back to admire my work. It's a lovely rose color and will look great when I get the crown molding painted white again. It feels good to be personally involved in restoring my childhood home. It relieves some of my guilt for having neglected it for so long.

Wielding the paintbrush has also helped ease my anger at Jarrod's deceit and my anxiety over facing Ira Peabody in court. I laugh grimly, remembering something else Grandnana had liked to say: "Busy hands are happy hands." I wouldn't exactly call mine happy hands, but they are for the moment distracted from my troubles.

Painting the hall has also rendered me ravenous. It's been a long time since the middle-of-the-night Chinese food. "Want to go see if Kisha would like to have lunch with us?" I ask Michaela, who jumps at the offer, thrilled to get to see her new friend again. I look up Rosalie's phone number and in minutes, using my new cell phone, make arrangements to pick them both up for lunch. I admit I'm glad to have a new friend, too. I wish I felt comfortable enough with Rosalie to confide in her about Jarrod. But on a personal level, he's history as far as I'm concerned.

To my surprise and delight, since coming to Shadow Haven Michaela has developed a taste for Cajun food, and I've been able to use some of Grandnana's recipes. Today, she asks if we can have jambalaya at the local restaurant that's become her favorite. Better that than Mickey D's, I think.

Rosalie and Kisha live in a modest house not far from Shadow Haven, on the road into Tibonne. They are waiting on the front porch when we arrive, and I wonder if the two of them need friends as badly as Michaela and I do.

"How you doing, Gabriella?" Rosalie asks when she and Kisha get into the car. I wonder if Danny has told her about my midnight shooting incident.

"I'm okay," I tell her. "I painted the hall this morning. It was a huge job, but it looks great now. The graffiti's gone, thank God. I can't wait to get to the rest of the house."

"You doing all that fixin' up by yourself?"

"Hardly," I laugh. "I hired Willie Johnson and a couple of other guys who're doing most of the heavy work. They're supposed to be coming over this afternoon to install some new locks on the windows.

Jarrod . . . uh, Mr. Landry, my attorney, thinks the house isn't secure enough."

"Your attorney? What've you got an attorney for?" It's the first time Rosalie has pried into my business, but it's my own fault. I shouldn't have slipped and mentioned anything about an attorney. I haven't told Rosalie about the custody suit. I'm not sure I want her to know. It's painful and embarrassing, and I'd like to start over here in Tibonne with a clean slate. Of course, she may already know if she and Danny Comeaux share gossip at the courthouse drinking fountain.

"He's helping me tie up some loose ends," I tell her, which is true. "There are a few details that need to be worked out with Charles's estate."

"Sounds like your husband was rich."

I didn't mean to imply that, but I guess Rosalie figures that only rich people have big enough legal problems with their estates that they have to hire a lawyer.

"He came from a wealthy family. They're . . . uh . . . contesting part of his will." Actually, I suppose technically that I'm the one doing the contesting. They have the codicil on their side.

"Was that your lawyer who came into my office the other day?"

"He wasn't my lawyer then."

"If I'd known he was looking up something that could hurt you, I'd've run his sorry backside off," Rosalie says.

I smile at her enthusiastic loyalty. "As it's turned out, I've hired him to represent me. It was a good thing he found out that I owed those taxes. It gave me a chance to take care of them before—"

I break off. I almost said, "before the custody case goes to court."

But Rosalie is tenacious. "Before what?"

We arrive at the restaurant, which thankfully interrupts the conversation. The girls want to sit at a table by themselves, and the waitress accommodates them by seating them at a table for two, with us nearby in a booth.

"It's fun to watch them grow up, isn't it?" Rosalie says with a laugh. "I'm glad you moved back to Tibonne. Kisha is crazy about Michaela."

"And vice versa," I agree. "Michaela was so excited to get to see her again. Why don't you let her come and play on the new swing set after lunch?"

"I would, but we're supposed to go to a picnic at our church later. Raincheck?"

"Sure."

We order lunch, and the waitress is barely out of earshot when Rosalie picks up where the conversation left off.

"What kind of trouble is your husband's kinfolk givin' you, Gabriella?" She sips her tea and looks at me thoughtfully, waiting for an answer, but I don't know what to say. Finally, she adds, "You don't have to tell me if you don't want to, but it seems to me you're mighty lonely and maybe you need a friend to talk to."

I desperately need a friend to talk to. I thought I had that friend in Jarrod, but I was mistaken. So, hesitantly but with a need to unload my burden, I tell her everything—about my miserable marriage, my husband's accusation about my mental health, about the codicil and the Colquitts' threat to take Michaela away from me. When I'm finished, I'm nearly in tears.

"Dear sweet Jesus," Rosalie says and reaches over and pats my arm. "I don't know how you're standing up with all that goin' on and tryin' to fix up your place and all. Listen, how can I help? Tell me what I can do. Nobody ought to have to face all that alone."

Her kindness summons the tears at last. I'm sniveling when the waitress arrives with steaming bowls of jambalaya and gumbo. If she notices anything is wrong, she doesn't let on. I don't care that she sees me crying, but I don't want Michaela to notice, so I turn my back to the girls' table and dab at my eyes with my napkin. In a few moments, I manage to say to Rosalie, "Thanks. I don't know what you can do, but it helps to know I have a friend."

Before dropping Rosalie and Kisha back at their house, I give Rosalie my cell phone number, and we promise that we'll get together soon. Michaela waves and waves out the back window, and I know we are both grateful for our new friends.

My little crying jag helped me release the tension that has been my constant companion since coming to Shadow Haven. I glance in the rearview mirror, however, and see that my face is red and blotchy and looks like hell. It doesn't matter. I'm not expecting to see anyone but Willie Johnson.

Willie is at the house when we arrive, busily installing the extra window locks.

"Afternoon, Ms. Deveaux," he calls, stopping what he's doing to come greet me.

"Hi, Willie. Everything going okay?"

He has a curious look on his face. "I suppose so. But . . . why'd you leave the house all open? It ain't going to do you no good to put in all these fancy locks if you go away with your front door and all your windows wide open."

I don't know what he's talking about. "Willie, I locked this place up tight before I left, except for the deadbolt. I knew you didn't have a key to it yet."

"Well, when me and the guys got here, every window in the place was open, and both front and back doors. I figured you must've wanted to air it out after painting it. The hall looks great, by the way."

Somebody has been in my house. Somebody broke in, just as Jarrod had before. Unless Jarrod had made himself a set of keys when he went to the hardware store. Had he come back and opened everything up? That makes no sense, when he's the one who insisted on the deadbolt locks.

"Have you seen anybody around?" I ask Willie.

"No, ma'am. Just me and the boys."

"Well, maybe I'm losing my mind," I say in a joking manner, but not thinking it funny. "Maybe I did open it up to air it out. Thanks for closing the windows again. I hate paying to air-condition the outside."

Michaela goes to her room to play, and I consider who might have done this. It seems most likely it would have been the intruders from the other night, but I would have expected them to ransack the place. I move quickly through the downstairs, but nothing appears missing or even disturbed.

Were they just trying to frighten me? Mess with my mind? Well, if that's the case, they've succeeded. My nerves are taut and singing once again.

I go into the parlor where the stone for Charles's monument seems to mock me from the carving table. I haven't even thought about touching it since the day the marble chip cut my cheek. I peer around the room, and again find nothing out of the ordinary.

Until I look up at the broken mirror that hangs above the mantel.

There, etched in what appears to be lipstick, in a frail handwriting is written: Find Marie Françoise!

CHAPTER

Twenty-eight

❧

NEW ORLEANS IS LIKE A SAUNA WHEN WE FINALLY arrive and find a parking space near the French Quarter. I'm not really quite sure what I'm doing here, but when I saw the message scribbled on the mirror, I knew I could no longer ignore Grandnana's directive.

Grandnana must have written it, although I never knew spirits could manifest in such a physical way. But who else could it have been? No one but Michaela knows about Grandnana's spirit and Marie Françoise.

After seeing the cryptic writing, I knew exactly who'd opened all the doors and windows. It wasn't returning intruders. It was my grandnana. I guess it was her way of getting my attention. She must have figured I'd wander into the parlor to shut the windows and find the message.

I left Michaela playing in her room, knowing she was safe with Willie in the house, and went to the enchanted garden to try to get some focus on the task at hand. I tried once again unsuccessfully to summon Grandnana's spirit but instead received a clear mental picture of where I might find Marie Françoise. It was the image of a small shop in the French Quarter where Grandnana had once taken me. In my mind's eye, behind the counter of the store I saw the tall woman with silver hair and indigo eyes whom I met in my first dream. It won't be hard to identify Marie Françoise when at last we meet for real.

I'm hoping to find that shop on this run into New Orleans. There's no telling whether Marie Françoise is still in town; it was many years ago when I went there with my grandmother. But it's the only place I know to start looking for the enigmatic Marie Françoise.

Except for when we arrived at the airport, it's been years since I've been to the Crescent City, but like with Tibonne, nothing much appears to have changed, at least not in the Quarter. That is, I think, part of its charm. It's a timeless place; some would say a magical place. I could use a little magic on this venture.

"Come on, *chérie*," I say, helping Michaela out of the car. "Let's go see what we can find."

It's nearly four o'clock, a little late to start this search, but the fear and uncertainty that surround me urge me to get on with it. Grandnana's efforts to warn me have been staggering and are not to be ignored.

For Michaela's benefit, I've disguised this journey as a shopping trip. I *am* shopping, in a manner of speaking. Shopping for Marie Françoise.

We wander down several of the narrow streets in the *Vieux Carré*, past all kinds of shops and boutiques, making stops here and there, looking at the wares. In one gallery, I see an artist's interpretation of the *loup-garou* depicted as a rather harmless-looking blue dog. He's kind of cute and cartoonish and looks nothing at all like the snarling creature in my nightmare.

Along the way, I make discreet inquiries about Marie Françoise, but no one seems to have heard of her. She must have been gone from the Quarter for a long time. Neither do I come across a storefront that looks like the one I envisioned in the enchanted garden.

Then we turn a corner, and suddenly I feel a tingle shimmer down my spine. I gaze down the tiny street and know intuitively this is where I came with Grandnana all those years ago. But does Marie still have her little store here?

We pass several shops, but none of them looks or feels like the one I'm seeking, until we come at last to a small perfumery. I know immediately this is the right place.

But Marie Françoise hadn't sold perfume. I remember abruptly that she'd been a psychic reader. What she sold were votive candles and incense, tarot cards and talismans. But her main stock in trade—I remember Grandnana trying to explain Marie's mysterious wares to me—had been giving her customers hopes and dreams for a better life.

Obviously, Marie is no longer here, but maybe

whoever has the place now will know of her whereabouts. "Let's go in here and take a look around," I say to Michaela.

The atmosphere in the shop is redolent with perfume, knockoffs of the expensive fragrances advertised in slick magazines. Bottles of beautiful golden liquid shine in the sunlight from the glass shelves and displays. "May I help you?" the shopkeeper asks as she approaches. She's a pleasant-looking woman, in her fifties, I guess. But she's not Marie Françoise.

"I may be mistaken," I say, "but I think I once came here, long ago, and there was a woman who told fortunes."

The owner of the perfumery smiles. "Yes, of course, Marie Françoise. She's retired. I bought this place from her more than five years ago."

Five years is a long time. She could be anywhere. Dead even. "Do you know where I might find her?"

The woman thinks for a moment. "I don't know where she went, but I have an address on the paperwork from when I bought the shop. If you'll wait just a minute, I can get it for you from my files."

I thank her and send up a little prayer that the address will prove to be a current one. We've spent a long time wandering the maze of streets and alleys in the Quarter. It's growing late, and Michaela is getting tired. "How about some perfume, *chérie?*" I offer as a reward for her stoic patience during our long search.

There's a section of the store that offers lighter

scents designed for children, and Michaela chooses one in a decanter shaped like a frog. When the proprietor reappears, Michaela hands it to her. "I'm getting frog perfume," she explains with great seriousness.

"It's a wonderful scent," the woman says, taking the green bottle. "Shall I wrap it for you, or would a bag be sufficient?"

"A bag would be fine," I reply and hand the woman a twenty-dollar bill. In return, she gives me a small slip of yellow paper with an address written on it. "This is where she lived when she sold the place. It's not far from here. Are you familiar with New Orleans?"

"I used to be, but I haven't been here in a while."

The shop owner gives me directions while she rings up the sale. "You could walk from here," she says, handing over my change, "but it's a little far. You might want to go in your car."

I thank the woman and take Michaela's hand as we leave the shop. Outside, I study the address. It's a fair distance, and my feet hurt. "Let's get the car."

The address proves to be that of a rather ramshackle two-story cinder block and stucco house that once was probably respectable but which has now been subdivided into apartments. I gaze at it from the sidewalk, wondering if it's safe to take Michaela inside.

Inhaling deeply, I search for guidance from within, but before I can feel anything, I get a nudge in the middle of my back, sending me forward. A shove like the one I felt in my dream that sent me into and through the figure of Marie Françoise.

So that *had* been Grandnana's spirit communicating with Marie Françoise in the dream. And she's here with me right now, making it clear that I'm at the right place. I have the power to know these things if I'll just let myself trust in it. Suddenly, I'm no longer afraid. I take Michaela's hand and give it a squeeze.

"Let's see if we can find this Mary Frances you've been telling me about."

CHAPTER

Twenty-nine

❧

THERE ARE FOUR DOORBELLS, NONE OF WHICH HAS A name beside it. I pick the top one and press hard.

"Who's there?" A voice sounds from a small intercom, and Michaela and I both jump.

"Uh, my name's Gabriella Deveaux, and I'm looking for Marie Françoise."

There's a long silence. "What d'you want with Marie?"

My heart skips a beat. Whoever this is knows the psychic. Maybe she *is* Marie.

"I'm . . . the granddaughter of an old friend of hers, Ariella Deveaux. I'm in New Orleans for the day, and I thought I'd stop by and say hello."

There comes a low grunt from the speaker, then, "Marie's not here."

"Do you know where I can find her?"

"She doesn't want to be found."

It isn't the answer I'm expecting. Nor one I want to hear. "Why not?"

"Go away," the voice says.

"Please, wait . . ." But there's no reply. "How rude," I mutter. But I can't give up. This person knows where to find Marie Françoise.

And Marie Françoise apparently holds the answers I desperately need. I poise my finger over the bell again, press it, and don't let up.

The wrought-iron gate leading into the center courtyard of the old house creaks as it swings open, and I feel Michaela hesitate. "Come on, *chérie*. It's okay." I place my hand reassuringly on her shoulder, and we go inside, but both of us jump as the metal gate clangs shut behind us.

Large philodendrons with dark, serrated leaves like the hands of giants pick at us as we walk down the flagstones to the doorway to which we've been directed. Faded yellow stucco is peeling away from the walls, exposing the gray concrete block beneath. A lizard skitters across the path in front of us, and Michaela lets out a little cry in the quiet afternoon.

The door opens before we reach it, and a small, bent woman peers out at us. She doesn't have silver hair and indigo eyes, but her features seem familiar. It's been a long time since I last saw Marie. This could be her, I suppose, the aged version.

"What'd you say your name was?" she asks, looking from me to Michaela.

Whoever she is, I get the creepy feeling this woman is like the witch in Hansel and Gretel, and that Michaela and I might soon become dinner.

"Gabriella," I reply, forcing a smile and extending a hand. "Gabriella Deveaux. And this is my daughter, Michaela. My grandmother, Ariella, was a friend of Marie Françoise." I hesitate, then ask, "You wouldn't happen to be her, would you?"

The woman ignores my proffered hand. "No. I'm not Marie," she snaps. "I'm her sister, Nicola. Marie's not here." Nicola studies me for a long moment, then stands aside and gestures for us to come in. "Marie's retired, you know. Doesn't do the psychic thing anymore. Drained her, that's what people did. Drained her till she wore down to a nubbin. I thought she was going to pass this plane for a while. I'm the one made her retire."

"I . . . I'm not after a psychic reading," I say, although I'm not totally sure it's the truth. Since the spirit of my grandmother has sent me in search of Marie Françoise, the old psychic is likely going to have to put her powers to use on my behalf in some way. If she will. I remember from my dream her reluctance to become involved. She seemed, in fact, as crotchety as her sister Nicola. I hesitate to impose myself on them.

Nicola turns her back on us and shuffles into the dark interior of the small apartment. "You come looking for Marie, means you're in trouble," she says. "What kind of trouble are you in?"

"Trouble?" I try to act innocent. "I don't know about any trouble. Like I said, we were in town—" But Nicola cuts me off.

"Let's get to the bottom of this," she says gruffly, going to a bookshelf and taking down a small rectangular object wrapped in a silk kerchief. "Here. Sit." She pokes a bony finger in the direction of a dilapidated black Naugahyde couch.

Nicola unwraps the silk covering, revealing a deck of cards. I recognize the tarot instantly. I have a deck like it myself, packed away somewhere. I hadn't thought about the tarot the whole time I was away from Shadow Haven, but I recall now my Grandnana using it from time to time to gain "clarity" on certain situations, as she put it.

I could certainly use some clarity on this situation. I'm totally confounded by it all. But I worry what a reading just now might foretell. I consider leaving, but some force compels me to stay.

Nicola shuffles the cards with the proficiency of a Las Vegas dealer, then begins to slap them facedown on the table.

"What's she doing, Mama?" Michaela whispers in my ear.

"She's . . . uh . . . playing cards, sort of." I wince to think what Elizabeth would make of this visit. She'd probably accuse me of being a witch or something.

Not wanting Michaela to be frightened by anything bad that might be revealed in the reading, I take her into the adjoining room where I can keep an eye on her. I'm glad I brought some of her favorite books. Hopefully, they'll keep her occupied for a little while.

When the cards are arranged in the order that seems to satisfy Nicola, the woman peers up at me. "I can feel a strong energy through the cards," she says, then adds darkly, "not good energy."

I swallow. This weird woman is unnerving me.

"That's why you've been sent to Marie Françoise."

"But you said she's retired. Maybe you can help me instead."

Nicola clucks her tongue. "I doubt it. My power is nothing like Marie's."

The first card she turns over shows a blindfolded and bound woman surrounded by a fence of swords. Nicola whistles softly. "That would be you, my dear. Hemmed in by what you don't know, or what you refuse to see."

I frown. There's nothing I'm refusing to see. That's why I came here, to try to get the answers I need to protect myself and Michaela. But I keep quiet.

The next card shows a monstrous figure. It reads "The Devil" at the bottom. "This card is in the position that shows what brought you to this moment. You are here because you are bedeviled by something or someone."

My mind flashes instantly to Elizabeth Colquitt. "You can say that again," I mutter.

Nicola studies the card more closely. "See there, at the foot of the beast, there's a man and a woman chained together. You have been linked to the one who besets you. Until you sever the link and dispatch your devil, you will never be free."

I can hardly wait to completely and forever sever my link to the Colquitt family.

The next card is the "High Priestess," who sits on her mystical throne, guarding the gate of knowledge. "This represents your 'Hopes and Fears,'" she says. "I should have known Marie would show up here."

"Marie?"

"She's always the High Priestess whenever she shows up in a reading." She looks up at Gabriella. "She is your hope, *chérie*. Could be your only hope. You must seek her out."

Icy tentacles of fear begin to spread through me once again.

The following card shows a big red heart stabbed through with three swords. "Well, that's good," Nicola says.

Nothing about it looks good to me. "How so?"

"It's present, but passing, your heartbreak. You've had some sad times in the past months, but soon, this will pass away. Beware, though, as this card also indicates deceit."

The woman's accuracy about my months of heartbreak is astounding. I hope her prediction that it will soon end will come true. I lean forward, eager for Nicola to go on.

The next card is a strange one, showing a frowning face in the moon, with howling dogs and a scorpion dredging itself from a lake. Nicola shakes her head. "Not good. This on top of the Devil card. The Moon represents the forces working for or against you and as you can see, they aren't good forces. I'm afraid there is much evil surrounding you. I understand now why the spirits have sent you to Marie."

I blink in surprise. How did Nicola know a spirit had sent me? But I guess there isn't much one can hide from a strong psychic such as Nicola is proving to be. I wonder how much more powerful Marie Françoise can possibly be.

Nicola turns up a card with a yellow background, showing a figure in a red hat and boots making off with five swords, while two remain planted in the ground behind him. "Interesting," she says. "Is someone trying to steal something from you?"

I suppose Elizabeth's attempt to gain custody of Michaela could be considered theft. Or was she referring to something else? "Perhaps." The accuracy of the reading is chilling. I wish she'd hurry. I want to know the outcome of all this.

Next comes the six of swords, a card showing a woman and a child in a boat being poled by a man across a body of water. "You are soon to go on a difficult journey across the water," Nicola tells me. "But it is a journey you cannot avoid."

"Journey? To where?"

"To find Marie, of course. On this journey you will encounter many disturbances. You will be left to your own devices and will have to master the situation internally."

The Queen of Swords comes next. "This shows the influence of Others in your reading," Nicola says.

"There is a woman with a sharp tongue and a strong will who can either help you or harm you."

Oh, she'd never help me, I think, gazing at the card that to me represents Elizabeth. The figure of the Queen sits in a fancy chair, with an upright sword in one hand. She's making a commanding gesture with the other hand, as if she rules the world. That's Elizabeth all right, looking strong and commanding. Does this indicate that she will rule in the end?

"This one will be an important card," Nicola says, turning the next card over. "This is you again, in the future." This card, too, has a yellow background, and it shows a woman dressed in white with one hand on a lion's head, the other near its mouth. "Strength," Nicola reads the word at the bottom of the card. She squints up at me. "You have greater powers than you can imagine, Gabriella. Powers that have never been revealed to you. This cards tells me you're going to have to learn to use those powers. You must develop them until you have the strength to literally tame the lion. Your survival depends upon it."

Powers? What powers? Is there something Grandnana didn't teach me? I remember fleetingly the feeling of exultation and heady power that came to me the night I conducted the ritual in the enchanted garden. And just a little while ago I had the distinct feeling that I had the power to know things, such as Grandnana's presence, if I would only let myself see.

The final card of the reading is another from the Major Arcana. There are many important cards on this table, and I know I'd better pay attention to their message.

This card is The Fool. It shows the figure of a jester looking cheerfully up to the sky. He carries a hobo's bag on a stick over his shoulder, and a little white dog frisks at his feet. He appears happy and carefree, even though he's about to step off a cliff.

"Trust is the issue here," Nicola says. "In the end, you will have to trust in yourself, even when you're not sure about your next step." She clucks her tongue. "It's damn near the only hopeful card in the deck, if you can get your act together. At least it's in the Outcome position. But you've got a lot of rough water to travel before you ever get to this place."

Even her hopeful reading of this card sounds nebulous. If the tarot can be believed, I'm in for it.

Nicola reviews the cards, shaking her head from time to time. Then she raises her aged eyes to meet my gaze. "The spirits are right to send you to Marie," she repeats grimly. "You need her wisdom, her power, her guidance, and her protection. She can help you like no other."

This at last undoes me. "But where can I find Marie?" My confidence is shaken, and fear lurks at the edges of my consciousness.

"She's become a recluse. She lives in the swamp."

"The swamp!" Was that the hot, wet, dark place of my dream? I shudder. I have no desire to go into the swamp. In fact, I've always been afraid of going too far into the dark shadows of the bayou country.

Nicola gathers the cards back into a pack, rewraps them in the silk cloth, and ties them with a leather cord. "Marie doesn't want to be bothered with people anymore," she says matter-of-factly. "She won't be particularly happy to see you."

I'm not particularly anxious to see her either. "Are you sure this is necessary? I don't want to intrude on her."

"You must go. There is no question. If you don't, great harm could come to you." She hesitates, then lowers her voice and glances at Michaela in the next room, "and to her."

Another chill shudders up my spine. Harm to Michaela? I think giving up custody to the Colquitts would be harmful, but not in the sense I believe Nicola means. "What harm?"

"There is one who is watching you," she says. "I can't see who it is, but I believe it is a man. He is watching, and waiting, and when the time is right, he will bring great harm to you and your daughter. He must be stopped, but only you can do it. It is your destiny. But you will need to strengthen your powers to overcome his threat, and Marie's the one who can help you most."

A man. Watching us from the woods. Maybe that's who opened all the doors and windows at Shadow Haven—it wasn't Grandnana after all. Was he toying with us, like a cat with a mouse? When, I wonder with alarm, will he strike at us directly? And what kind of power must I have to defeat him?

Michaela has grown bored and comes to my side. "I want to go."

"We're going now, baby. Thanks for being such a good girl."

"Just a minute. I have something for you."

Nicola places the tarot cards back on the shelf and goes to a small bureau. From the top drawer she takes out what appears to be two rocks attached with wire to leather cords. But the stones are not ordinary rocks. They're white and polished and have a mysterious glow about them.

"My magic is not as strong as Marie's," Nicola says. "But these talismans may protect you until you reach her. Here, put them on."

She steps forward and ties one around my neck, the other around Michaela's. "There. Now," she says, reaching for a notepad, "here's how you will find Marie."

CHAPTER

Thirty

❦

My teeth are on edge by the time we leave Nicola's apartment. I tell myself her warnings are just figments of an old woman's imagination, based on nothing but her interpretation of the tarot cards. Still what she told me has deeply disturbed me. Nicola is a psychic of great power. Grandnana must have known I'd have to find Nicola before I could reach Marie; perhaps somehow she even managed to guide me to her. To ignore Nicola's warnings would be both foolish and dangerous.

Nicola had said a man is watching me. Someone of great evil. Ira Peabody? He seemed like a schmuck, but not necessarily evil. There's another possibility, one I don't wish to entertain but that I can't ignore. Nicola could have been speaking of Jarrod. In spite of his professed desire to help me, he could be deceiving me on that score just as he deceived me with his kiss.

Nothing is as it seems.

I sit quietly in the car for a long moment before I

start the engine. I wish I could trust Jarrod. I wish I could go to him with all this and let him help me sort it out. More than anything, I wish to God I'd never looked in his date book or found out there was a Valerie. The truth would have surfaced eventually, however, after I'd made a royal fool of myself.

My throat is tight and my nerves are tense. I'm alone and frightened and being sent into the bowels of the Louisiana bayou country by spirits and fortune-tellers. Maybe Charles was right. Maybe I am crazy.

I look down at the paper crumpled tightly in my hand. Directions to Marie's hideout in the swamp. If what Nicola told me is true, Marie has retired to one of the darkest, most remote corners of the bayou, unreachable by land. Nicola also warned me not to return to Shadow Haven, claiming that it's too dangerous. Whoever is watching me is ready to spring. She instructed me instead to go directly to Marie's.

I believe she might be right, that it's risky to return to Shadow Haven, but I left in such a hurry to make this trip to New Orleans, I didn't pack an overnight bag or anything. It's not far from Tibonne to New Orleans. I hadn't planned on making this an overnight.

I glance at Michaela, who is watching me intently with wide brown eyes, as if she senses the intrigue in the air. One thing is certain in my mind. There's no way I'm going to take her on the dangerous journey into the swamp. But where can I leave her? There's no Mrs. Bolton at hand. No family. No one I can trust.

Therefore, I simply won't go, I think resolutely. There must be some other way to resolve this. I'll let Danny handle it. He's the sheriff, after all.

What feels like a charge of electricity suddenly zaps through me, leaving me with the sensation that I've just been slapped. Someone in spirit—Grandnana?—heard my thoughts and attempted to strike them away. Obviously the spirits aren't going to let me out of this. I start the engine at last, but I'm unsure where I'm headed.

I have to force myself to concentrate on negotiating the New Orleans traffic during rush hour. It seems like a maze to me, and for a while, I make turns at random. My heart beats heavily as I try to decide what to do. Eventually, I find myself heading down the highway back to Tibonne, simply because I don't know where else to go.

Suddenly, my phone starts blaring a musical tune from somewhere inside my car, and I jump, jerking the steering wheel to the left. A horn blares, and I turn to see a large pickup truck swerve to miss my car. The driver glares at me, and as he speeds by, he motions to me with a rude gesture. The phone keeps up its abrasive bugling, and I pull off the road into a parking lot, shaking. Whoever thought it was funny or cool for a phone to ring like that ought to be shot. I take the phone from my purse and look at the caller ID. I recognize the number; it's Jarrod.

"Aren't you going to answer it, Mama?" Michaela asks.

The phone rings again.

There is one who is watching you . . . watching, and waiting, and when the time is right, he will bring great harm to you and your daughter.

"No." I turn the phone's power off.

"But someone wanted to talk to you."

"There's no one I want to talk to at the moment. Besides, it's dangerous to talk on the phone while you're driving. I almost had a wreck when it rang."

Unnerved, I slide the car back into the traffic, which thins as we drive away from the city. I'm torn by my dilemma. According to Nicola, it's dangerous for us to return home, but I don't want to take Michaela with me in search of Marie. I'm not afraid to undertake the perilous journey through the swamp, but not for a minute would I consider taking a six-year-old along. There are snakes and quicksand, mosquitoes and muck in there. It's easy to get lost. A person could die and no one would ever find the body.

It's not a fate I anticipate, but I'm certainly not willing to put my daughter at such risk.

I reach across and run my fingers through Michaela's thick brown hair. "Want to stop for some supper, *chérie?*" I need time to think.

"Okay," Michaela says, stifling a yawn. It's been a big day, especially for a kid who's been dragged all over the Quarter. I'm exhausted as well, from the trip, the stress, and having had only a few hours' sleep last night. I make a sudden decision.

"I have an idea. Let's make a little vacation out of this. What do you say we find a nice place to spend the night, get some supper and have a good night's sleep before we go home?"

"Whatever," Michaela says, her little head beginning to nod.

The next village we come to is too small to offer accommodations, but a few miles farther along the road, we reach a larger town, and I see an advertisement for a Victorian style bed-and-breakfast. Michaela is sound asleep by the time I pull into the parking lot. It's almost seven o'clock. I turn off the engine, roll down my window, and drink in the quiet. I become aware that I have a pain in my jaw from clenching my teeth. I try to relax it. I rotate my shoulders and inhale deeply. Before me the imposing, turreted old home that is the B&B looms in the fading light.

What am I doing here? This is solving nothing. Nicola said it was urgent that I get to Marie's right away.

I gaze at my sleeping daughter, and my heart wrenches. What have I done to put her in such danger? I think back over the chain of events that led us back to Shadow Haven and try to come up with an explanation for why we're supposedly surrounded by evil. But I come up with nothing other than the Colquitts' attempt to take custody of Michaela, and that, mean-spirited as it might be, can't be considered evil or dangerous.

And yet, I am beginning to feel the danger now myself, like electricity coursing just under my skin. I know Grandnana and Nicola are right; the evil around us is coalescing into a pure, physical threat to our lives, but its source remains elusive.

I'm clammy with perspiration, and I rub my hands down my arms as my mind wraps around the question of what to do with Michaela. I'm not sure how long it will take me to find Marie's remote cabin, how long I will be there, and what actions I might have to take afterward. I need someone I can trust to look after my daughter, but I know of no one.

And then I remember Rosalie Odette and her offer to help. No one must know where I leave Michaela. Can I trust Rosalie to hide and protect Michaela for a few days while I go on my quest?

I drum my nails on the steering wheel. It's getting stuffy in the car, and it's hard for me to catch my breath. Michaela stirs but doesn't wake. I'm overcome by a creeping sense of urgency. I don't have time to dally here overnight. Something's afoot in the energy field of my world. I can feel it. To put off this journey even one more day might bring disaster.

I take my small address book from my purse and look up Rosalie's number.

CHAPTER
Thirty-one

ROSALIE'S PHONE RINGS THREE TIMES, THEN TO MY surprise, is answered by a man. I almost hang up. Maybe I dialed the wrong number. "May I speak to Rosalie?"

"Just a minute." I hear a muffled sound, like his hand covering the receiver, and he hollers, "Rosalie, it's for you."

I've made a bad mistake. I can't leave Michaela with Rosalie if she has company. Especially a man.

"Hello?" Rosalie's voice is strong and warm.

"Uh, hi, Rosalie, it's Gabriella Deveaux calling."

"Gabriella! It's good to hear from you. I enjoyed our lunch today. Let's do it again real soon."

"Sure, I'd like that." So much has happened this afternoon, I feel like our lunch with Rosalie and Kisha was days ago rather than hours. "I . . . I was calling to ask you a favor, but I see you have . . . uh, company."

Rosalie laughs. "Oh, that's not company. That's my little brother, Ambrose. He drives a truck for a pipeline supply company. He was passing through and stopped by for a free meal. I took him to the picnic. But he's getting ready to leave. What's the favor?"

I take a deep breath. It's not easy for me to ask favors, especially of this nature. "I . . . I was wondering if Michaela could sleep over with Kisha for a couple of nights? I have some business I need to take care of, and I don't want to take her along."

"I told you I wanted to help you. Of course Michaela can stay with us. When?"

"Could I bring her over in about an hour?"

"An hour?" Rosalie sounds surprised but adds quickly, "Sure, I mean, why not?"

"Thanks, Rosalie. I owe you big-time for this."

I hang up and start the car. When she awakens, I smile at Michaela. "I have a surprise for you. How would you like to spend the night with Kisha?"

Michaela's eyes widen. "Cool!"

"We'll stop by the drive-in for burgers, then do a little shopping before I take you over there."

Michaela looks at me quizzically. I guess she must be wondering about our odd afternoon and my indecision about where to stay the night. But she's obviously excited at being able to spend the night with her new friend and isn't going to question the decision that has been made.

When we finish our meal, I head to the nearby Wal-Mart. It's the only place open at almost nine o'clock at night. I'm not going to take a chance on going back to Shadow Haven with Michaela, so I plan to purchase pajamas and new clothes and some toys and games for the children to play with before dropping Michaela off at Rosalie's.

Afterward, however, I have to return to Shadow Haven. I could buy clothes and other things I need for the journey, but I want my gun. It might be dangerous to go home, but I think it would be even more perilous to go into the swamp unarmed.

When we reach Rosalie's house, Michaela dashes to the front door just as Kisha runs out of it. The two little girls squeal in delight when they collide, and I smile. At least something good has come out of all this. Rosalie follows her daughter onto the front porch, smiling too, but I see a look of concern in her eyes.

"Come in, Gabriella."

I gather the large Wal-Mart bags from the backseat and go into the house.

"What're those?" Rosalie asks, nodding at the shopping bags.

"I . . . uh, I didn't have time to go to Shadow Haven to pick up Michaela's things, so I bought what she'll need, and some toys for both the girls."

Rosalie eyes me suspiciously. "Sit down a minute. Want some sweet tea?"

I feel a brush of panic. I don't have time to be social, but I can't be rude to Rosalie, whose help I so desperately need. "Sure. I can't stay long, but . . ."

Rosalie takes two glasses from the cupboard and heads to the fridge. "This . . . business . . . you got to take care of, is it about your in-laws and that custody thing? Nine o'clock on a Saturday night seems an odd time to be meeting with your lawyer." She raises a speculative brow. "Unless he's more than just your lawyer."

My cheeks flush. "It's . . . not that." I can't tell Rosalie the truth about the mysterious journey upon which I'm about to embark at the urging of spirits and psychics. She might decide I'm crazy, too. "I don't have a hot date, Rosalie," I add, forcing a smile and accepting the tea she offers. "I wish I did. I just have to do some . . . uh . . . research, and I think it would be boring for Michaela." It's only sort of a lie, but I'm no better than Jarrod. I'm lying by not telling her the truth.

"You don't have to explain. It's your business. Can I reach you on your cell phone if Michaela changes her mind and decides she wants to go home in the middle of the night or something? They're awfully young, you know. She ever stayed over with anyone before?"

I hadn't thought of this, but Michaela could become frightened, or homesick, or even actually sick. Maybe this is a bad idea, I think. But it seems my only option. I raise my eyes to meet Rosalie's. "No, she hasn't stayed overnight with a friend before. I think she'll be all right or I wouldn't leave her, but of course, call me if anything comes up."

I don't tell Rosalie, but I seriously doubt my cell phone will work in the backwoods. It's a risk I have to take, that if anything were to happen to Michaela, Rosalie could and would handle it.

"There's something else I need you to do, Rosalie. Please, you must keep Michaela out of sight while I'm gone. Don't let anyone know where she is."

Rosalie's large brown eyes widen, then she frowns. "What's going on, Gabriella? Are you in trouble?"

I try to come up with a reassuring smile. "Not with the law or anything. It's just that my life is, well, like I told you, pretty messed up right now, and I have some things I have to do to try to get it sorted out. I can't tell you where I'm going, Rosalie, or even how long I'll be gone. I don't think it'll take long, maybe a couple of days. Call my cell phone in case of an emergency. But please," I reach over and grasp her arm, "if you want to help us, keep Michaela out of sight."

"Why? Is someone trying to hurt you two?"

I try to think of a reasonable explanation. "I . . . uh . . . believe that the Colquitts might try to pull something on us, like having Michaela placed in a foster home until the custody case is over. If they can't find her, they can't take her."

Rosalie studies me for a long moment. *Oh, please, God, don't let her change her mind.* Then she pats my hand and says, "Nobody's going to find her while she's with me. Tomorrow's Sunday. We'll just stay home and lay low. I'll have to take her to work with me if you're not back by Monday morning. But I think I can keep her out of sight."

I don't want anyone to know where Michaela is, but with Rosalie's office being next door to Danny's, I guess she'll be safe. "Okay. I'll try to be back by Sunday night."

Before I go, I jot a note giving Rosalie written permission to seek medical care for Michaela in case of emergency.

"You going to the moon?" Rosalie frowns again when she sees what I've written.

"No, it's just a precaution. I know nothing's going to happen, but just in case . . ."

Rosalie looks at the paper, then back at me. "You sure you don't want to talk about this? I mean, this sounds serious. You're kind of scaring me."

"I'm sorry, I can't," I reply in a low voice. "I promise, I'll tell you everything when I get back."

If I get back . . .

I finish my tea and rise to go. Rosalie comes to me and puts her substantial arms around me.

"Thanks for being such a good friend," I tell her, returning her hug.

I go into the living room where Michaela and Kisha are happily playing with the new Barbies Michaela picked out at Wal-Mart. I kneel next to Michaela and touch her hair.

"I have to go now, *chérie*. You're going to stay with Miss Rosalie and Kisha tonight, and maybe even for a little while longer. Would you like that?"

Michaela looks up, suddenly hesitant. "Where are you going?"

I pause, then answer as truthfully as I can. "I have to take care of some business outside of Tibonne. You don't want to be dragged along on some old dry boring errand, do you?"

I can see questions in Michaela's expression, but she doesn't press the issue. She stands up and comes to me, Barbie in hand. "Thank you for the new dolls, Mama," she says, and my throat tightens. I draw Michaela into my arms. "You're welcome, *chérie.* I love you."

Michaela holds on to me as tightly as she did the day she was stung by the fire ants. "I love you, too, Mama. Come back real soon, okay?" It's as if she senses that I'm going someplace dangerous.

"I will, baby," I promise, and mean it. Nothing but my death will keep me from coming home to Michaela, not the dark of the swamp, not whatever dreadful information might be imparted to me by Marie Françoise. I will be back, and soon. I don't make promises lightly, especially to my daughter.

"'Bye," I say again to both girls and Rosalie, then dash through the door before I change my mind.

CHAPTER

Thirty-two

SHADOW HAVEN LOOMS LIKE A PALE APPARITION lurking behind the shroud of the moss-laden trees as I approach the circular drive. Willie left no lights on, and the moon hasn't risen, but there is enough starlight to reflect faintly on the weathered boards, and the old house seems to glow in the dark.

Blood courses heavily in my veins, sending fear to every cell of my body. The evil is nearby; I can feel it. Is someone in the house, waiting for me? Do I dare go in there and get my things or do I turn tail and run?

I kill the engine and listen to the night. There's no sign that anyone is nearby, and yet, I feel the danger.

I want that gun. I need that gun.

Before I lose my courage, I dash to the front door. Of course, it's locked. Swearing beneath my breath, I fumble to locate the keys. My hand is shaking so hard I have trouble inserting them into the locks.

Inside, I move stealthily in the dark, figuring that if anyone is in here, they'll have a harder time attacking me in the darkness. Swiftly, I hurry on tiptoe down the hall to my bedroom.

I reach beneath the bed and snag the little travel bag. Opening it, I toss in a few clothes. I hurry to the bathroom and throw in my toothbrush and other toiletries. Then on to the kitchen where I add mosquito repellant, a flashlight, and some candy bars to my stash.

I stand still for a moment to catch my breath. Listening to the sounds of the house, I hear nothing extraordinary. With a little whimper of relief, I sense I am alone inside Shadow Haven. There's no one else in the house. I relax my shoulders and am about to go out the front door when I see headlights approaching.

"Damn." I wasn't fast enough in my getaway, and now I'm caught. My gun isn't even loaded.

Maybe it's the sheriff, I think hopefully, but then I decide that I might not want a late-night visit from Danny; he might be bringing me something I don't want, like a subpoena from Ira Peabody.

But when I peer out one of the windows in the front parlor, my heart nearly stops beating when I recognize Jarrod's car.

There is one who is watching you. . . .

I suddenly find it strange that Jarrod always seems to show up at these odd times, like the night he found me doing the ritual in the graveyard. Last night, he'd admitted he'd been parked nearby. For a week now he's been dropping in on me unannounced.

Is he the one who's watching me?

Panicked, I try to think what to do. I don't want him to know I'm about to flee, whether he comes as friend or foe. I see his headlights go out and hear the car door slam. I race back to my bedroom with the travel bag and stuff it under the bed again as Jarrod's knock sounds at the door. I decide to pretend I've been asleep, even though I'm fully clothed. I guess I was too tired to change into pajamas.

"Who's there?" I call out, trying to slow my rapid breathing. I flip on the lights in the hall.

"It's me, Jarrod. Are you all right?"

I unlock the door and lean against the doorsill. I don't invite him in. This is a far cry from the way he was received last night.

"Why wouldn't I be all right, Jarrod?" I try to sound irritated and groggy. "I'm just trying to get some sleep. I thought I told you we could do our business on the phone from now on. What are you doing here?"

"I've been trying to call you all day and never got an answer." He sounds really pissed off.

"I turned my phone off."

"I figured that." He studies my face. "But it was on when I called this afternoon. You must have seen my name or number on the caller ID."

"I did."

"And you didn't want to talk to me."

"No. Not at that moment. I nearly had a wreck when the phone rang in the car."

Jarrod steps past me into the hallway and turns to

face me. His face is almost as red as the rose-colored wall behind him. "Gabriella," he says my name brusquely, "what's going on? Why didn't you call me back if you knew I'd tried to get in touch with you?"

I close the door behind us. "I . . . was going to call you back. I've . . . been busy."

He shakes his head. "It's not that. Something else is going on. Why are you acting like this?"

"Like what? A grouchy, exhausted woman whose sleep's been interrupted one too many nights in a row? Jarrod, it's late. Way beyond business hours. Go home and let me get some rest."

"I'm not here on business." He takes me by both arms. "I want some personal answers. What's with you, Gabriella? Last night you kissed me . . . well, in a way that led me to believe maybe you had some feelings for me. Now, you'll hardly talk to me. What did I do, walk in my sleep and make some big mistake that's got you all upset?"

He made a big mistake, all right, in making a pass at me when he's involved with another woman. I stiffen and shake his arms away, although the temptation to allow him to hold me against him is great. I could use some warmth and physical comfort.

"I can't afford to have feelings for anybody right now, Jarrod. Not until this custody thing is resolved."

And I can't have feelings for anybody who isn't free.

And I can't even think about having feelings for Jarrod or anyone else until I find out who, or what, is threatening me and my daughter.

As disappointed as I was in Jarrod when I discovered his weekly dates with Valerie, standing here so close to him, I don't sense anything evil in him. The evil that I've felt lurking nearby didn't come in the door with him. But that doesn't make this late-night call right. "Please, just go, Jarrod, leave me alone."

"I'm not the enemy, Gabriella," he says, his jaw tight. "I'm on your side, remember?"

I vacillate just a little. He is my lawyer, after all. "Yes, but I don't need you popping in at Shadow Haven just because you can't reach me every minute. I told you I'd call you, and I will."

He glares at me, and I manage to glare right back. "Look, Jarrod, I'm sorry if I've offended you. But I'm really tired. I need you to go and let me get some sleep."

He doesn't budge. What can I say that will convince him to leave?

I sigh heavily, turn away from him and cross my arms over my breasts. I take a few steps toward the back of the house, then face him again. "Jarrod, I came back to Shadow Haven to find my soul, and that takes time. Time alone with myself. With Michaela around, I don't get much of that these days. She's spending the night with a little friend. I appreciate your concern, I truly do, but I just want to be alone tonight."

Jarrod's fists are clenched at his sides, and the look on his face is thunderous. He reaches for the front door knob, then glances back at me.

"Okay, I'll leave you alone, Gabriella," he growls. "I just hope Ira Peabody will do the same."

I watch him drive away, wondering if he'll go very far or if he'll park down the lane like he did last night and keep watch from there. I'm torn between my desire to believe in him and the fear that clutches at my heart. I can't afford to believe in him, not just now, even though it would be so easy to fall into those strong arms and allow him to carry part of my burden.

But what if those strong arms turned against me?

I wait until I can no longer see his taillights, then go into my bedroom and pull the travel bag from beneath the bed again. My hands are shaking. When I return to the kitchen, I take a bottle of water from the fridge and drink deeply of the cool, bracing liquid. It works, sort of, to calm my nerves. I dig in my purse for the slip of paper Nicola gave me with the directions to Marie Françoise's bayou hideaway. I place it on the table and take a seat, trying to pull myself together after my encounter with Jarrod.

And then I hear a voice.

"Gabriella."

Someone is calling my name. "Gabriella," it comes again. I jump up and whirl around, but nobody is there. And then I realize that the sound is coming from inside my head.

"Gabriella."

It's Grandnana's voice, reaching through to me at last. "Oh, thank God, Grandnana," I whisper, and I can feel my grandmother's spirit all around me. It soothes my frazzled nerves and fills me with peace. "I knew you wouldn't forsake me."

"You must go, child. Go now. Listen to the spirits. Trust what you've been told. Go, before it's too late."

The urgency in her tone shatters my momentary serenity and frightens me all over again. Grandnana was always the essence of calm wisdom. She never panicked or went off the deep end. I've never heard her speak like she is now.

"Go with me, Grandnana," I plead to the invisible presence. "Guide me."

Once again I feel a physical nudge from the spirit world. "There are many who are with you," my grandmother's voice continues, but it's growing faint. "God bless and protect you."

With that, a cool breeze strokes my cheek, and Grandnana's spirit is gone.

Suddenly, I hear another noise, this one not so benevolent. It sounds like a footstep on a creaking floorboard at the back of the house. Oh, dear God, maybe there *is* someone else in here! Someone corporeal and not benign.

I grab my purse and the bag containing my gun and make a run for the front door. My only thought is to get out of the house and away from Shadow Haven before the unseen stalker, my dreaded *loup-garou*, can strike.

Gravel sprays from beneath the wheels of my car, which careens dangerously as I take the circle drive too fast. As I scream down the lane and out onto the highway, I keep an eye out for Jarrod's car, but if he's still around, he's found a good hiding place.

When I approach Rosalie's driveway, I slow down, wondering if I've done the right thing in leaving Michaela there. For an instant, I think perhaps I should have brought her along.

But then I remember my destination. I'm headed into dangerous territory, no place for a child. Michaela would probably be terrified by the journey. There are, after all, real alligators out there. And nasty mosquitoes and water moccasins. Michaela could fall into the bayou and get sick from the foul waters. . . .

I step on the accelerator and pass by Rosalie's house. Michaela will definitely be safer here. And if anything does happen to me, I trust that Rosalie will take care of her. I pray nothing will go wrong, that the journey will be short and successful, and at its end, I'll return to find Michaela happily playing Barbies with Kisha Odette.

CHAPTER
Thirty-three

WHEN JARROD LEFT, I DOUBTED HE WOULD GO FAR, and my suspicions are confirmed when I pass by the Sonic hamburger drive-in in Tibonne and spot his car parked there. To my dismay, he seems to have spied me as well, and I watch in my rearview mirror as he pulls out and begins to follow me north on the main street through town.

I swear under my breath. He *was* watching me. Now he's following me. Hot bile rises in my throat.

Steady, I tell myself. Think. I have to ditch him, but how? Jarrod is persistent, I have to hand him that.

I pass the last stoplight at the edge of town and drive on into the night. I think I'm going to scream in nervous frustration. With Jarrod on my tail, I can't turn onto the road that leads to the bayou. My best hope is to go past my turnoff, get on the interstate and try to get lost in the traffic. When I lose Jarrod, I'll turn around and double back to the bayou road.

I check the rearview mirror again and frown. That's odd. There's no one behind me after all, not a single set of headlights in the darkness behind me. Had I only imagined that Jarrod was following me?

Still, I'm taking no chances. Imagination or not, I have to be sure Jarrod is nowhere around before continuing on my journey. I pull into an all-night truck stop near the entrance to the freeway, park in the shadows of the building, and wait, engine running. Keeping my eyes on the road, I fumble in my purse, searching for Nicola's directions. I want to make sure one more time I know where I'm going. My fingers find my checkbook, hairbrush, comb, lipstick, coin purse, wallet.

But no paper. The directions aren't there. I shut my eyes and cringe as I realize I must have left them on the kitchen table when I thought I heard the footsteps.

Geez, Louise, can't I do anything right?

I wonder momentarily if I really heard those footsteps, or if I was just so spooked I imagined them. At any rate, I can't go back to Shadow Haven to get the directions. I'll have to try to remember what was on that paper and trust that I'm being guided by the spirits.

In the meantime, I wait, scanning the night highway with keen eyes, looking for Jarrod's BMW. Ten minutes pass. Fifteen. I'm getting cold with the air conditioner blowing on me, and I see that my car engine is beginning to heat up. I need to be on my way again. Letting out a long breath, I run my fingers through my hair. I guess it's safe to turn around now.

If Jarrod's the one who's been watching me, he's either given up or decided to wait till another time to strike.

I turn off the air conditioner and roll down my window, rubbing my arms and considering my next move. Can I find Marie's place without those directions?

I close my eyes and envision the heavy, almost childlike handwriting on Nicola's note. I concentrate on seeing the words until they start to focus and become clear in my mind's eye. I mentally draw a map of the lonely lanes that wind through farms and fields until they end in the black waters of the bayou. A few moments later, when I finish the exercise, I believe I can make my way without the written directions. Hoping for the best, I swing out onto the highway and backtrack several miles before turning onto the small road I believe Nicola had indicated.

By this time, my stomach is tied firmly into a knot. I wish I'd gone into the truck stop for a sandwich or something. I was so nervous when Michaela and I ordered our burgers earlier, I could hardly touch a thing. I laugh at myself. What makes me think I could eat anything now? I'm even more nervous than I was before. I'd probably just throw up.

I drive deeper into the rural countryside, glancing frequently into the mirror to make sure no one is following me. *Had* Jarrod been following me, or had his "pursuit" been nothing but coincidence? If he'd meant to follow me, why had he backed off? I'm being paranoid again. It's possible that Jarrod hadn't even seen my car pass by the drive-in.

I turn on the car radio for company, but all I get is scratchy rock 'n' roll music that fades in and out, so I finally click it off again. The lanes get narrower as I go, and midsummer crops rise on either side of the road, closing me in. My heart begins to pound harder. Am I going the right way, or am I becoming hopelessly lost in the maze of country roads?

I come to a small intersection and hesitate, considering turning around and heading back to Tibonne. If I can find my way back. But an unseen hand brushes against mine, guiding me to turn left. I blow at my bangs. "Okay, Grandnana. Stay with me," I murmur, and obediently turn left.

Although my destination is remote, it isn't far, at least the part I can reach by car. Nicola directed me to a small grocery that serves the bayou people, from which she said I could rent a boat to go on to Marie's cabin.

I poled a pirogue on the bayou when I was young, but I never went very far or felt very comfortable in the narrow, traditional bayou craft. Maybe I can rent a motor boat, although I know they can be dangerous if the motor catches on the many unseen hazards that lurk below the surface of the shallow waters. Nothing about a boat trip on the bayou appeals to me, but Nicola insisted it's the only way to reach Marie.

It's nearly eleven o'clock when I reach the end of the road. Quite literally, the rough asphalt ends abruptly at a tiny shack that leans precariously out over the waters of the bayou. In the light of the car's headlamps I can read the sign: Boudreaux's Corner. Food. Gas. Beer.

Not surprisingly, considering the hour, Boudreaux isn't here. The place is closed and dark, and suddenly I wish I'd had the good sense to spend the night in town at a motel and embark on my journey by daylight.

But Grandnana's spirit had been adamant that I get on my way, and so now here I am, miles from nowhere, outside this little country store in one of the most desolate places in south Louisiana. My shoulders ache with fatigue and tension, and a headache threatens just behind my temples.

I turn off the engine, douse the headlights, and sit in the quiet darkness, assessing my situation. The waning moon has finally begun to rise, and it filters light through the trees. I watch it glimmer on the dark waters of the bayou. As undone as I am, I find some small peace in its beauty.

I remember times, years ago, when Grandnana and I went down to the bayou on nights when the moon was full, and she'd tell me wonderfully shivery stories about *le loup-garou* and the ghostly lights that people often saw in the misty swamps. Those stories had been fun then, not threatening, because I knew I was safe with Grandnana.

But I shiver now, not feeling one bit safe. Somebody is after me, but I don't know who. Or why.

I recall my dream in which Charles shape-shifted into the yellow-eyed *loup-garou* and chased me through the swamp. My pursuer can't be Charles, of course, since he's dead.

So who is my real *loup-garou?*

I lean back against the car seat, wondering what kind of real monster I face. I don't believe Elizabeth Colquitt's attempt to gain custody of Michaela is a mortal menace, although her actions could ruin my life. That leaves Jarrod. And Ira Peabody.

Or someone I don't know.

Oddly, I hadn't considered that possibility before now. But sitting here in the quiet darkness, feeling relatively safe because no one knows my where-abouts, I think about it. Why would a stranger, or strangers, be after us?

Because they think we're rich.

It's that simple. Anybody could have read of Charles's death in the newspaper, and if they knew of the Colquitts' vast wealth, might have planned to kidnap me and Michaela and hold us for ransom. Might have followed us to Louisiana. Might have been watching us. But why hadn't they made a move? We've been living in a remote place, virtually unprotected, for nearly a month.

And then I realize they *have* made a move. Those two men who'd come onto my porch hadn't been your average, everyday burglars. With those ski masks on, they'd come to do some serious crime, such as kidnapping. Obviously, I thwarted their plans when I shot the one, but Grandnana's spirit must have thought they'd be back.

But why didn't my grandmother's spirit, when she came through at last just a short while ago, tell me what danger I face instead of giving me cryptic, enigmatic messages and sending me here to the outback swamp and Marie Françoise? What can this psychic friend possibly offer that the police can't?

For that, I have no answer.

My head is pounding now. For whatever reason, I've done as I was told. I'm here, it's late, and I'm exhausted. Making sure the doors are locked, I reach into the backseat and find the small pillow I keep there for Michaela to sleep on when we travel. Tucking it behind my head and reclining the back of the seat, I shut my eyes.

Sleep overcomes me at once, but it's an uneasy sleep. A shadow lurks in my dreams, a wolflike figure who walks upright, with a face I can't see, but whose long fangs glint in the moon-washed darkness.

CHAPTER

Thirty-four

I AWAKEN TO THE SOUND OF SHARP KNOCKING ON THE car window. Daylight floods my eyes, and I squint into the rays, trying to make out the face of a man whose silhouette shadows my car. It takes me a moment to remember where I am, and when I do, I bolt straight up in my seat, my heart racing.

"*Bonjour, madame. Ça va?*" the man asks in a thick Creole accent.

I roll down the window, reluctant to get out of the safety of the car. "*Bien, merci,*" I reply, although I don't feel very "*bien.*" "Are you Monsieur Boudreaux?"

He steps away from the car, and I can see his face better. He's a tall man, although not as tall as Jarrod, and has a complexion the color of *café au lait*. His dark eyes are lined at the outer edges from hours in the sun. His hair is the color of midnight, long and tied at the nape. His arms are muscular, those of a man used to physical labor. He's a Creole, a Cajun, a bayou man.

"I'm Boudreaux. What you want here?" He's eyeing me suspiciously. I guess they don't get many strangers here, especially women sleeping in their cars.

"I . . . I need to rent a boat."

His frown deepens. "A boat? What you want a boat for?"

I consider replying that it's none of his business, but he looks like a man I don't want to cross. Besides, I might need his help in finding Marie Françoise, since I've so brilliantly left my directions behind.

"There is a woman who lives deep in the swamp," I tell him. "Her name is Marie Françoise. I must see her. Today. Do you know her? Where she lives?"

His expression darkens even further. "What you want with ole Marie?"

So he does know her! I suddenly become more optimistic. "I . . . she has a message for me."

But the man shakes his head. "Ole Marie don't talk t' nobody. She don't want no one comin' round."

"I . . . I know that. But she's . . . ah . . . expecting me. Her sister sent me." *Her sister and a spirit from beyond this plane.*

He looks skeptical. "I take her food, and she leave money on the dock. Won't come outta that ole shack t' see me. Some folk say she's a witch, you know."

Grandnana failed to tell me that. "She . . . she's a friend of my grandmother," I explain, trying to make this bizarre quest sound normal to a man who obviously believes in witches. "Please, I must find her. I was told you have boats for rent."

"You ever take a boat out in that there bayou?"

I shake my head again and can't conceal the shudder that rumbles through me at the thought. "No. But maybe you could give me directions. I'm not afraid."

"You oughtta be," Boudreaux growls. "The swamp's *trés dangereaux*. It no place for a learner. Or a lady by her own self," he adds.

I swallow hard, silently agreeing with him. But I'm not sure I want to get into a boat with him either. Kids from towns like Tibonne grew up hearing disturbing stories about the bayou people. I've always been told they're on the wild side, that they live by their own code, that their laws are different, looser, than those on the books.

But without a guide, I might end up hopelessly lost in the labyrinthine bayou. Boudreaux is big and muscular, but he doesn't look, or feel, evil. "What would you charge to take me to Marie?"

He scratches his head. "Can't do that. She'd be gettin' real mad if I brought a stranger t' her door, might stop trading wi' me."

I look at the dilapidated store. "I take it this is your place?"

He nods.

"Besides your grocery, where's the next nearest store?"

Boudreaux frowns, not getting my drift. "There ain't noplace close by here," he replies. "Gotta go into town."

"And where else could Marie get home delivery out here?" I continue.

Boudreaux finally sees what I'm getting at. Marie isn't going to quit trading with him; he's too convenient. Still, he hesitates. "I don't know. I sure don't want t' get on her bad side. She might put th' bad ju-ju on me."

The day is already growing warm, and a trickle of sweat runs down my spine. I've got to get on with this before I lose my nerve. "Look, Mr. Boudreaux, I'll pay double your going rate if you'll take me there. I'm certain she is expecting me, and I don't think she'll be mad at you for bringing me there safely." I give him what I hope is a guileless feminine smile. "Please, won't you help me?"

Boudreaux looks at me intently, a scowl on his face. I suspect he knows I'm playing on his masculine sympathies. But the offer must interest him, because he replies, "Double?"

"Double." I hope I have enough money to cover my offer. "How much would that be?"

"Seventy. Usual charge is thirty-five t' outsiders, them boys who come back in here looking t' fish. So it'd be seventy t' you," he says, frowning, as if making sure his math is correct.

"It's a deal." I hand him the money. "Can we go now?"

Three boats are nestled into the marshy mud at the edge of the bayou near the grocery store: a traditional pirogue, a wooden rowboat equipped with a small outboard motor, and a much larger craft with what appeared to be a huge fan rigged to one end. I've seen airboats before, but I've never been in one. I heard they're fast because they skim over the top of the water. "Can we take that one?"

But Boudreaux shakes his head. "Not where we're going. That for open flats. Marie, she live on an island way back in th' swamp. We gonna have t' snake around th' creeks and avoid th' quicksand down below in th' shallows. Trees hang too low back there for th' airboat. Gotta go slow, real careful like."

It's the long, narrow pirogue that Boudreaux chooses for the journey, and I say a silent prayer for our safety as I step into the scruffy-looking craft. Boudreaux hands the travel bag to me, and I stow it under the forward seat, hoping it won't get wet. The big Creole man shoves the pirogue into the black waters of the swamp, then wades in after it and climbs aboard. I squelch a shriek as the boat lurches beneath his weight.

Using a long pole and his lifetime of experience navigating the treacherous waters, Boudreaux guides the boat away from shore with swift, sure strokes that leave inky stains on the water in their wake. We go around a bend, and I lose sight of the little store.

Suddenly it seems like we're miles from civilization, and I begin to have second thoughts about having hired Boudreaux. It occurs to me too late that because he's obviously afraid to take me to Marie's, he might not. Maybe he's pretending to, but when we get out of sight, he's going to ditch me somewhere in the dark swamp where no one will ever find me.

Get a grip, I silently tell myself. Grandnana's spirit is leading me to a place of safety, not danger.

Still . . .

NEITHER BOUDREAUX NOR I SPEAK AS WE MAKE OUR way through this surrealistic waterscape. I feel like I'm on a movie set, or on some kind of jungle ride in a fantastical theme park. I almost expect to come upon Tarzan and Jane.

Although it's hauntingly beautiful, I'm too frightened to enjoy the scenery. I glance over my shoulder at Boudreaux from time to time, but he doesn't look at me. His eyes are on the bayou, which he scans for hazardous hidden obstacles. He seems harmless enough, but I'm as frightened as a rabbit cornered by a hound.

My mind flits back to one of the images on Nicola's tarot cards—that of a man poling a woman and a child across a body of water. I am that woman; Boudreaux is that man. Thank God there's no child in this picture.

Boudreaux's strokes are steady and even, but every now and then we hit a little bump.

"'Gator," Boudreaux says once as we veer off a

creature half-hidden beneath the water. How can he be so calm about it? I'm about to jump out of my skin.

Sometime later, we scrape beneath a low overhanging branch, and I hear a thump on the floor of the boat just behind me. I turn to see what it was and am unable to stifle a scream. A large snake has dropped in on us and is writhing on the bottom of the pirogue. Boudreaux lays his pole across the gunwales of the boat and nonchalantly picks the snake up behind its head and throws it back into the water.

"What . . . what kind of snake was that?" I think my heart is going to beat itself out of my chest.

"Moccasin."

I was afraid he was going to say that. "Aren't they poisonous?"

"*Oui.*"

"But, you . . . you just picked it up like it was nothing."

"Takes practice."

My reticent guide doesn't seem to want to talk about it, so I turn to face the front of the boat again. My teeth begin to chatter despite the oppressive heat, and I keep a warier eye than ever on the low branches we pass. I notice at one point that my knuckles are white where I'm gripping the sides of the boat.

After traveling for over two hours through the dark waters of the bayou, my back aches from sitting in the same cramped position, I'm soaked in sweat, and I have to go to the bathroom. If we don't reach our destination soon, I might lose my nerve and ask

Boudreaux to take me back. If, that is, he has any intention of getting me back alive.

"How much farther?" I ask him.

"Not much. Up round the next bend, then on about a mile."

A mile! I doubt that the little boat is going even half a mile an hour. I rub the back of my neck and swat at a fat mosquito. I look at my watch. It's almost eleven-thirty. I never thought about bringing something to eat. I'm thirsty, too, but I'm afraid taking another drink from the large bottle of water Boudreaux provided will only aggravate my other urgent problem.

Finally, embarrassed but desperate, I say to Boudreaux, "I need to make a rest stop. Is there anywhere we can pull over for a few minutes?"

Without a word, the big Cajun nods, and moments later he eases the pirogue onto the shore, if the squishy, muddy embankment can be called a shore. "Go that way," he says, indicating a stand of small trees about twenty yards away that could provide some privacy.

"Thanks."

He helps me out of the boat, and my feet sink an inch into the marshy land. "You gotta be careful now and watch where you . . . step," he advises. "There go snakes here just like on th' bayou."

Face flushed from heat and embarrassment, I half-walk, half-wade toward the stand of trees. I glance over my shoulder once to see if Boudreaux is following me, but he's facing the other direction in a posture that says he's taking advantage of our little pit stop as well.

The trees surround a small open space, and I quickly answer the demands of Mother Nature. I'm about to zip my jeans and return to the boat when from the corner of my eye I see something move in a patch of sunlight. At first I think it's the sun-washed marsh grass, moving in a light breeze.

And then I realize that the grass has eyes.

Great golden eyes.

Feline eyes.

I've never seen a bobcat or a panther except in a zoo, but I'm certain this creature is something like that. I stare at it in horror. It looks huge and muscular . . . and hungry. It stares back at me, crouching and twitching its tail, its eyes feasting on me, gleaming in anticipation.

I think I'm about to die.

I manage to scream, but the rest of me is unable to move. I can't seem to tear my gaze from the predator. My heart is beating so fast I'm growing dizzy. My knees are as mushy as the boggy soil beneath my feet, but at last they decide to work. I turn and run.

Behind me, I hear the hiss of grass as the great cat launches itself. Then the blast of a shot explodes so nearby that the reverberation rocks through me. Breathless and weak with terror, I crumple to the ground. The world starts to fade to black, and I decide it's the end of me.

Moments later, I discover I'm not dead after all; I just passed out. When I come to, Boudreaux is bending over me, wiping my face with a damp bandana. "I shoulda known better," he says, scowling. "Shouldn't'a let you go in there without looking on it first."

I struggle to sit up. My heart rate is still up there, but my breathing has slowed somewhat. My fear, however, clings to me as if the animal had been successful in its hunt. I can see the cat's bloody carcass on the grass just a few feet away. Boudreaux must have shot it barely in the nick of time.

"I . . . I think I'm going to be sick."

"I'll fetch you water." Boudreaux sprints the short distance to the pirogue, leaving me to my misery. I fight to control my nausea, and he returns in moments. Thankfully, the water settles my stomach, saving me from further embarrassment.

"What was that?" I ask, not looking at the dead animal.

"Bobcat."

"Thanks for shooting him. I couldn't run fast enough."

"You shouldn't'a run."

"What?"

"You can stare 'em down. It's when they see your fear they come after you."

I gape at Boudreaux, incredulous. "That's not true, is it?"

For the first time, I see the stoic Cajun laugh. "Don't know. Never tried it."

I don't find his joke very funny.

He takes out a long hunting knife, and instinctively I recoil. "Too bad I had t' kill him." Boudreax says. "But . . ." He holds up the knife. "Th' pelt'll be worth money to someone."

I'm not inclined to watch him. What he does to the bobcat he could easily do to me. But since he just saved my life, I doubt if I have to worry about his intentions anymore. "I think I'll go back to the boat and wait for you."

"*Bien.*"

Boudreaux has the decency to wrap the pelt in a tarp from the boat, and soon we're on our way once again. The sun blazes overhead, but the swampy forest grows denser the deeper into the bayou country we travel, offering us a steamy kind of shade. I'm still shaky, but I'm no longer afraid of my Cajun guide. My fear is now focused on the danger that lies ahead, the reason Grandnana sent me here in the first place.

CHAPTER

Thirty-six

✤

"OLE MARIE'S PLACE'LL BE COMIN' UP ON TH' LEFT," Boudreaux says sometime later. "That there little dock belongs t' her."

I spy a small, rickety wooden structure that's half-hidden beneath a bough thick with leaves. If he hadn't said something, I might not have noticed it as we passed by.

"That's Marie's place?" The dock looks as if it's about to fall into the water. Behind it stands a weathered shack that leans precariously as well.

"*Oui*. You sure you want off there?"

I'm not sure about much of anything at the moment, except that I'll be glad to be back on dry land. "*Oui, merci.*"

With silent expertise, Boudreaux guides the long, narrow boat alongside the pier and grabs hold of one of the pilings. He secures the boat on both ends, then helps me onto the dock.

"You want me t' come again for you?" he asks, handing me the slightly soggy travel bag.

"Yes, please, but I'm not sure when. Do you have a phone?"

He looks at me as if I've lost my mind. "Sure, I got a phone. But ole Marie don't."

I reach into my purse and take out the cell phone. "You suppose this works out here?"

Boudreaux shrugs. "Ain't never tried one of them."

I turn it on and see that there's a signal, although it looks as if it fades in and out. I'm not sure it's usable. "Give me your number," I tell him anyway, "and I'll try to call you when I'm ready. If you don't hear from me in twenty-four hours, come get me."

I think that sounds rather melodramatic, like something out of a Clint Eastwood movie, but it gives me comfort to know someone will come to my eventual rescue. If it isn't too late, and this swamp witch hasn't already eaten me or something.

Boudreaux tells me his phone number at the little store, and for lack of anything else to write on, I jot it down on the back of my hand.

"You call, and I'll come fetch you soon's I can," he promises.

I hesitate for a moment, then reach for his calloused hand. "Thanks, Mr. Boudreaux. And . . . thanks for saving my life back there."

He glances a little anxiously over my shoulder and beyond to where Marie's derelict swamp hut stands. "You rather I hang around here in case you need saving again?"

* * *

I watch the tall Cajun pole the pirogue swiftly away from Marie's small island, leaving me stranded in the wilderness. I think about the card in Nicola's tarot reading that showed a woman with her hand on the head of a lion.

You have greater powers than you can imagine. . . .

What powers can she mean? She said I must develop my powers to have the strength to "tame the lion." I think ruefully about the bobcat's attack. Obviously, I had no power against that beast.

The damp heat of the bayou is suffocating. In the distance I hear the call of a bird, but otherwise, the bayou flows silently in the noonday sun. I turn and face the small wooden shack, electric tension singing in every nerve.

"Okay, Grandnana," I mutter, "I'm here. Now what do I do?"

As if in reply, the front door opens slowly, and a tall, elegant woman with long, silver hair and indigo eyes stands before me. She wears a flowing purple robe, trimmed in silver and adorned with amethyst stones.

"Well, I see you made it."

When I see her in person, I remember Marie Françoise instantly. In fact, she looks exactly as I remember the day I met her as a child. It's been more than twenty years, but she appears not to have aged a day.

So what I'd told Boudreaux, that she was expecting me, was true. But how did she know I was coming? I wonder if Nicola called her, but then I remember that Boudreaux told me Marie Françoise didn't have a phone.

I don't have time to ponder it further. Marie Françoise beckons me inside with an impatient wave of her hand. "Get in here. There's too many damned mosquitoes outside." The old woman swears as she swats the air and closes the door behind us.

The shack appeared derelict from the outside, but inside it's homey, if small. It's dimly lit, with the light of only one small lamp enhancing the daylight filtering in through grimy windows. An air conditioner hums from a window on one side of the main room, and although I'm grateful for the instant relief from the sweltering heat, I wonder how she comes by electricity out here in the wilderness. Are these appliances powered by magic?

"No," the old woman answers me with a low laugh, even though my question was unspoken. "I've got one damn big generator out back. I had to go to a lot of trouble to get it delivered out here from New Orleans. Tea?"

Her answer elicits a nervous laugh from me in return, in spite of my apprehension about this whole affair. Marie Françoise is gruff like her sister, but I like her nonetheless. I thought I'd be afraid of her; instead, I find I'm drawn to her. For a woman who is supposedly a powerful psychic, she seems remarkably down-to-earth. Other than an ethereal aura about her and the odd clothing she's wearing, she could be anyone's grandmother. I realize she's offering me refreshments. "Tea? Yes, please."

"Hot or cold?"

"Cold would be good." My eyes slowly become accustomed to the low light inside the cabin, and I watch Marie move into the kitchen. She's a tall woman, and her head nearly brushes the low ceiling.

Along the walls, interspersed between odd-looking cooking utensils, I see bundles of herbs hanging upside down to dry. Lined up along a shelf on one wall are numerous small jars filled with different colored powders and unidentifiable substances. The effect is both charming and disturbing. It looks every bit a witch's kitchen. I wonder where she keeps her eye of newt.

"I'm glad to see you're wearing Nicola's talisman," Marie says. "It's protected you on your journey. Now I suppose I have to take over."

Protection. Both Grandnana's spirit and Nicola told me this mysterious woman hiding out in the swamp could protect me. But how? We're just two women alone and isolated. Seems like we're more vulnerable to an attack here than someplace where we could call for help.

"The evil ones'll have to find us first," Marie says, startling me again with her mental powers. "That's why I told your grandmother to send you out here. Hiding is a form of protection, you know."

"Who . . . who are the evil ones?" I ask. "I've had trouble contacting Grandnana's spirit, and she hasn't been very specific in her warnings, other than being adamant that I find you."

Marie chuckles as she finishes pouring the tea over ice into two tall crystal glasses. Garnished with lemon and mint, the presentation is elegant, as if we're in some fancy tea room in New Orleans, not huddled in a swamp hut talking about evil ones and spirit warnings.

"She didn't tell me either, but we'll soon find out."

Marie offers no further explanation, but leads me back into the sitting area that is cluttered with magazines, books, unlit candles at various stages of meltdown, a box of chocolates, and one very large cat reposing on an afghan at one end of the sofa. "That's Amelia, my familia'." Marie laughs at her little rhyme.

Amelia looks a little too much like a smaller version of the golden bobcat that attacked me, and I take a seat in a rumpled but comfortable chair on the far side of the room. "Thanks for the tea." What did she mean, *we'll soon find out*? I thought she just told me I was being protected by hiding out here.

Marie eases onto the sofa and strokes the cat. Her hands are large, her fingers long and slender. I imagine she could easily mesmerize someone with them.

"Your grandmother was a wonderful woman," Marie says after a thoughtful silence, taking the conversation in an unexpected direction. "She loved you very much. Still does, in fact."

A lump forms in my throat. "I know. She raised me after my parents were killed in an accident when I was small."

"We spoke often about you." Marie laughs. "Apparently you were quite a handful."

I shift in my seat. I hadn't been a difficult child. Had I? I'd never meant to be.

"Oh, you weren't difficult," Marie comments on my thoughts. "Your grandmother was just a little on the old side to handle a bright young girl like you." She leans forward and adds, "But I think you kept her young, you know?"

I smile. I appreciate Marie bringing Grandnana so clearly to mind. I'm suddenly filled with memories of the happy times when my grandmother would sing the songs handed down in our family from the days of old Angelique, when she'd get up and dance like a young woman. "We had many good times. I miss her."

"She's still around, *ma chère*. But she's worried about you." Marie leans forward. "You see, there was work left unfinished in your upbringing when Ariella died. You have powers the strength of which you can't imagine, Gabriella," she says in a voice so low it's almost a whisper. "Another reason, besides protection, that Ariella sent you to me is that she wants me to help you learn about your full power, how to take command of it, for it is the Deveaux power that will save your life."

I'm getting nervous again. "How?"

"Nicola's reading indicated that only you can destroy the evil ones, that it's your destiny."

"She . . . uh . . . mentioned that. Are you saying I'm going to have to kill somebody?" I cringe that the spirits would suggest such a thing.

"There are other ways to destroy evil," Marie tells me. "If you assume the power that is your birthright, if you let it guide you, the evil will be taken care of."

Marie's making my head swim. "How did you know about the reading?"

"I was there, the High Priestess, remember?"

Good grief. But why should I be surprised that somehow Marie Françoise was in that room yesterday?

"I thought Nicola was speaking figuratively when she said you were the High Priestess."

Marie finds this highly amusing. "It's how I use my power these days. But let's talk about your power, Gabriella. You must claim it, and claim it now. You will be called upon to use it sooner than you think. The evil ones are fast approaching."

The hair at the back of my neck bristles. "They're coming here? How did they know to come here? I thought you said I was protected by hiding here."

Marie gives me a disgusted look. "You left the directions for them, right there on your kitchen table."

CHAPTER

Thirty-seven

I NEARLY SPILL MY TEA. "WHAT ARE YOU SAYING? HOW do you know they found that slip of paper?" I curse myself again for my stupidity.

"I saw them," Marie answers. "Two men broke into Shadow Haven in the night, while you slept in your car. That's why Ariella was so insistent that you get out of there. She knew they were coming to harm you, and you weren't yet ready to face them."

Now Marie's scaring the heck out of me. "Did you see who they were?"

She shakes her head. "I'm not sure. They both are surrounded by auras of such great evil, I didn't want to dirty myself by penetrating them to learn their identities. Like I said, we'll find out soon enough. One of the men was limping. Their intention was clear; they were after you and your daughter. And," she hesitates, staring into space as if she's watching the scene on some invisible screen, "they tore through your house, looking for valuables. They seem to think you have things of great worth."

One man was limping. I was right. The intruder I shot the other night and his companion were robbers and kidnappers. In an odd way, I'm relieved that my threat is from strangers rather than people I know, like the Colquitts. At the moment, their threat seems tame.

"I have nothing in that house worth stealing," I tell her. "But they must know that I'm the widow of a wealthy man. I guess anyone would assume I'd have some good jewelry and silver."

"They seem to know a great deal about you, Gabriella, and the one with the limp seems bent on your destruction. He was furious last night when he came up with nothing but that piece of paper with Nicola's directions."

"I never meant to leave that behind. I was so upset and in such a hurry—"

"Perhaps it's for the best," Marie goes on in a low, calm voice. "This evil that pursues you is tenacious. It won't go away until it is eliminated. Facing it here, on our own turf, gives us an advantage."

I shiver. Earlier I'd been so hot I thought I'd die. Now I can't seem to get warm. "Why is it my destiny to destroy the evil, Marie?" I squeak. "This has gotten way out of hand. I should have turned it all over to Danny Comeaux. Seems to me attempted robbery and kidnapping are police matters."

"You tried, as I recall, and he didn't take it seriously."

Hmmm. She's right. The thought offers no consolation.

"I suspect there's something karmic going on here," Marie continues enigmatically. "Some kind of bond between you and the evil ones that must be severed, or you will be lost to their power forever."

"Bond? But I don't even know these people. I'm sure all they're after is a big ransom."

"Maybe so. But I sense there is more to it than that. Their evil intentions are focused on you."

"Maybe we ought to at least try to call the sheriff," I suggest again as my panic mounts, threatening to take away my breath.

But Marie shakes her head, then surprises me by asking, "Do you want to find your soul again, Gabriella?"

The old seer knows that's what's in my heart. That it's one reason I returned to Shadow Haven. Perhaps she heard me tell that to Jarrod last night. "Yes. Desperately," I reply with a catch in my voice. "But what does that have to do with the men who are after me?"

"It has to do with standing up to your devils, Gabriella. It has to do with reclaiming your power. Only when you face your fears and banish them will you find your soul once again."

I think about the bobcat, and Boudreaux's advice to stare it down. *It's when they see your fear they come after you.* He might have been kidding, but it underscores what Marie is getting at. I have been afraid for so long. Afraid of Charles, afraid of losing Michaela, afraid of the unknown danger that stalks me. My fear has clearly undermined my power, stolen away the rich gift of my ancestors.

I have allowed fear to creep insidiously into my soul, like a deadly, poisonous snake. I'm hit with a thought so clear it rocks me.

It isn't the kidnappers I must destroy.

It's my fear.

Understanding my true enemy brings new courage into my heart, and I begin to feel lighter. It's as if a dark shadow is passing out of my soul and is being replaced with shimmering golden light. I inhale deeply, absorbing this heady sensation.

My fear is my *loup-garou*. And I will not let him win. "I'm ready, Marie. Will you help me?"

"Of course, I'll help you. I'm with you, as are many in spirit. But it's your inner power you must trust and call upon when the battle engages."

My heart is thundering. "I can do that. But I need to know for sure that Michaela is safe."

"She is," Marie assures me. "She's in strong, loving arms. She is protected. She is hidden from the evil, at least for the moment. But you must be swift and sure in your combat and never in doubt of the outcome. This evil is wily and cunning. It will try to fool you."

Nothing is as it seems. . . .

My throat is parched, my tongue feels swollen. I'm stunned and shaken, yet invigorated as never before. I had been holding on to my glass of tea without partaking of its refreshment as Marie spun before me the magnitude of my challenge. Now, I take several long swallows, grateful for its soothing coolness. Almost immediately, a peaceful calm replaces my anxiety, and I feel a little light-headed. I look down into the tea glass. "What's in this?"

Marie laughs gently. "Nothing that will harm you. You've had a long and terrifying journey, and you've learned some astounding truths along the way. You need to rest now and regain your strength for the challenges that are to come."

I fight the encroaching cloud of unconsciousness but lose the battle. I feel Marie come to me and take the glass from my hand. "Sleep well, *ma chère.*"

In a dream state, I think I hear her talking to someone else in the room, an invisible presence. "You happy now, Ariella?"

"*Merci, ma vieux amie,*" comes a gravelly voiced reply. And with that, I lose all consciousness.

CHAPTER
Thirty-eight

IT'S LATE AFTERNOON WHEN I FINALLY AWAKE TO FIND myself peering into other eyes—golden, feline eyes. For a moment, I think they're rushing at me, flying through marsh grass. I scream and jump out of the chair before I get my wits about me and discover it was just Amelia staring at me curiously from the arm of the chair where I'd slept.

"Got ants in your pants?" Marie Françoise asks, watching in amusement.

"That's not funny," I sniff. "I didn't tell you I was attacked by a bobcat in the swamp on my way here."

"Attacked? By a bobcat?" Marie frowns. "I should have felt that happening. Must be getting old."

"Boudreaux shot it."

"Boudreaux's a good man. Brings my groceries and things by boat. Kind of like Meals on Keels." She chuckles at her little joke.

I smile as well. I'm enormously refreshed after my deep sleep, and I can almost forgive Marie for putting a potion in my tea. I'm also ravenous.

"Have something to eat," Marie says, pointing to a large platter of cold cuts and cheeses that sits in the middle of a low table. I guess I'll have to get used to having my mind read by this woman.

While I slept, I sought in dreams for a face, an identity of those whose evil threatens me, but to no avail. I tried to connect with Grandnana, to see if she could give me some clue, but she wasn't to be found in the misty world of my subconscious. I glance at Marie, wishing she would help me. But she'd said she didn't want to dirty her psyche by penetrating their evil auras to learn who they are. I can't help but wonder, however, if she has any hint or gut feeling about who they might be. I decide to "think" my question to her, since she seems to hear my every thought anyway.

Who are the evil ones?

Marie doesn't answer. She takes a piece of cheese from the platter and offers a bit of it to Amelia. Then she looks over at me. "Who's Charles?"

Charles? That was the last thing I expected to hear. "He . . . was my husband. He was killed in April, in a plane wreck."

"Are you sure?"

"What do you mean, am I sure? Of course I'm sure. He got on his company's airplane in Toronto, and a few hours later, that plane crashed in Montana. No landings in between, no survivors."

"I see," she says, frowning.

"Are those men somehow connected with

Charles?" I can't imagine him being aligned with such lowlifes, but then, Jarrod suspects Charles to have been involved in criminal activities. Perhaps he's right. How little I must have known my husband.

"Could be," she says, then leans forward abruptly. "You've brought something with you, in your bag, something that attracts evil like a magnet. They want it."

"There's nothing in my bag except some clothes and things, and a gun. Are you speaking of the gun?"

"No, there's something else. Bring your bag here. Let's take a look."

Curious, I pick up the small travel bag from where I'd left it by the front door and take it to Marie. I can't imagine what she's talking about. I watch as her long fingers unzip the bag and reach inside. She fumbles around in it for a minute, then draws out the golden torc. My eyes widen when I see it. Of course.

"That's what I thought." Marie drops the torc on the table beside the salami like a hot potato, then flicks her hands in the air, as if to rid them of something nasty.

Instinctively I step backward when I see the golden circlet. "I forgot I had that in there."

"I'd want to forget that thing too. It's filthy."

I frown. "Filthy?" It shines in the rays of late afternoon sunlight coming in from a nearby window. It doesn't look dirty.

"It is. It's filthy with the guilt of a thousand murders."

I grimace. "Murders?"

"Whoever wore this was responsible for the deaths of multitudes. I can hear them screaming as I speak." She covers her ears and shakes her head. Her face contorts, likes she's in physical pain.

I hope I never develop my own psychic gift to be as powerful as Marie's. The old woman is definitely suffering from whatever impressions she's getting from the torc. I take a seat beside her to try to comfort her, but when I touch her arm, she jerks from beneath my fingers.

"It's okay," Marie says after a long moment. She composes herself, although she looks pale. "It's passed, whatever 'it' was. Where'd you get that thing?"

"Charles gave it to me, but I've never worn it. It . . . stung like fire when I put it on."

"I can imagine. Nipped my fingers just then too."

"Do you know what it is? Charles told me it came from Tiffany's."

She scowls. "He didn't buy this in any store. It came from the darkness of time. It's been hidden away somewhere for centuries."

So Jarrod's suspicion had been correct. It's an ancient and probably valuable artifact. But is it stolen?

Marie Françoise closes her eyes and appears again to enter into a trancelike state. "It was forged for a queen of an ancient land, but she was killed by invaders, and the torc was seized by their leader. He proceeded to murder her people in a brutal butchery, and with each death, evil was absorbed into the torc. Those who have possessed the torc through the centuries have died violent deaths."

I shudder. "Like Charles."

Marie opens her indigo eyes and gives me a piercing look. "Like you could, if you don't get rid of that thing. The torc has been attracting evil into your life ever since your husband gave it to you. No wonder you've experienced such tragedies this past year."

Her story about the curse of the torc sounds a little melodramatic, but who's to question it? I *have* been plagued by tragedy since Charles gave it to me. "What should I do, toss it in the bayou?"

"Not in my backyard." Marie frowns, thinking hard. "I promised Ariella I would protect you, but I didn't know I was going to be up against something such as this."

"I'm sorry. I never meant to bring trouble to your doorstep. If I'd known about the torc, I would have left it in New York." A mean thought crosses my mind. *Maybe I should have given it to the Colquitts.*

"Don't give in to evil thoughts like that," Marie warns.

"Sorry. I didn't really mean it."

"The Colquitts are the least of your worries, *chère*. The danger you face comes from the evil ones."

It occurs to me that perhaps I face more than one danger. "What about Jarrod Landry?" I ask. "Does he pose any threat?"

Marie smiles gently. "Not Jarrod. He's your friend. He wants to help you fight the Colquitts. He's also frantically trying to find you right now. He cares a great deal for you, you know."

"Humph! He acted like he cared for me in a special way," I admit morosely, "but then I found out he keeps a steady Saturday night date with somebody named Valerie."

Marie cocks her head slightly. "Valerie? How did you know about Valerie? I sense that Jarrod keeps that side of his life very private."

"I bet he does. Does Valerie know he cheats on her?"

"Things aren't as they seem, *ma chère*," she reminds me with a small laugh. "But it's not up to me to tell you about Valerie. That must come from Jarrod."

I start to object. Obviously she's tuned into some psychic source of information about Jarrod. Why can't she just tell me who Valerie is? But she shifts the conversation in another direction.

"Jarrod is trying to keep the Colquitts from gaining custody of your daughter, but you can't seem to trust him. Why not?" she asks.

"There are things he's keeping from me. Some sort of problem he had with Charles and the Colquitts years ago. And he certainly hasn't been honest with me about Valerie."

"Forget about Valerie. Jarrod has his reasons for not telling you about her. He's in a tough and vulnerable position at the moment, but he's working through it with integrity."

How can Marie stick up for him like this? But she sounds irritated at me for doubting Jarrod, and I decide not to press her further. "So you think I can trust him?"

"Absolutely. You may even have a future with him. Here, let me see." She takes my hand and turns it palm-up. "Yes, there, you see, there are going to be two men in your life. See those parallel lines. How old are you?"

"Twenty-nine."

"That would be about right. See how this line stops about halfway across your palm? That indicates the end of a relationship at about your age. But the other line keeps going until your end."

I don't know what to think. A future with Jarrod? I doubt it.

"You'll have time to sort things out with him," Marie says, then adds, "But you have your own soul to set straight first. Let's get to it."

CHAPTER
Thirty-nine

I'M ALONE IN THE CABIN. MARIE HAS BEEN GONE FOR
some time, saying she had things to take care of
outside, and Amelia followed her out the door. I'm
glad to have a little time to myself. I desperately need
to clear my head, and to cleanse myself—body, mind,
and spirit—of the fear that has apparently insidiously
become an integral part of my daily existence.

Marie has talked to me at length about the legacy
of power that has been handed down in my family.
She claims I have everything I need to face my
adversaries, and she's given me some exercises that
are supposed to help tone my "psychic muscles." She
left me with the admonition to work hard and fast at
assuming my true power.

It's a daunting challenge, because I'm not used to
being powerful, in any sense. I pace restlessly, trying
to focus on the matter at hand, but I keep thinking
about Michaela. I pray that Marie's vision is true, and
that Michaela is safe and out of harm's way. After the
treacherous journey here, I know I made the right

decision not to bring her along. But she's not entirely safe, not yet. I am about to face the evil that threatens her as well as me, and I must succeed in destroying it, for if I don't, it will then go after Michaela.

The other obstacle that keeps bumping into my thoughts and disrupting my psychic work is Jarrod. My thoughts about him are not so clear as they are about Michaela. Jarrod is not in danger. But my heart is. Marie said Jarrod is my friend. . . .

He cares a great deal for you. . . .

I want to believe that. I want to trust him. Perhaps I even want to consider a future with him. But I have so many unanswered questions. . . .

The main question at the moment is, Will I live to see Jarrod again?

The golden torc glints from where it lies on the nearby table, and its mystery taunts me. Is it a relic from antiquity? Is it cursed? I see the plane crash in my mind's eye, and wonder suddenly if Charles's violent death was in any way related to the curse of the torc. Charles would not have believed in any such curse. Most people wouldn't. But I don't doubt Marie's story.

I consider Jarrod's suspicion that Charles stole the torc. It seems improbable, but not impossible. Like Jarrod said, Charles would do anything if it suited his purpose, but what could his purpose have been in stealing the torc?

Money? Revenge against someone at his company? The thrill of getting away with it?

It could be all of the above. Charles worshipped money. I know he didn't particularly like the president of the company. And he took chances sometimes.

My mind is racing down the road of possibilities, and I can't stop it.

What if he stole it for a specific client, someone who didn't care how he'd obtained it? Maybe he'd given it to me only temporarily, hiding it in plain sight so to speak, until he could deliver it to his private party. Was that person still waiting for delivery? Had the buyer hired the men who broke into my house to get the torc since Charles was no longer around?

If that's the case, I'd be happpy to just give them the damned thing and be done with it. I don't want it. It's cursed, it attracts evil, and it's apparently putting me, my daughter, and Marie at great risk.

The solution is so obvious, my heart leaps with relief. I go to the front door, anxious to share my revelation with Marie. The sun has dipped below the tree line, and dusky afternoon shadows slant through the cypress trees. "Marie!" I call out, not seeing her at first. And then out of the corner of my eye I see a figure move just beyond an old live oak. It's Marie Françoise, and to my amazement, she's tending a roaring fire in a circular pit, looking for all the world like a witch in a Disney movie. Hanging over the fire, suspended on a rod between two poles, is a large black pot. "What are you doing?" I call out, going to where she stands, stirring whatever's in the cauldron.

"Experimenting. I've always been interested in alchemy."

"Alchemy?" I have a bad feeling about this.

"We'll see if it works. Wait here."

Marie goes into the house, but I'm too curious to stand by and wait to see what she's up to. I follow Marie through the door in time to see her coming from the kitchen with a broom. She goes to the torc and maneuvers it onto the wooden broomstick, careful not to touch it with her skin.

"What are you doing?" I ask again as Marie carries the precariously balanced object outside.

"I'm going to give this bad boy a little bath."

It takes a moment to register Marie's intentions—she's going to immerse the torc in whatever chemical witches' brew she's concocted in her pot. There's no telling what damage it might do to the torc, my one hope, short of murder, of getting rid of those who pursue me. "No! Don't! Wait!"

Marie hesitates, holding the torc precariously over the boiling liquid. "What?" she asks crossly.

My breath is coming in short gasps. "Look, Marie, what if whoever is after me only wants the torc? Why not just give it to them, no questions asked, and send them on their way?"

With a scowl, Marie plonks the torc into the solution that bubbles over the fire. I hear the metal sizzle as it sinks to the bottom, and my earlier euphoria fizzles away with it.

"I told you," she scolds, "it's not just the torc. It's

you they're after, believe me. And your daughter. Are you willing to take that chance?"

I stare glumly at the cauldron, my hopes dashed. "What's in there?"

"Mostly stuff the EPA wouldn't like to know I have."

I wrinkle my nose, smelling the acrid odor emanating from the steam. "You sure it's safe to do this? I mean, should we be breathing this in?"

"Probably not. But it's not safe to leave the torc as it is. I'm hoping the chemicals in here will cleanse the evil energy it holds. Right now, that thing's guiding those men to you like a beacon."

Troubled, I watch as she complacently stirs the pot with the broomstick. When she removes the stick, I see that the solution has eaten away at the wood.

"The torc needs to stew in here for a while," she says as nonchalantly as if she were cooking turnips. Turning to me, she adds, "I promised your Grandnana I would protect you." She takes my hand. "Ridding the torc of its evil, if that's possible, is a start, but there's more we must do." She glances over her shoulder at the darkening bayou. "It won't be long now."

Inside, Marie bids me to stand in the center of the small main room. "Your powers are growing, but we must cleanse your aura and throw an extra mantle of protection around you. Are you willing to do as I say without question?"

My pulse is beating hard. If Charles thought my

ability to speak with the dead was weird, he should have met Marie Françoise. But I'm not going to question the mysterious ways of the old woman. I've always trusted the spirits. This is no time to doubt. "I will do as you tell me."

Marie goes to a large cupboard and takes out a white feather and something that looks like a clump of sticks. "First, we're going to purify you before we begin the protection."

I've had on the same clothing for two days and figure I could stand a bath, but that isn't what Marie has in mind. Instead, she has me extend my arms and stand with my legs apart. She lights the bundle of sticks, and the scent of sage permeates the room. Using the white feather, she wafts the smoke from the sage over every part of my body, from head to toe. While she works, she whispers things unintelligible to my ears.

"Close your eyes and think of those you love the most," Marie advises.

Behind my eyes comes the image of my daughter, with her sunny smile and grown-up ways. How could anyone want to hurt my baby?

"No negative thoughts," Marie reprimands. "Think of those you love, see them protected and in safety."

I quickly banish any speculation of someone hurting Michaela and see instead the stout arms of Rosalie Odette encircling her.

The next image to rise in my mind's eye is of Jarrod, with his broad shoulders and handsome tanned face.

"That's more like it," Marie commends as she continues her ritual.

I blush that I've been caught thinking about him. I'm not sure he fits in the category of someone I love, but he came to mind nonetheless.

Marie said Jarrod is looking for me. I wish he were here with me now, to help me face whatever demons are coming my way. But perhaps it's better he's not. I've put enough people in jeopardy.

Besides, according to Marie, these are demons I must face alone. And destroy.

"I can see your thoughts are getting too deep into the moment," Marie says, finishing her ritual. "Yes, you must face this evil, but not alone. I'm here with you, as are others in spirit."

"Grandnana?" I haven't felt or heard from my grandmother since our communion last night.

"Of course, *ma chère*," Marie says. "Perhaps when this is all over, it'll be easier for you to connect with her."

Marie takes a long white garment from a cedar chest and brings it to me. "You must wear this until the danger is past."

It's a white silk kimono-like robe that under other circumstances would have enchanted me with its beauty. Unfortunately, it looks like it might be hard to run while wearing it. There's something in the texture of the fabric, however, that makes me feel as if I have on armor.

Silken steel.

Marie goes out the door, closing it behind her. I stare after her, and briefly, doubts beset me again. What if Marie is just a crazy old crone, not a seer with magical protective powers? What if this is nothing but a pretty bathrobe she's given me to wear?

I cast out these thoughts and close my mind to any other doubts before they can take hold.

No negative thoughts.

I hear a thump at the door. "Open up. Hurry!" Marie calls, and I dash for the door. She enters the cabin, carrying the torc again balanced on the wooden broomstick. The thing seems to glow.

"Turn on the faucet," she instructs me. "Cold water only."

I head for the kitchen and do as she says, and Marie passes the torc beneath the cooling waters. The sizzling sound is clear, and in it, I hear the sighs of hundreds of souls being released from purgatory. My skin prickles. "What did you just do?"

"I'm not quite sure." Marie continues to let the water sluice over the torc, and I watch in amazement as the golden piece fades and turns to shining silver. "Well, I'll be damned. Reverse alchemy," Marie utters. "You can turn the water off now."

Marie tentatively touches the torc, cooled now after its boiling chemical bath. She runs her slender fingers around the inner edge of the circle, then around the outer. She eases it off the broomstick and into her palm.

"Nothing," she tells me. "I feel nothing." She

holds it out. "Will you touch it? See if you feel anything?"

With a trembling hand, I touch the cool silver metal, and I no longer feel the evil. Gone are the burning vibrations that once were so strong they'd seared my skin. Instead, a cool serenity floods me, washing me with peace and hope. I raise my eyes to Marie.

"I'm sorry I ever doubted you."

The old woman smiles in amusement. "Maybe I am, as you thought, just a crazy old crone, not a seer with magical protective powers. But I believe in the power of good and," she winks, "in better living through chemistry."

CHAPTER

Forty

MARIE PLACES THE SILVER TORC AROUND MY NECK, and still I feel nothing but a cool, peaceful sensation. "Are you okay?" she asks.

"Yes." I touch the torc with one finger. Going to a nearby mirror, I draw in a sharp breath when I see my image. "It's exquisite."

"And it's going to help save your life," Marie adds. "You must not take it off, let no one touch it, until the threat has passed. It was for this purpose that it was forged in the first place, but the queen was deceived by her attackers, and she allowed them to come too close."

She leans close to me and gazes directly into my eyes. "I don't know why your husband would give you such a wretched gift, but now that I've inverted the curse, it will serve as a talisman of protection. Its powers are strong, but you cannot depend solely upon it. You must hold strong to your own personal power, Gabriella. I don't wish to penetrate the veil of evil to know who approaches, but I can tell you this, you are about to face deception of monstrous proportions. Something that will throw you off, cause you to doubt," she warns. "Whatever happens, trust in your power, and it will not fail you."

How can I trust in power I'm unsure I know how to use?

Marie hears my thought. "The power will guide you, *ma chère*. You only have to trust in it and let it take you where you need to go. You've had this power your whole life, you know. You've just never known you had it." She leans so close I feel her breath on my cheek. "Gabriella, now is not the time to doubt the heritage of the Deveaux women. You must have faith in yourself like you've never had before. Accept your power, and use it now."

She pauses, then frowns slightly. "If you want proof of what you're capable of doing with your power, try this." She steps away from me, picks up a small crystal from a basket on the table, and holds out her arm with the crystal on her upturned palm.

"Shoot it," she commands.

"Shoot? I don't have a gun, and I wouldn't shoot at you if I did."

"Not with a gun, with your power. Blow that crystal right off my hand."

I stare at Marie in amazement. "Are you saying I'm telekinetic?"

"Why's that so hard to believe? You've always been able to talk to the spirits. If you can do one, why not the other?"

Why not indeed? I wonder what other powers I might have lying dormant inside me.

"Start by concentrating on the crystal," she instructs.

I focus my gaze on the little stone, slowly shutting out the rest of the world until I'm conscious only of the stone.

"Good. That's good," Marie whispers. "Now, see it explode. See it just pop like a firecracker. Don't worry. It won't hurt me."

I'm vaguely aware that my whole body has become feverish, and there is a tingle, like a surge of electricity, emanating from my solar plexus. Up it comes, and out it goes, shooting with invisible energy toward the crystal. In less than a heartbeat, the stone pops loudly and flies off Marie's palm.

The sound of the tiny explosion rocks me back to full consciousness. Stunned, I turn to Marie, who has a big, satisifed smile on her lips. "See?" she says. "I knew you could do it."

I'm in shock. For a moment, I can't speak, and I don't know what to think. "Grandnana never told me about this kind of power," I manage at last. "Did she have it?"

"Of course. All you Deveaux women have it. Your daughter will have it, too. You never knew about this power because Ariella passed into the Otherworld when you were still too young to be trained in its use. She told me that she didn't dare turn you loose on the world as a teenager with that power in hand. Her plan was to wait until you turned twenty-one, and then to introduce you to it. But she died before she had the chance. And then you married that Northern boy and left Shadow Haven, so she gave up, even in spirit."

I go to where the crystal shards sparkle on the floor and take a few in hand. They're still hot, and I have to roll them like dice on my palm to keep from burning myself. I stare at them, slowly accepting the enormity of the power it took to blow them up.

"Marie, this power could kill somebody. I don't know if I can do that."

"Use it indirectly," she advises. "Use it to deflect the evil back onto itself."

"How?"

But before she can answer me, we hear noises from outside.

"They have come," Marie says gravely, and I turn toward the door, half expecting a yellow-eyed swamp wolf to burst through it.

Quickly, Marie douses the lamplight, and darkness descends upon the cabin. The sun went down some time ago, and the sky carries only the deep purple residue of the day that has passed. From the front of the house, firelight still flickers in the circle. I peer out of the glass windowpanes, and through the gloom I can see the shadows of two figures tying a boat to Marie's dock.

My pulse pounds, and I can scarcely dare to breathe. I'm nervous but unafraid. I have no idea what is about to transpire, but I'm relieved that at last

I'm going to face the nameless enemy whose threat has brought me to this place and this moment.

"Are you ready?" Maries asks.

"I think so." For a brief moment I consider taking my gun, just in case. But if I did that, it seems to me I'd be weakening my power simply by not trusting it.

Trust in your power and it will not fail you.

I'm clear about one thing—if I wish to reclaim my soul, I must trust my power and use it now.

Only when you face your fears and banish them will you find your soul once again.

I once allowed Charles and his derision to erode my identity and self-confidence. I became fearful of him, and I've lived in fear for many years. It was my own fear, not Charles, that stole away my power and cost me my soul.

Tonight, by facing whoever this is and calling upon my power—and only my power—to destroy the evil, I will find myself, my true Deveaux self, once again.

The thought is joyous, freeing, and it floods me with courage.

"Remember," Marie admonishes, "just listen to your heart and flow with your power. Trust that the spirits are with you, and I'm here as well, should you need me. But I doubt that you will. You have the power and you know how to use it. Turn the evil upon itself, and it will be destroyed."

I reach for the door handle, feeling strong and calm and ready for whatever awaits me. I straighten my back and hold my head high. I am a Deveaux, and whatever lies outside, I will use the power of my heritage, not a gun, to transmute this evil, just as Marie transmuted the evil locked into the torc.

I step out into the wet heat of the night and take a stance near the fire, waiting. The intruders seem to be fumbling as they make their way toward the house. As yet, they've not seen me.

"What the hell was that?" I hear one of them say. "Felt like a dog or a wolf ran by. Nearly knocked me down."

The second man doesn't answer. I see that he favors one leg as he walks, and I know this one is my enemy. The other serves him, but he is the one I must destroy.

Who is this man?

Suddenly, he raises his head and sees me, and I stare back at him, my eyes straining to identify him, to put a face to the evil. He comes a few steps closer, then gives a growling laugh. "Well, well, if it isn't the little Cajun witch, all dressed up for Halloween. I see you've decided the torc is good enough for you after all."

My heart ceases beating. My skin turns cold. I don't recognize the face, but I know that voice. How can this be? "Charles?" I think I might faint.

He laughs again as he watches me struggle to comprehend the incomprehensible. "Sur-pri-ise," he taunts, stretching the word into three syllables. "You like my new face? I have a great doc in the Caymans. Made me more handsome than ever, don't you think?"

Time stands still. Reality fades. This can't be Charles. Charles is dead. This man doesn't look like Charles, and yet his voice and his actions are the same. But Charles had been polished. This character looks rough, haggard, as if he hasn't slept in days. I rarely saw Charles wearing anything other than expensive business attire. This man is dressed all in black, like a burglar.

This man, I quickly surmise, must have known Charles and is trying to impersonate him. Unless, I think uneasily, I've somehow managed to conjure Charles's ghost.

Impersonator or ghost, he stirs the rage within me that has festered against Charles for years, an anger that turns white-hot and bursts to the surface with volcanic intensity.

"You sorry son of a bitch," I utter. "I don't know who you are, but I should have killed you when I had the chance."

"Whoa, baby, look who's gotten feisty," he taunts, but he comes no closer.

That voice.

I wish for a moment that I had brought my gun, after all. I'm so enraged I don't know if I can focus my power sufficiently to blow him away.

I don't have the gun, but he doesn't know that. Something tells me that I need a ruse to give me time to regroup and channel my power. Marie warned me that he would try to fool me.

Nothing is as it seems. . . .

I raise my arm beneath the folds of the robe and point at him, as if concealing a weapon. "Leave now, before I take this opportunity to finish the job," I command with full authority in my voice.

At this, he draws his own, very real, gun and turns it on me. "You should have aimed better the first time, Gabby. You hurt me just enough to piss me off."

. . . *deception of monstrous proportions* . . .

My stomach lurches. No one has ever called me Gabby, except Charles, when he wanted to antagonize me.

The man comes closer, and I see a malicious gleam in his eyes. I recognize that gleam, and those eyes. They're the eyes of the *loup-garou* that chased me through the swamps in my dream. The eyes of a man I knew well, a man I once thought I loved, a controlling, obsessive man, demented now, and bent on evil.

This is Charles, in the flesh.

My worst nightmare has come true.

Forty-one

"SURPRISED TO SEE ME, GABBY, MY DARLING, LOONEY wife?" Charles takes another step toward me, and I feel my power waver. Charles always managed to do that to me.

Used to do that.

I clench my fists. I will never give in to him again, no matter what. I don't understand how he can be standing here before me, alive and well except for a gunshot wound in one leg, but I won't let him intimidate me again.

"Yes, you might say that," I reply evenly, working to pull myself together again. I have no weapon against him except my newfound power. If I can blast a crystal from across the room with it, there's a chance I can somehow use it to face down my personal *loup-garou.*

"Use it indirectly." I hear Marie's voice in my head. "Use it to deflect the evil back onto itself."

"I thought you were dead," I say to Charles.

"You sure I'm not?" he mocks. "You claim you can talk to the dead. Are you certain I'm not a ghost?"

"The thought crossed my mind. But no, Charles, I can see you are clearly flesh and blood. And you're the same arrogant bastard you always were."

At that, the other man guffaws.

"Shut up," Charles snaps, and the man silences instantly.

Briefly, I shift my attention to Charles's companion. He's shorter than Charles, with a broad nose, dark eyes and hair, and teeth that shine white in the night. I sense that he, too, is evil, but he's not the source of all that threatens to destroy me.

The evil incarnate is my own husband.

"Let's get on with this," Charles says to the other man. "Check out the house. Get my daughter and get rid of whoever else is in there. Hurry."

The man trots off in the direction of the house, but I'm unafraid for Marie. In fact, I wonder what fate she has planned for him. He has no idea of the power he's up against. Will she kill him? A chill shivers through me.

Will I kill Charles?

My focus returns to the moment when Charles starts toward me. I wave my concealed hand in warning. "Stop right there, Charles, or whoever you are. I mean it, I'll shoot." He could, of course, easily shoot me instead, but I sense that he doesn't want to physically harm me, not at the moment, at least. Not until he's gotten what he wants from me.

My ploy works. Charles stops and studies me, a frown on his too-smooth face. He must be surprised . . .

and irritated . . . to find that I'm not the same submissive creature he lived with for eight years. The notion charges my power, which surges through me in a warm wave. My skin begins to turn feverish, as it did when I destroyed the little crystal.

"What is it you want, Charles, if that really is you? Why are you here?"

"It's me, Gabby, and I've come for what's mine. I want what you've stolen from me."

"Stolen?"

"That's right. That torc, for starters. And my collections. What have you done with my collections, you stupid bitch? The house is empty."

If I'd had the gun, no doubt I would have shot him on the spot, this time in both knees. Instead, I choose to use his own weapon—words—against him.

"Why, Charles," I say in a silky, Southern-girl voice, "you know those things never meant anything to me. I got rid of them in a big ole garage sale after you supposedly died." I lie on purpose just to goad him, and I can tell it worked. A red aura flares around his body.

"You . . . you . . ." He lurches toward me again, but I shake my head.

"Uh-uh, Charlie. Remember, I won some medals in shooter's school." Just for fun, I try sending a little jolt his way. He jumps back and clutches his arm, almost dropping his gun.

"What the hell?" He thinks I've shot him, but there's no blood. "What . . . ?"

"Apologize."

He glares at me and raises his gun. "No. You're a stupid bitch. Always have been. I don't know what I ever saw in you."

I zap him again, this time with a little stronger energy. I hear him snarl, and I expect him to shoot at me any moment now. I'm successfully staving him off, yet my destiny is to destroy him. But how?

Turn the evil on itself. . . .

I touch the torc, and something inside of me urges me to lure him forward. I shudder to think what might happen if he actually reaches me, but the feeling is strong that he must come closer before he can be destroyed.

"So, what's your plan, Charles?" My tone is mocking, derisive. "You're going to kidnap your own daughter?"

"And my wife. I said, I came to collect what belongs to me."

I feel as if he's slapped me, but this time I take it as a wake-up call. If I don't destroy him, he will most certainly destroy me.

"I don't belong to you, Charles. Not anymore. You don't own either of us. I can't believe I was such a fool to let you control me like you did."

"You've always been a fool, Gabby. At first, it entertained me. But it didn't take long for me to grow tired of your silly ways."

Before, such hateful words would have stolen any power I might have had, but now his derision merely fuels my determination to rid the world of his evil tongue.

From out of the darkness comes a mournful cry, the howl of an animal, like the baying of a hound from hell. Charles jerks his head toward the sound.

"What's the matter, Charles? Afraid of the *loup-garou?*"

"You and your stinking patois."

But he's unnerved, and I use his fear to my advantage, as he once used mine against me. "You *should* be afraid of the *loup-garou*, Charles. He's a creature of the swamps, sometimes a dog, sometimes a man, a werewolf sort of fellow with fangs and claws that will tear you apart."

"Give me a break."

I'm not about to give Charles anything. "The *loup-garou* is an evil shape-shifter, Charles, kind of like yourself. Monstrously deceitful." Suddenly, I wonder if the *loup-garou is* only a legend, or if the swamp creature is real and has come to somehow play a part in destroying the evil brought to my doorstep by Charles and his henchman.

The howling sounds again, this time closer, and Charles jumps.

"He's coming for you, Charles. You can't escape the *loup-garou.*" As nervous and unsure of my stragegy as I am, I'm also enjoying taunting this man who so often used his words to batter me.

"Shut up!" he screams.

Behind him, there's a shout, and we both turn to

see yet another boat approaching Marie's dock. "What the hell?" he snarls again. Seems like this is a night of surprises for the supposedly deceased Mr. Colquitt, as well as for me.

The "hell" is his, not mine. My knees go weak with relief as I see Jarrod and Danny Comeaux jump onto the dock and run in my direction. With them is a woman I don't recognize who remains in the boat.

Charles spins to face them, gun leveled at Jarrod, who is closer. "Well, well, if it isn't good old Jarrod. You just made your last mistake, buddy."

Jarrod stops short. "Charles?"

"I warned you not to get involved in this."

"So it was you on the phone the other night," I murmur, incredulous at the enormity of the scheme Charles has plotted. Somehow he faked his death in that plane crash. Who did he send in his place that fateful day? And how did he know the plane would crash? He must have planted a bomb on board himself. He must have known other people would die.

Charles Colquitt is far worse than a common thief.

Charles Colquitt is a murderer.

And if he's committed murder once, he'll do it again. And at the moment, his gun is aimed at Jarrod's heart.

CHAPTER

Forty-two

JARROD IS OBVIOUSLY AS SHOCKED AS I AM TO SEE Charles, very much alive, standing before us, gun in hand. "What, surprised to see me, Landry?" Charles laughs, and his voice has an hysterical edge. He accused me of not being in my right mind, when clearly, he's the one who's insane.

"What are you doing here?" Jarrod demands.

"I might ask you the same question. What brings you out to these godforsaken swamps? Couldn't be you've gotten sweet on my little wife, could it?"

"What do you want, Charles?" Jarrod's voice is cold steel.

"Only what's mine. You keep your hands off what's mine or I'll—"

"What? Destroy her like you did Valerie?"

This brings Charles up short. He hesitates, then laughs again, this time nervously. "How is old Valerie, by the way?"

I feel as if I'm watching some kind of surrealistic play, the plot of which escapes me. Who the hell is

Valerie, and how does Charles know about her? What did he do to harm her? And why does Jarrod have dinner with her once a week?

"I didn't destroy Valerie. It was an accident, and we both know it," Charles snaps. "But you managed to come out of it okay, as I recall."

"You destroyed her by leaving her when she needed you most, you bastard," Jarrod says and takes a step toward Charles. He is taller, broader, and I'm certain much stronger than Charles. The only problem is, Charles is the one with the gun. And he raises it, ready to shoot.

"Wait! Stop!" I shout. I feel hot power rise up from deep within me, and I send it, as I did toward the crystal, directly into Charles's hand that holds the gun. I see the energy strike; his whole arm veers suddenly, and when he pulls the trigger, the bullet misses its mark.

The next few seconds seem to pass in slow motion. There is Charles, turning in my direction, as if he knows I'm the one who fouled his aim. His face is contorted in rage, and his gun is now pointed at me. I hear the sound of a shot explode in the night.

But it's not me who goes down. It's Charles. I watch in stunned horror as he falls forward, stumbling into the fire. His head strikes the black iron pot, tipping it, splashing a wave of hot liquid onto his new face. The flesh singes, then before my eyes, it begins to dissolve. He emits a primal scream, an anguished keen that surely can be heard in the darkest reaches of the swamp.

The death-cry of the *loup-garou*.

His face is eaten away in an instant, shifting his countenance from human to a grotesque skeletal mask. His body writhes in agony, shudders violently, and then is still. The smell of burning flesh begins to permeate the air.

I have no breath left in me to scream. My stomach threatens to heave, and my knees give way. I crumple to the ground, gagging and sobbing.

Someone comes to me and lifts me into his arms. I look up to see Jarrod's face etched with alarm and confusion. "Gabriella," he says, "dear God, what is all this? Are you . . . all right?"

I turn my face into the breadth of his chest and continue to sob. Behind my closed eyes, I see the image of Charles's face being eaten away, and I can't shut the sound of his scream out of my mind. This can't have happened. This has to be yet another nightmare from which I will gratefully awaken. Horror too deep to imagine seeps through my soul.

"I think she's going into shock," I hear someone say. "Take her into the house."

I'm aware that Jarrod is settling me onto the couch, and I hear Marie's distinctive voice. "Go back and help the sheriff. I'll take care of her."

There is the taste of a metal cup at my lips and then a warm, pleasant-flavored liquid on my tongue. I swallow it gratefully.

"There, that's good," Marie says when I've finished all I can manage. "Now, just rest. The worst is over."

Soon, my stomach calms, and the concoction starts to numb the images of Charles's violent death. My breath begins to return to normal. Outside I hear voices.

"There were two of them." It's Danny speaking. "I'll check around back. You go inside and make sure the women are safe."

I hear the front door open and shut, and I see Jarrod's huge frame hunkered in the small cabin. He looks at me and sees that I've been cared for, then turns his gaze to Marie, who is sitting calmly in a chair across from me as if nothing has happened.

"Did you see the other man?" he asks.

"What other man?"

I sit up straighter. "The one who came in here to kill you." I remember Charles's horrible directive to his lieutenant.

But Marie just smiles enigmatically. "Well, obviously he didn't." Before either Jarrod or I can question her further, there's a knock at the front door. "Would you please let Mrs. Boudreaux in?" Marie says to Jarrod.

I wonder if he's caught on to Marie yet, that she knew who was at the door before it was opened. I wish she'd be more discreet in his presence. Of course, she's always openly acknowledged her powers, and therefore her weirdness, and the fact that she doesn't care what other people think only empowers her more.

Hmmm. That's food for thought. But I'm not as brave as Marie, or as experienced in this power thing. I must go slowly and carefully, especially where Jarrod's concerned. Charles actually called me a witch. I think now that I might be. Charles called me crazy. Would Jarrod think the same?

A woman about Marie's age comes into the room. She looks a great deal like the bayou man who brought me here. "Is she all right?" the woman asks Marie, nodding toward me.

"Ask her," Marie says, seeming unsurprised at the arrival of yet another stranger invading her reclusive shores.

"I . . . I'm . . . okay," I tell her. "Thanks."

"I'm Boudreaux's ma," she introduces herself. "I knew he carried you out here. Then later those two fellas came in the store, sayin' they were private investigators, and they showed us your picture with a little girl. Told us you'd kidnapped the child, but my boy, he knew they was up to no good. He rented them a boat, figuring they'd get lost and take care of themselves. I thought he trailed them, just to keep an eye on his property. He was gone when the sheriff and the other fella came looking for you, too, so I carried them out here as well. I wonder where that boy is?"

"He's here," Marie says, nodding toward the front door again. "Big night on the island."

There's another knock, and Jarrod opens the door to a man who stands almost as tall as he. Boudreaux is carrying a rifle. "Ma? What you doin' here?"

His mother gives him a scornful look. "Somebody had to get the sheriff out here. Couldn't find you so I had to bring him myself."

"Well, all of you, come on in and shut the door," Marie says gruffly. "Don't want to waste good air-conditioning."

"I'm going to help Danny," Jarrod says. "He's out there by himself looking for that other guy."

"He won't find him," Marie assures us, holding up one hand as if to keep Jarrod in the room. "When he heard that shot, the second one ran off like the coward he is. A mealy-mouthed little twit, that one. He's probably been swallowed up by the bayou by now."

Jarrod looks at Boudreaux. "Did you see which way he went?"

But Boudreaux shakes his head. "Didn't see him at all. All's I saw was th' critter I shot."

"Critter?" I ask, recalling the howling sound I'd used to frighten Charles.

"It was hard to tell in the dark, but it looked like a wolf to me." His dark eyes bore into mine, and he adds in all seriousness, "Coulda been th' *loup-garou*, you know?"

Danny bursts into the room through the back door. "I don't see anyone out there," he exclaims, breathless, "but I'm not inclined to go far into the swamp until daylight."

"Unless he know his way 'round th' bayou, he won't live t' see th' sunrise," Boudreaux states. He frowns slightly. "I didn't know th' one who died, but th' other little weasel seemed kind of familiar this afternoon. I might've seen him in these parts before. It good he's gone now."

"Could be," Danny says. "But I'd appreciate it if you'd come back in the morning and help me search the area."

"Glad to, Sheriff, but don't hold out no hopes that we'll find him."

Danny turns to me. "I saw that man attack you, Gabriella. Your shot was definitely in self-defense. Guess you took a better aim this time," he adds with a small smile. Then the smile vanishes, and he holds out his hand. "I'll have to take your gun anyway, until all the questions are cleared up."

I turn my palms to him. "I didn't shoot him, Danny. I was only pretending I had a gun." I hear Jarrod swear as I demonstrate how I'd faked having a gun beneath the folds of my gown. "The gun's still in there," I say, pointing to the travel bag that sits next to Marie's chair.

I catch Marie's eye, and I can see she's trying hard not to grin. She gives me a wink and a small nod. We both know I didn't need my gun, and we both know I can't tell the sheriff that.

In spite of the horror of this night and the obscenity of it all, I have come through stronger than I could have imagined. My skin is still warm, and power continues to hum through me, giving me courage and hope that after this, I can face anything, and win.

But who killed Charles? I had feared it was my destiny, but that didn't prove to be the case. Someone else shot him.

Danny voices my question. "Okay, if Gabriella didn't do it, who did?"

No one says a word. Danny scratches his head. "Guess we'll get to that later. At any rate, I'm going to call it self-defense, no matter who pulled the trigger. Anyone know who the dead man is?"

I straighten my shoulders. It's still hard to wrap my mind around the ugly truth. "It . . . it was my husband, Charles Colquitt."

Danny looks at me incredulously and frowns. "I thought you said he was dead."

I swallow to ease the strain in my throat. "I thought that too."

"Are you sure it was him?" Danny presses.

"It was him," Jarrod says, his jaw tight. "The rotten bastard."

Only then do I recall the bitter exchange between Jarrod and Charles. "Jarrod," I blurt, "who's Valerie?"

Jarrod's answer is a silent, long, measured look into my eyes. Then he says, "Let's get you out of here."

I'm too tired to argue. But tomorrow, if Jarrod's still around, I *will* get an answer.

CHAPTER

Forty-three

EXHAUSTION AT LAST SETS IN, THREATENING TO STEAL away my consciousness as Boudreaux steers his motorboat through the inky bayou. He'd been unwilling to take me in it by the light of day, saying it was too hazardous, but I guess he has no choice tonight. There are too many of us to fit in the pirogue, and he didn't want his mother taking more risk than she already had.

Mrs. Boudreaux sits in the front of the boat, aiming a powerful battery-powered light ahead of us to show the way. Jarrod holds me tightly against him, and I try to relax in the safety of his arms. My muscles, however, feel as if they're tied in hard knots.

Danny Comeaux remained with Marie on the island to await backup to help in tomorrow's search and the removal of the body. He's asked Jarrod to summon other area law enforcement officers once we reach Boudreaux's Corner, since the signal for cell phones proved to be too weak that far back in the swamps.

Before we left, I provided Danny with all the information I could about Charles, his family, and the plane crash. I know he doesn't believe the dead man is my husband. And without a face on the corpse, we'll have to wait for DNA tests to prove I'm right.

When we boarded the motorboat for the trip home, we discovered that one of the two pirogues that had been tied to the dock was missing, and Danny surmised the accomplice had stolen it in an attempt to escape.

I hoped silently that an alligator would eat him.

No negative thoughts.

Marie's voice reverberated through my mind at that instant, and I understood what she was trying to tell me. She wasn't admonishing me to be nice. She was warning me against those things that would erode my power. Negativity was one of them. Anger another. And fear.

No negative thoughts.

That's not so easy at the moment. It's negative to wish someone dead, but I am glad Charles is dead. Really dead this time. Because his death means Michaela and I are safe at last. He'll never hurt us again.

It's negative to wish ill on other people, but when DNA proves that it's Charles Colquitt's body lying out there on that island, there will be plenty of potential scandal with which Jarrod can threaten the Colquitts and get them to leave Michaela and me alone. I wish I could be a bug on his shoulder when he tells them.

I want them for once to feel pain and shame such as they were fond of inflicting on me with their superior ways and condescending manners.

I have to work hard to shake off that negative thought, but I manage. I will not let the Colquitts, even thoughts of them, steal away my power ever again.

In spite of the power that is building within me and my determination to overcome the bleak years of living with fear and anger, shock and disbelief at the night's events still rock me, and I jerk spasmodically from time to time. Jarrod strokes my hair, and I lean into him. Marie's palm reading indicated that we might have a future together, but I'm not so sure. It depends on the secrets he's been holding from me. And why he hasn't already shared them. But for the moment, I'm content to let him comfort me.

I must have dozed off, because I awake with a start some time later as the boat nudges against the shore. "We're here," Jarrod says quietly, stirring me gently. With a motorboat, the trip was far faster than in the pirogue. It's barely midnight.

While I slept, the horrors of this night faded in my mind, but when I return to full consciousness, they come screaming back. My earlier equanimity has fled, and my nerves feel as if someone is pulling them out of me right through my skin.

I know Charles can't hurt anyone now, but I must make sure Michaela is safe, that he didn't somehow manage to snatch her and hide her away before coming after me. "I have to call Rosalie," I say, clambering out of the boat. *Dear God, how can I ever tell my daughter what happened?*

Maybe I won't, certainly not until she's older. I won't tell her anything ever, I decide, unless and until I understand the full depth of Charles's deception and his motivation for it.

My cell phone works from here. I dial the number and a sleepy Rosalie answers the phone. "'Lo?"

"Rosalie, it's me, Gabriella."

"Oh, my God, girl, where the hell are you? Are you all right?" I can see her bolting upright when she hears my voice.

"Yes, no, oh, I don't know. Yes, I'm all right." *Physically, that is.* "I'm with Jarrod Landry, my lawyer. I'll explain what happened later." *If I can.* "Is Michaela okay?"

"She's fine. She's missed you, but I think the girls have had a fun time. She's sound asleep now. You want me to wake her up?"

"There's no point in doing that. I'll come by first thing in the morning and pick her up." I pause, then add, feeling it an incredibly inadequate statement: "Rosalie, thank you for taking care of her." *You very well might have saved her life,* I add silently.

"It's okay, Gabriella. I'm glad I could do it for you. But you owe me some big damn explanations when all this dust settles. I take it Danny and Jarrod found you in time?"

"How'd you know they were looking for me?"

"Jarrod may be your lawyer, honey, but you'd have

to be blind not to see how he feels about you. It's a long story. Ask him. But you're a thousand kinds of fool if you don't give that man a chance."

With that, Rosalie says good night, and I disconnect the call. While I talked, I paced the small, dusty parking lot outside the store. Now I look through the night and see Jarrod sitting on the store's front porch rail, talking on his cell phone. Inside, Boudreaux and his mother are busily at work placing the items they'd borrowed from their store for the trip back on the shelves, ready again for sale.

"Yes, there's one fatality," Jarrod is saying when I come up to him. "Bring what you need to transport the body. Male. Caucasian. Identity . . . ," he glances at me, "not confirmed."

I shudder. I don't need any confirmation. There's no doubt in my mind the body belongs, or belonged, to Charles Colquitt.

Jarrod ends his call and comes to me. He put his arms across my shoulders. "How's Michaela?"

"She's fine. Sound asleep. I'll get her in the morning. Will you take me home?" I'm unsure whether I want Jarrod in my house again overnight, but I'm so weary I don't think I can drive.

Jarrod hesitates. "Of course. I rode out here with the sheriff. My car's at your house."

A long silence stretches between us. "Gabriella, did you have any idea Charles wasn't really dead?" he asks at last.

I feel hollow, and cold. "No. I can't imagine . . ." I

think about my dreams, the first in which Grandnana warned me that evil was coming my way, and the second in which I saw the face of that evil . . . Charles. If I'd been aware then of the extent of my powers, perhaps I would have known to take the dreams literally. Perhaps. But even the powerful psychic, Marie Françoise, had declined to penetrate the evil to determine its source.

You are about to face deception of monstrous proportions was the closest she could come to it.

Charles's deception was so monstrous I doubt if I could have conceived of it even with all the power I could conjure.

"He must have faked his death in that plane crash." Jarrod is thinking out loud. "But why? And why was he after you?"

"He told me he'd come to get what I'd stolen from him."

"What?"

"He seemed to think I was hiding all those hideous things he'd collected, and he wanted them back." I bite my lip. "He also said he'd come back to get Michaela and me. He seemed to think he owned us as well. I guess to him we were just more items in his collection."

Jarrod places his index finger beneath my chin and raises my head until our eyes meet. "We'll get to the bottom of this," he says. "I promise."

This, and other things, Jarrod.

We thank the mother and son who so selflessly

came to our aid and get in my car. But before Jarrod starts the engine, he turns to me. "There's something you need to know."

A fresh wave of alarm washes over me. "What? What is it now?"

"Charles and his sidekick went to your house again last night. . . ."

I already know this—Marie told me that they'd gone to Shadow Haven, where they'd found the directions to her swamp hut. She'd also said they'd torn the house apart looking for valuables. I have a premonition that Jarrod's about to tell me something bad. "And?"

He clears his throat. "I spent last night in Tibonne," he explains. "I just had a bad feeling about leaving you alone at Shadow Haven, even though you made it clear you didn't want me around. I went to see you this morning and . . . well, the place was trashed and you were nowhere to be found. I called the police and the sheriff, and I started looking for you. The police have your house cordoned off as a crime scene, Gabriella. I don't think we can go there, at least not tonight."

When is it going to end? I wonder, fighting the fury that threatens to consume me again. Is this to be Charles's final outrage against me? Or will he find some way yet again to come back from the dead and torment me? I've had all of Charles Colquitt I can stand.

"Let's go. That bastard has hurt me for the last time. He's not going to keep me from staying in my own home."

I HAD HOPED TO GET JARROD TO TELL ME ABOUT Valerie on the way home, but I fell asleep almost as soon as the car turned out of Boudreaux's driveway.

The crime scene tape is still wound around the columns in front of the house when we drive up, but everything is dark. I figure all the law enforcement officers in this and the neighboring parishes are headed toward Boudreaux's Corner about now.

"You sure you want to go in there?" Jarrod asks as he turns off the engine.

I stare for a moment at the silhouette of Shadow Haven outlined against the starlit midnight sky. "I'm sure. It's my home." I open the car door and head toward the house. Jarrod follows a few steps behind. I expect things to be topsy-turvy, but after all I've faced and conquered tonight, I think I can contend with any damage he might have done.

When I flip on the lights, I let out a little cry. This is not just topsy-turvy. This is a brutal, premeditated attack on my home. Red paint has been sloshed in the hallway, running down the freshly painted rose-colored walls like dripping blood. The hardwood floors are stained as well with the thick, red ooze. To my right, in the parlor that served as my temporary studio, the black marble has been smashed to bits.

We make our way to the kitchen, where we discover the furniture looks as if it's been butchered with an ax, and all my dishes and glassware are in shards on the floor. The bathroom is a complete gooey mess from shampoos and lotions that have been poured all over, and my bedroom has been ransacked as well. But it's when I come to Michaela's room and see that he's even desecrated her toys that I lose it at last.

"Damn him," I cry. "Damn his soul to hell!" I kick at the debris underfoot. "Oh, dear God, why'd he have to do this?" I wail when I see that he's torn Mandy's head off.

Jarrod takes the doll in hand and stares at it for a long moment. Oddly, he cradles it tenderly in the crook of his elbow. "Let's get out of here, Gabriella," he says in a low voice. "I'll get you a room at the motel."

But I shake my head, trying to control the rage that burns in my belly. "No. If I do that, Charles wins."

"Charles is dead," he reminds me. "It's late. You're tired. You've had an appalling experience. I probably ought to take you to the emergency room and get you checked out."

He's right that I'm tired, but not nearly so much as

he thinks. Power continues to hum within my breast, and I'm charged with a determination to clean up the last vestige of Charles's sick perversion before I can go to bed.

"No way. I'm okay. I want to get this mess out of here. I promised to bring Michaela back tomorrow, and I'm not about to let her come into Shadow Haven and see that our home's been torn apart once again."

It's nearly four in the morning when Jarrod hauls the last trash bag outside. We've managed to straighten Michaela's room to an acceptable degree. Her toys, except for the unfortunate Mandy, have been arranged in their usual places, her books lined up on the shelves. I've hidden Mandy in a shoe box on my closet shelf, hoping I can find a doll doctor in New Orleans.

The kitchen, bathroom, and my room weren't so easy. I swept up the broken glass while Jarrod took the destroyed furniture to a junk pile at the far edge of the property. We cleaned up the goo that had been poured all over the bathroom.

I tackled my room while Jarrod worked at getting the red paint off the hallway floor. It was latex paint and not completely dry, so a lot of it washed up, but I suspect I'll have to lay new hardwood. I grieve for the ruin of the beautiful cypress floors that had been so carefully laid when Angelique's loving husband had built this home for her.

I'd hoped to be able keep this latest invasion of our

home from Michaela; it's bound to frighten her. But there's no way. Although the bedrooms have been made habitable once again, the kitchen is practically barren. How do we explain all that missing furniture?

I'm so tired now I think I'm going to collapse. I see dark circles beneath Jarrod's eyes, and his face looks haggard. I suddenly realize that he's been on a rough journey as well, a dangerous trip into the bayou—to rescue me. Whatever questions I have for him can wait.

"I think we've done all we can do for tonight. I'm going upstairs and soak in a hot bath for a little while. Want a shower?"

He doesn't argue as I point him toward the small bathroom beneath the stairs. I wonder if he can fit in that little cubicle. "You can have my bed again."

"No. I'll sleep in Michaela's room. You've been through hell the last couple of days. You need to be in your own bed."

I'm too tired to argue. "Okay, well, see you in the morning."

The night is hot and still, and I can hear a swamp creature baying in the wet darkness. Its howl is wolflike and becomes louder as I listen. The sound sends terror into the depths of my heart. I am on the bayou again, alone and vulnerable. I peer through the inky night, searching for the *loup-garou*, whom I know with dead certainty is coming for me again.

"No!" I cry out. "You can't! You're dead!"

But I can see his yellow eyes in the distance, like

flickers of malevolent marsh gas. I hear the sound of footsteps approaching, and I try to run, but my own feet are bogged in quicksand. And then I see him, his deadly fangs poised as he leaps through the air, charging toward me.

"No!" I scream. "Leave me alone!" I feel the creature shaking me, and I claw at it to free myself.

"Wake up, Gabriella. Wake up. It's only a dream."

I open my eyes to find that it's Jarrod who is shaking me awake, but my consciousness is still fuzzy. "Don't let him get me!" I scream. "Don't let him touch me!"

Jarrod encircles me with his arms. "I won't let anyone hurt you ever again," he says, and I feel him kiss the top of my head.

My heart is pounding a thousand times a minute, and my skin is drenched in a sheen of cold perspiration. I cling to Jarrod, try to burrow myself into his protective embrace. "Hold me," I beg. "Hold me." My power has vanished in the wake of the dread and fear generated by the dream, and I feel as if I'm on the edge of hysteria.

Jarrod does as I ask. He holds me, in fact, so tightly I begin to have trouble breathing. But his steady presence at last works to calm me.

That, and something else.

I lean into him, suddenly wanting him— desperately, sexually, and now. I ease my way up his body until my lips are upon his. I part his lips with my tongue.

"Gabrie . . . ," he starts but I steal away his words with my kiss. I want no words. I want . . . I need . . . to be loved. I need the feel of someone's strong arms holding me, protecting me from the horrors that lay outside my door. I crave the touch of someone's hard body against mine, around me, inside me, warming me, bringing back my power. I want this man to make love to me, to restore me as a woman.

I push him backward and pin him against the sheets with my body. Kissing him fiercely I strip off his boxers, pausing only to slip off my nightshirt. I slide one leg over his belly and balance my weight on either side of him. His hands caress my breasts, inflaming my desire until I can bear it no longer. I move against his hardness, feel him enter me. Slowly I ease down upon him, surrounding him, drawing him inside me. And as he fills me, the darkness and the terror subside.

Sensations spark and explode in brilliant swirls of light and color behind my closed eyes. I feel myself soaring to a place where I'm forever safe and loved, where no one can ever hurt me again. Too soon, I reach a pinnacle of exquisite release, and as I crest, I feel his body pulsing with mine.

Spent, we lie together, breathing hard in the hours before dawn. I don't want to think about what I've just done. I know it was wrong to use Jarrod like this. But at the moment, all I want is to lie here in his arms and know that the *loup-garou* threatens me no longer.

CHAPTER
Forty-five

THE SUN IS HIGH WHEN I'M AWAKENED BY A MUFFLED musical sound; it takes me a moment to realize it's my cell phone, playing "Dixie" from inside my purse on a nearby chair. Reluctantly, I roll away from Jarrod and reach for my handbag.

"Mama?" Michaela's small voice rings happily in my ears. "Can I come home now?"

My heart does a little flip at the sound of her voice. "Oh, baby, it's so good to talk to you. I'll be there in a little while." I speak briefly with both Michaela and Rosalie, then hang up and turn to Jarrod.

"Time to go back to the real world." I snag my sleep shirt that got tossed during our passionate lovemaking.

"Don't . . . put that on just yet," he says, and pulls on it, drawing me back into the bed.

"Jarrod . . ." I feel awkward and apologetic. "I . . . I don't know what made me do that last night—"

His lips cut off further words. His kisses arouse me in no time, and we make love again, this time more slowly, luxuriously exploring each other in the summer morning sunshine.

"What is this, Jarrod?" I whisper when we have sated each other once again. I could rationalize my behavior last night as a reaction to the terror and fear of all that had happened. But this morning is another matter. . . .

He strokes my hair. "Maybe it's the real world."

Unsettling emotions stir within me. After Charles's shocking reappearance, I'm no longer sure what is real and what is not.

Things are not as they seem. . . .

What feels real at the moment is that I think I've fallen in love with Jarrod, even though I don't know him very well, and even though we haven't resolved the Valerie issue yet. Intellectually, I know I could be setting myself up for a fall, but it seems my heart is overruling my mind. "I . . . I really do have to go pick up Michaela now." Reluctantly, I slip out of bed.

When I come out of the shower a short while later, I find Jarrod dressed and ready to leave. My disappointment is almost palpable.

"I have to go into the office," he says, "but the matters I have to take care of shouldn't take all day." He comes to me and rests his arms on my shoulders, the way he's done several times since he came into my life. I like the weight of him, the feel of him so close. I don't want him to go.

"Do you think you'll be all right out here now," he asks, "or would you like to go to New Orleans with me?"

Charles is dead, and Marie believes his crony is fatally lost in the bayou. That leaves only the Colquitts, and I suspect they're on Jarrod's list of "matters to take care of."

There is nothing to be afraid of now.

"We'll be fine. I plan to do some serious shopping today, see if I can get some new kitchen furniture and some more paint. But . . . would you like to come back for dinner?"

He lowers his lips to mine. "If you insist."

I return his light kiss, feeling breathless. "I insist. Call me before you leave New Orleans, so I'll know when to expect you."

"I'll call if you promise you'll keep your phone turned on."

I'm the one who's getting turned on standing here in his embrace. I'd better go before something gets started again. I can't help but eagerly anticipate him coming back tonight.

"I promise. I've got to get rid of that silly musical ringer, though."

He kisses me again and turns to go. "See you tonight."

Michaela is standing beside the large Wal-Mart sack on Rosalie's front porch when I arrive. I grin and wave to her through the windshield as I turn off the car. She comes flying toward me, and I feel as if my heart will burst.

"Hi, *chérie.*" I whirl Michaela into my arms and

hold on tightly. It's beyond my comprehension that this beautiful child could be Charles's daughter. Maybe Charles hadn't fathered her. Maybe I'd been visited by fairies when Michaela was conceived.

"Did you have fun with Kisha?" I ask, releasing her at last.

But Michaela isn't interested in talking about her playmate. "Mr. Jarrod found you! He came here, and I told him about Mary Frances and showed him the frog perfume, and then he found you!"

It's the first time I've stopped to consider how Jarrod and Danny had known where to look for me. "You told him about Marie Françoise?" I ask, marveling that Michaela, age six, could remember enough of our trip to New Orleans to provide Jarrod and Danny with a lead. "That was a very smart girl."

"Yeah," Rosalie says, coming out onto the porch. "You might think she's a fortune-teller or something. Come on in, Gabriella." She gives me a shrewd smile. "I got coffee waiting, along with a thousand questions."

Over coffee, I answer some of those questions, and I learn what happened here while I was away.

"The girls were in the living room playing with their new Barbies," Rosalie tells me. "I was flipping through magazines, not paying much attention, until something Michaela said caught my attention. She was talking real spooky-like, and she said something like, 'There is much evil surrounding you. Someone is trying to take something from you. You must be strong.'"

I feel my face start to flush as Rosalie talks.

"I looked over to where they were playing to see what was going on. They had their Barbies standing on either side of a low footstool, and Michaela had laid some playing cards out on the stool. Her Barbie was the 'fortune-teller,' and Kisha's was the one whose fortune was being told. I asked them what they were doing, and Michaela told me they were playing a game that you'd played that day with some old woman in New Orleans."

I can tell Rosalie didn't like this one bit, but I don't interrupt her.

"Michaela told me the woman had scared her," Rosalie continues. "She said the fortune-teller said somebody was trying to steal something from you, and that you had to go on a long trip over the water."

I'm appalled that Michaela overheard this. I thought I'd moved her out of hearing distance.

Rosalie stops and laughs a little sharply. "I have to tell you, for a moment I had the bad feeling that you'd left Michaela here with me and run off for good or something. Then I decided you wouldn't do a thing like that, but that you must be in a heap of trouble. I know you asked me to keep it a secret that Michaela was here, but I decided you needed help, so I called Danny."

I learn that early Sunday morning, after both Rosalie and Jarrod had called Danny for different reasons, the sheriff, accompanied by Jarrod, had come to Rosalie's to question Michaela. She'd told them about Nicola and the tarot reading and showed them the bottle of "frog perfume." The name of the shop where we bought it was on the bottom.

A phone call to the shop had produced Nicola's address; a search of the New Orleans cross-directory gave them her phone number. According to Rosalie, Nicola had been reluctant to reveal the location of the mysterious Marie Françoise, but gave in when she learned Danny was the law.

"Danny knew where Boudreaux's Corner was, of course," Rosalie continues. "Those two hightailed it out of here so fast it made my head swim." She leans closer. "I'm telling you, that lawyer of yours was acting more like a husband with a missing wife than a lawyer who's lost a client."

I don't want to go there right now. I can't deny my feelings for Jarrod, but there's still the Valerie thing hanging between us.

And my own secret as well, I realize with a start. I'm determined he's going to tell me about Valerie, but am I willing to risk telling him about my Deveaux powers?

"Well, I'm glad Michaela remembered all that," I say, shifting the direction of the conversation.

"She's a smart one. Now, tell me, who trashed your house this time, and why on earth were you out there in that godforsaken swamp?"

The truth about Charles is too ugly and enormous to be believed. Neither do I want to tell Rosalie that it was the spirit of my grandmother who sent me to the safe haven of Marie Françoise's island. But she deserves to know something.

"I only told you a half-truth," I admit to Rosalie. "I said I thought Michaela's grandparents might be trying to get her put into a foster home. But the real reason I left Michaela with you is that I suspected someone might try to kidnap her. That's why I didn't want anyone to know where she was."

"Kidnap?!"

"I guess you've figured out by now that Michaela's father was . . . very wealthy. I'm afraid I made us sitting ducks by moving out into the boonies like I did. Anyway, I believe the men came to the house to kidnap Michaela, maybe both of us, and when we weren't there, they got mad and did a lot of damage."

"That poor old house has seen some violence," Rosalie mourns.

"Yes, it has." *All at the hands of Charles Colquitt, directly or indirectly.*

"So, do you think they'll come back?"

"No. Rosalie, I did a real stupid thing. I left the directions Nicola gave me lying on the kitchen table. The kidnappers obviously found them, then followed me to Marie's."

"Dear God in heaven! So what happened?"

I relate the grisly tale, withholding only the identity of the kidnappers. "One's dead, the other probably will be if he isn't already. City folk don't stand much of a chance wandering around in the bayou." I recall the 'gator, snake, and bobcat I'd encountered. Had it been only yesterday?

"But I still don't understand why you went out there."

I give a rueful laugh. "I don't quite understand it myself. The woman I went to see, Marie Françoise, was a friend of my grandmother's. I . . . I can't really explain why, Rosalie, but I had this . . . uh . . . strong feeling that I needed to see her. You're not going to like this, but I knew that Marie was a psychic in her day. Maybe I went there thinking she could tell me who was after us. I don't know. . . ." My words fail. How can I explain the inexplicable?

"Guess you must've wanted to see her real bad," Rosalie says with a wry laugh. "According to what Michaela told us, it took you a trip to New Orleans and a visit to Marie's weird sister to find out she was living way out in the middle of the swamp." Rosalie shakes her head. "Listen, you don't have to explain. It's enough that you're both safe now. Have some more coffee."

Forty-six

AFTER LEAVING ROSALIE'S, MICHAELA AND I PAY A visit to the insurance agent in Tibonne who recently wrote my homeowner's policy. She isn't particularly happy that her new client is already filing a claim, but when she learns the circumstances, that vandals have struck Shadow Haven again, I have her full sympathy. She's a local, and although I didn't know her when I lived here, she knew all about the drug raid and the damage to "that lovely old plantation house." She assures me the claim will be filed right away. I leave her office, gratified that at least I'll have a little extra money this time to restore this latest trespass against my home.

Our next stop is the furniture store where we bought the kitchen table and the fireplace chairs. We're lucky that they have identical pieces in stock, and I make arrangements for them to be delivered later in the afternoon. Then we're off to the home improvement store, where I buy another bucket of rose-colored paint. I'll be damned if I'm going to let Shadow Haven suffer one day from the ravages of Charles's attack.

Charles. The thought of him nearly makes me sick. I have to keep going, keep moving, keep doing things to hold on to my power and overcome the habitual fear he engendered. But he hovers at the edge of my consciousness, like a coiled snake. I know he's dead. I saw his body. But I can't seem to shake the notion that somehow he'll manage to reach out from beyond the grave and strike again and again until he at last succeeds in destroying me.

Wal-Mart has dishes and glassware to replace what was destroyed, and I indulge Michaela in the toy department once again. She asks why we're buying new things, since we made these same purchases a short time ago.

"Some things got broken last night," I answer her briefly, then change the subject. "Look, there's a set of jacks. I used to play jacks when I was a girl. Want me to teach you?"

We stop for a hamburger at the Dairy Queen, then head home, when suddenly I'm overcome with an irrational apprehension. When we reach the twin pillars at the entrance to Shadow Haven, I slow the car. I know, I *know*, that someone is on this land.

"What's the matter, Mama?" Michaela asks.

"Oh, it's . . . nothing." I continue up the lane, but the shivery feeling won't go away.

Someone is on the land, but I relax when I see

Danny Comeaux's cruiser parked in front of the house. He's sitting on the verandah talking on his cell phone, but hangs up when we arrive.

"Hey, Danny." I wonder if I've broken the law by taking down the crime scene tape and cleaning up the house.

He stands up. "Hello, Gabriella." His expression is grave. "You doing okay today?"

I nod. "I guess so. Michaela, why don't you go play on your swing set while I chat with the sheriff?"

She darts off, and I turn to Danny. "Thanks for coming after me last night. Rosalie told me how you figured out where to find me."

Danny hands my gun to me. "I brought this back. I've got no use for it. When I dragged the body inside last night after you left, I examined it closely. Gabriella, there was no gunshot wound."

The blood drains from my face. So I killed him after all. I didn't think my energy zaps were that strong, and he seemed to remain on his feet after I deflected his gun away from Jarrod. But I don't know the strength of my power. Maybe I electrocuted him, in a manner of speaking. "What . . . was the cause of death?"

"We're doing an autopsy, but it looks like when he turned to shoot you, he stumbled over something, maybe his own feet. He hit his head on that iron pot in the fire circle, and the acid spilled on him." Danny shudders. "Hell of a way to die."

Turn the evil upon itself, and it will be destroyed. . . .

Danny thinks it was an accident. I don't. If I didn't cause Charles to lose his balance, something did. Or somebody. Marie? Grandnana? Even Boudreaux might have conjured his "critter," his *loup-garou*, to foil the attack. Bayou people are said to possess a little Cajun magic.

I am beyond questioning possibilities anymore.

"It's more'n I can reckon what you were doing out there in the first place," Danny goes on. "We were damned lucky to happen upon old Mrs. Boudreaux at the store. She told us that two men had come in earlier, making themselves out to be private investigators looking for a kidnapped girl."

I shrug. "Mrs. Boudreaux told us what happened. But it was Charles who was the kidnapper, Danny. I can't explain his actions, but he told me that he'd come for Michaela and me."

Danny takes a metal pen from his pocket and twiddles it between his fingers, as if he's nervous. Then he asks, "Are you really sure that was your husband, Gabriella? I mean, I called his family in Boston, and they assured me he'd died in that plane wreck. They're faxing me his death certificate."

I wish Elizabeth Colquitt could have been there to see her son's eyes. She would have known him in an instant. "It was Charles, Danny. He'd had his face altered, but it was him. He knew too much about me to have been an impostor."

"His mother suggested . . . uh . . . that you were hysterical when you thought you recognized him."

Ah, yes. The mentally unstable Cajun girl. "Why don't you make them come and view the body?" I snap. "Surely she'd recognize his hands or feet or something." And then I remember. "There's a big scar on his left leg, right at the knee. He told me he got it in a motorcycle accident. She'd recognize that."

Danny brightens visibily. "That'll be easy to check out. Of course, they're doing a DNA check, but that takes some time. If it really is Charles Colquitt, that'll open up a whole can of worms for you, I'm afraid. Got any idea why he would do all this?"

I shake my head. "Danny, none of it makes any sense. Charles was rich. He had anything and everything he ever wanted. I can't imagine why he would want the world to think he'd died."

"People don't take such desperate measures without strong motivation," Danny points out. "There must have been something he wanted. When you spoke with him last night, did he give you any clue where he's been or what he's been doing since the plane crash?"

I have to think for a moment, but I do remember one thing. "He said he had a good doctor in the Caymans," I reply. "I think he was referring to a plastic surgeon. He was talking about his new face."

Danny leans forward. "The Caymans. A good place to hide money."

"Hide money? Why would he want to hide money?"

"Depends on how he got the money. Maybe he was involved in drugs or something."

This is beyond believability. But then, so was Charles's little return from the dead last night. I think about the torc. "Jarrod seems to think maybe he was stealing antiquities. He was an attorney for a large liquidation firm in New York. He would have had access to rare and valuable items."

Danny stands up to go. "Could be that's it. Guess we'll find out as time goes along. You going to be okay out here?"

I wish people would quit asking that question. It makes me wonder if I am. "Sure. He was the danger, and now he's gone."

"Well, call me if you need anything. You *do* have a phone now. . . ."

Danny leaves and I gather my packages from the car. Michaela seems content to play outside, and I'm anxious to restore my household and get things ready for Jarrod's return this evening. I'm busy unwrapping dishware and glasses when Michaela comes running into the house.

"Mama!" she calls. "There's a man here to see you."

I frown. Now what?

I go into the hallway to see who's at the front door, when to my horror I realize the man is in my house. He has a broad nose, dark hair, and teeth that shine white against his light brown skin. Is it my imagination, or do his eyes have a strange yellow cast? I recognize him instantly—the other *loup-garou*, the goon who'd been with Charles last night.

Fear turns my mouth sour, and I lose all sense of my power. Marie had believed he'd never surface again from the swamps. How could she have been so mistaken?

The man gives me a wicked grin. "Good morning, Mrs. Colquitt. We meet again." He has a strong Latino accent and appears extremely nervous.

I have a large glass tumbler still in my hand from my unpacking chore. I clench the cool hard surface, breathing hard. "Get out of my house," I demand, heading for him, arm raised and ready to strike. He isn't much larger than I am, and my fear subsides. The power that sustained me last night surges once again in the nick of time. "Get out!" I shriek.

"Not before I get what I came for."

Only then do I see the gun in his hand. With his free hand, he grabs Michaela, who screams and struggles against him. I dare not throw the glass now, or an energy bullet. I might hit my daughter instead.

"Now I want you to listen real close, Mrs. Colquitt," the man utters. "I won't hurt your little girl here," he gestures at Michaela with his gun, "if you do just what I say. First, don't even think about calling the police if you want to see her alive again. Instead, call your rich in-laws. Two million will set her free. I'll call your lawyer friend with the details later."

With that, he's out the front door, carrying a screaming Michaela over his shoulder like a sack of potatoes.

Oh, dear God. I swear and run to the door in time to see him get behind the wheel of a late-model car, Michaela on his lap. Ignoring his warning, I pick up my phone and dial the sheriff's office. Maxine answers. "Danny's not here," she tells me. "I thought he was going to Shadow Haven."

"He's been here and gone," I scream. "Find him! Someone's taken my daughter! That bastard's stolen my daughter!"

Forty-seven

MAXINE PROMISES TO GET HOLD OF DANNY ON THE radio right away, but I can't wait on him. I grab my car keys, phone, and gun, and am out the door in a flash.

The dust from the kidnapper's hasty retreat from Shadow Haven hasn't settled on the lane, but when I reach the road, I don't know which way to turn. "Grandnana, where is Michaela?" I cry out loud. "Help me find her."

As I did on the lonely road to Boudreaux's Corner, I feel a nudge, and the wheel seems to want to turn to the right. Good. He's headed toward Tibonne. I dial Maxine again. "Tell Danny the kidnapper is headed into town. He's driving a dark blue Lexus sedan. I'm behind him by a couple of minutes."

Before she has time to lecture me about the danger of following him, I disconnect the call. I jump when the phone rings again almost immediately. "Hello?"

"Gabriella? It's Jarrod. What's going on?"

How did he know something was going on? "That

man, that other man, Jarrod . . ." I'm almost screaming into the phone. "He didn't die in the swamp. He came to the house, and he's taken Michaela." The hysteria of which I was accused earlier begins to rise. "Where are you?"

"On my way back to Tibonne. I got this really creepy feeling that something wasn't right. Like this voice inside my head was yelling at me to turn around and come back to you."

"Well, it was right, and I'm glad you're on your way back. But I don't know what to do, Jarrod. The kidnapper is driving a dark blue Lexus sedan. I've already tried to contact Danny, but I haven't talked to him yet." I'm driving as fast as I dare, but there's no sign of the Lexus ahead of me. I hope I didn't turn in the wrong direction.

"I'll meet you at the sheriff's office," Jarrod says. "But keep your phone handy, and call me if anything changes and I need to meet you somewhere else."

I hang up and put the phone in my lap. I don't know what good Jarrod can do, but it's a comfort to know he's here for me. That voice he heard . . . I wonder . . . No, it couldn't be. They say everybody has intuition; it's just that in some it's more developed. Whatever, I'm glad he was willing to listen to his today.

I pull up in front of the courthouse on the square and lean my head on my arms crossed on the steering wheel. Where is my baby? I begin to tremble. If that bastard hurts my baby . . .

I take several rapid, deep breaths. I have to stay in control. I have to call on my power. It won't help Michaela if I fall apart now. My phone rings. It's Danny. "I'm outside your office," I inform him, and he tells me to stay put. He's put out an APB on the Lexus and is calling in the Feds, as kidnapping is a federal crime. I'm astonished that he's acted so fast.

"I was afraid last night he'd gotten away," Danny says. "I guess Boudreaux was wrong. And that weird Marie. This guy must know his way around the swamps."

I wonder again how Marie had failed to forsee this. Why hadn't she been able to tune in to the fact that this thug was still alive and help Danny find him?

"Danny, the man said he wanted two million dollars for Michaela's release, and that he'd call my lawyer, I guess he meant Jarrod, with the details. But what will he do with her in the meantime? Where could he go to hide her?"

"The bayou comes to mind. If he managed to survive in it once, he might try it again."

I sit very still, breathing hard. My skin begins to grow warm, and there's a strange buzzing in my head. I allow my power to take over. I give in to it completely, not caring if it consumes me totally. In barely an instant, I know he's not headed for the bayou. In my mind's eye, I see an airplane. "He's not going to the bayou, Danny," I say with utter certainty. "He's got a plane. He's going to take her out of the country."

Danny's cruiser pulls up next to my car, and we hang up. He hurries to me. "What makes you say that?"

I can't tell him how I know, but I do, the same as I knew earlier there was someone on my land. It wasn't Danny that I sensed. It was this man, come to kidnap my baby.

"Remember I told you Charles had a doctor in the Caymans? That's where this guy's taking Michaela. Danny," I turn to him, "I have to stop him."

Jarrod's convertible screeches into the parking space on the other side of my car, and in an instant, he is running toward me. "I knew I shouldn't have left you," he says as he takes me in his arms.

"She thinks the kidnapper is going to take the girl out of the country," the sheriff tells Jarrod. "He said he'd contact you with the details for getting him the ransom. Have you heard from him?"

"No. Out of the country? Where?"

The three of us hurry into Danny's office, where Maxine is talking rapidly on the radio. She looks relieved to see Danny. "Nobody's seen that car," she tells us. "But I've got every sheriff in neighboring parishes looking for it. The main roads are covered."

Again the buzzing sound rumbles through my mind, and I see the car on a narrow road, not a main thoroughfare. And again, I get an image of an airplane. "Danny," I say, clutching his upper arm, "are there any small airfields near here? Private runways?"

He looks at me, frowning. "Yeah. In fact, there's

one not far from Shadow Haven, on Grant's pasture. Those drug-runners who ruined your house a few years back were using it."

I remember the Armands mentioning it. In the heart of my soul, I know that's where the kidnapper is taking Michaela. "He's there. Or he's headed there."

"How do you know?"

"Look, Danny, there are just times when . . . a mother knows!" I turn to Jarrod. "We've got to get to her before he has a chance to get off the ground."

Jarrod looks from me to the sheriff. "Well, let's go!"

Danny gives me an odd look, then shakes his head. "It's worth a try. Maxine." He turns to the dispatcher. "Keep me up with what's going on. I'm expecting an FBI team from New Orleans to show up this afternoon. You know that airfield out behind the rigs? That's where we're going. I'll let you know if anything turns up."

Jarrod insists on taking his car and following Danny to the airfield. I jump in beside Jarrod. He jerks the gearshift and spins the tires as he backs out. Neither of us speaks as we follow Danny, who's turned on his blue lights and is racing through town. My skin is burning now, and the focus of my inner eye is on that airplane.

The road to the airfield turns off to the left several miles before the entrance to Shadow Haven. I must have missed a signal here somehow. I passed this lane without feeling a nudge to turn down it. But now that we're traveling along it, I know it's the right way.

"There it is," Jarrod says as we approach. Ahead of us is the blue Lexus, and behind it is a Lear jet. On the tarmac in between is the man with the yellow eyes, holding my daughter at gunpoint. I hope like hell that Danny's calling for backup right about now.

Dear God, don't let that beast hurt her.

Turn the evil on itself. . . .

Before I can think, I hear the crack of gunfire and see Danny's windshield splinter into shards, and the cruiser careens out of control. "He's shooting, Jarrod. Stop!"

Jarrod pulls the small car behind the sheriff's vehicle as it settles to a stop, using it as a shield. To my surprise, he takes a gun out of his glove compartment. "Stay here," he says as he gets out.

I'm so shaken I can't think for a moment. Then I jerk my door open and bolt out after him. Jarrod can't shoot at the kidnapper while he's got Michaela in his clutches. "No, Jarrod, don't!"

But he's not headed toward the kidnapper. He's reaching for the door of Danny's car. I watch in horror as he opens it, and the sheriff, bleeding profusely, falls against him.

The sight of my childhood friend struck down by the evil brought here by Charles Colquitt turns my already hot blood to fire. My daughter will be taken by that evil, too, if I don't stop it now.

I don't think; I don't hesitate. I know what I must do.

Jarrod's attention is on Danny, and he doesn't see

me as I make my way past the cruiser. Power charges through me like electricity until I think that I must shimmer like an arc beneath the hot summer sun. I'm unafraid as I begin walking toward the man who holds my daughter. *He is a coward.* The message is clear though unspoken. *Use your power.*

I see him raise his gun. "Stop or I'll shoot," he growls.

"No you won't. You haven't got the guts." I don't know where the words came from, but they were meant to call his hand, challenge him into making a mistake.

His face contorts, and his mouth twists into a snarl. But he doesn't shoot.

"You're nothing but a mangy excuse for the *loup-garou,*" I deride him. "Go ahead, shoot me."

I focus all my power on his gun. In my mind, I can see the pressure of his finger on the trigger. I hold my stance and direct the force that shimmers through me to the barrel of the weapon. He squeezes the trigger.

An explosion rocks the afternoon, but no bullet slashes through me. Instead, I watch in stunned amazement as the man falls writhing to the ground. His right arm ends in a bloody stump. His hand has been torn off when the gun blew up.

I race toward Michaela. "Run, baby, run!" I shout, and Michaela dashes to me, her face red and her eyes filled with tears and terror. Together, stumbling and panting for breath, we flee to safety behind the sheriff's car.

I'm only vaguely aware of the sound of sirens approaching. I'm dazed, and I fall against Jarrod, clutching Michaela to me. The power that surged through me is spent, and I sag into his body. He picks Michaela up in one of his strong arms and draws me against him with the other.

"What the hell were you thinking, going after him like that?" Jarrod shouts over the din. I become aware that Danny is lying on the ground at our feet. He's bleeding, but he's alive.

"I told you last night, that bastard Charles has hurt me for the last time. I came for my daughter."

CHAPTER

Forty-eight

THE PARAMEDICS ARRIVE ON THE SCENE, AND ONE OF them, a woman with rosy cheeks and bright blue eyes, comes to me. "Are you all right, ma'am?"

I'm quaking and completely drained but otherwise unharmed. "Please, check out my daughter," I beg her. "She . . . she's the one who needs your help."

Jarrod gently eases Michaela to the ground, and she immediately throws her arms around my legs. I lower my body so our eyes can meet. "It's okay, *chérie*," I soothe her. "The lady won't hurt you. She's like a doctor, and she's here to make sure you're okay. Did . . . did that man hurt you?" The thought of his filthy hands on her makes me want to blow him up all over again.

"He . . . he scared me, Mama."

"Yes, I would have been scared too. But you were a brave girl, and he won't be able to hurt you ever again."

We decide that Michaela should be examined in

the emergency room at the small parish hospital, and I ride with her in the ambulance. If nothing else, she's been traumatized and may need to be treated for shock. Behind us, out the rear window of the emergency vehicle, I see Jarrod's car following closely. I'm grateful for his presence; he's giving me added strength to face this latest, and hopefully last, assault on my world, directly or indirectly, by Charles Colquitt.

Only now, when I believe my daughter is safe and being properly cared for, do I allow my mind to return to the scene of the explosion on the airfield runway. I'm drained of power now, but I recall the tremendous psychic force I delivered to that gun, causing it to explode.

Did I kill that man with my power?

Gustavo Torres didn't die, nor is he likely to. But he'll never threaten anyone with a gun in that hand again. The police believe the weapon accidentally jammed and exploded, and I'm not going to convince them otherwise.

He's in custody in a New Orleans hospital at the moment, and, according to Jarrod, who is keeping up with the case, is singing his heart out, hoping for leniency. Seems Torres has been a very bad man for a very long time. I hope they lock him in jail forever, and I don't consider that a negative thought.

It's been three days since I faced him across the airstrip, and I'm still in a state of shock. Or rather, a state of depletion. At first, I was so weak I could barely walk, although I'm feeling stronger this morning. Michaela and Jarrod have been watching over me like anxious nursemaids. I must have slept for twenty-four hours or longer when we returned to Shadow Haven.

"How about some breakfast in bed?" Jarrod says, peeking into my room and seeing that I'm awake. I smile at him.

"You're a saint. I'd like breakfast, but I'll come to the kitchen. I need to get my bum out of bed." He closes the door behind him, leaving me to reflect on the role he's played in this grisly misadventure.

St. Jarrod.

He's been here for me all along; I was just too fearful and scarred from my life with Charles to allow myself to trust him fully. But he's taken such tender care of Michaela and me since the horrors of the bayou and the airstrip, there's no longer any doubt in my mind. Valerie's still hanging out there as a question mark, but Marie didn't seem to think she's an obstacle to our relationship.

Of course, Marie also thought Gustavo Torres was no longer a threat.

I wonder if Marie knows she blew it on that call.

I shower and dress quickly, feeling refreshed and renewed, and when I reach the door to the kitchen, my heart is filled with pure joy at the sight that meets my eyes. Jarrod, tall and broad-shouldered, his back to me, is engaged with Michaela, standing on a stool next to him, making beignets. He's showing her how to roll out the dough so it'll keep its flaky texture. My eyes well when I see her look up at him with the sunniest smile I've ever seen on her face.

She catches a glimpse of me and hurls herself off the stool, rocketing in my direction. "Mama!" She careens into my arms, making floury handprints on my jeans.

"Hi, baby." I raise her into my arms and kiss her cheeks. She feels so good and warm and real in my arms.

"Mama, Mr. Jarrod's taken real good care of me while you've been sleeping."

I raise my gaze to meet Jarrod's. He's never looked so handsome, even with flour on his face. His grin eats me alive. "I know. He's taken good care of me, too." I smile at him. "Maybe you missed your calling," I tease. "Maybe you should've been a nurse instead of a lawyer. Seems like you have a knack for taking care of others."

The grin fades, and he becomes serious. "I take care of those I love."

The words fall between us, ready to be examined. Neither of us has mentioned the "L" word before now.

I go to him, and I let him encircle my daughter and me in a bear hug. "Thank you, Jarrod," I manage over the tightness in my throat.

"I love you, Gabriella, and I love Michaela. Please . . . let me." He kisses the top of my head.

I raise my face. "I think I can do that now." His next kiss lands on my lips, and Michaela squeals with laughter.

"He's kissing you, Mama."

As if I didn't notice. I draw away and grin at her. "Yes, he's kissing me. You got a problem with that?"

She giggles again. "Can he be your boyfriend now?"

I tilt my head and look up at Jarrod. "If he wants to."

"I want that very much."

"Then, okay. You're my boyfriend now. Officially." Then I frown slightly, remembering his other role. "But does that mean you can't still be my lawyer?"

He releases us, and I put Michaela back on the stool. "I don't think you'll be needing a lawyer," he tells me in an undertone. "We'll talk later."

I'm dying to know what has transpired while I was regaining my strength, but I don't push it. He'll tell me when Michaela is out of earshot. Together, we finish making the beignets, and Jarrod cooks bacon and eggs to go with them.

"You seem pretty handy in a kitchen," I remark, downing my second beignet with hot, dark-roast coffee. I'm eating as if I'm a starving person, and I realize I probably am. I can't recall taking a meal in the last few days.

"Being a bachelor all these years, I've had to learn a few tricks. But bacon and eggs isn't exactly *haute cuisine*." At the moment, nothing could taste better.

The mention of his bachelorhood brings my

thoughts to Valerie. Will he offer an explanation for that enigmatic exchange between Charles and him that night in the bayou? Will he volunteer information on the woman with whom he's apparently spending his every Saturday night?

The day is overcast and cooler than it has been all summer. "The weatherman says there's a tropical depression in the Gulf," Jarrod tells me. "It's going to rain for days. Do we need to do anything to secure Shadow Haven?"

I shake my head. "This old place has weathered lots of storms," I tell him. "It's far enough inland and protected by the trees, so hurricane winds haven't left much of a mark, and it's on high enough ground that it's never flooded, even though the bayou is nearby. But . . . I would like to walk the grounds before the storm hits. Things have been so . . . strange since we got here, I haven't taken much time to enjoy being home."

The three of us leave the dishes on the table and go out into the restless morning air. Low gray clouds scud above us, and wind shimmers through the live oaks, unsettling their burdens of Spanish moss. A thrill runs through me as I inhale deeply of the stormy air.

"I love it when the weather promises a storm," I tell Jarrod. We're walking across the flat land that stretches behind the house to the edge of the bayou. The wind brushes the grass beneath our feet, but the ground is dry, not marshy.

"It's not much fun when a tropical storm hits New Orleans," Jarrod replies grimly. "Everything's a soggy mess, and life pretty well comes to a standstill until the storm passes and the water drains away."

"Maybe that's one reason Angelique moved here," I think out loud. I turn and look back at Shadow Haven. It's stately even in its disrepair, and the rear of the house is as beautiful in design as the front.

"Did I ever tell you the story about your great-great-great-great-great-great-grandmother?" I ask Michaela, knowing that I have not. Charles would have been furious.

She shakes her head. "What's a great-great-great-something?"

Jarrod and I laugh. "That *is* a lot of 'greats,'" he says.

"Yes, but that's what makes Shadow Haven so special," I reply in almost a whisper. "Angelique's magic."

"Magic?" Michaela's eyes widen.

I grin down at her. "I told you that first day we came here that Shadow Haven was a magical place. That's because the woman for whom it was built had magic in her soul."

"Who was she?" Jarrod asks. We begin to stroll again, turning west along the edge of the marshes. As we walk, I relate the legend that's been handed down in my family for many generations.

"The story goes that my great-great-many-great-grandfather, Pierre Fontaine, a very wealthy, and very old, French businessman, went to Martinique to arrange for exotic spices to be shipped to New Orleans."

"Where's Martinique?" Michaela wants to know. I explain that it's an island in a beautiful blue ocean far, far away to the south. "I think I know it," she says matter-of-factly, and I don't question her. She is a Deveaux, after all, and who's to say she hasn't had dreams about the homeland of her ancestors?

I continue my story. "While Pierre was in Martinique, he met a young and beautiful Creole, Angelique Deveaux. After a whirlwind courtship, Pierre returned to New Orleans with his spices, and an exotic young bride as well."

Jarrod laughs. "I bet that set the tongues wagging in New Orleans."

"Oh, yes. The city's *société* was scandalized. The women accused Angelique of marrying Pierre for his money while the men, on the other hand, congratulated Pierre for making such a conquest. The story goes that Pierre built Shadow Haven for Angelique so they could escape the New Orleans gossips and live on the bayou in peace. That's why she called it a 'haven.'"

"What happened to them?" Jarrod asks.

"Apparently, in spite of all the speculation about their relationship, Angelique and Pierre were deeply in love regardless of their age difference, and when Pierre died, Angelique was heartbroken. She didn't live long after his death."

"That's sad. I take it they had children."

"They had one daughter who inherited the land, and after Pierre's death, Angelique mandated that Shadow Haven be passed down to the women of the family. She also bid her female descendants not to take the husband's names when they married, an ongoing tradition followed to this day."

"So that's why you're listed as Gabriella Deveaux on the tax papers, and even in Charles's will. You never were Gabriella Colquitt."

"Never. It's one of the few things I ever did to stand up to Charles. But Michaela carries the Colquitt name."

"My name is Michaela Deveaux now," she informs us. "I'm one of the Deveaux women, aren't I, Mama?"

I pick her up and give her a big hug. "That you are, *chérie*."

From somewhere inside my head, I hear a gravelly laugh.

CHAPTER
Forty-nine

THE FIRST RAINDROPS BEGIN TO FALL AS SOON AS WE reach the house. Jarrod picks up his briefcase and looks at his watch. "I'm sorry," he says, "but I have to go back to New Orleans. I hope I can make it before the brunt of the storm hits."

"You're going?" I'm devastated. "But . . . I thought . . ." I can't bring myself to say what I was thinking. I thought he was going to stay here and take care of us.

He comes to me and bends to kiss me. "I'd planned to stay longer, but I hadn't counted on a tropical storm coming in. Gabriella," he says, and I read an inexplicable agony in his face, "I have to go. It's . . . about Valerie."

I pull away from him and look him in the eye. "Who is Valerie, Jarrod?" I demand. Might as well face it and get it over with. If I'm to give my heart to this man, which obviously Michaela has already done, I have to know about the other woman.

I'm not expecting the answer he gives me.

"Valerie's . . . my sister, and she gets very upset during stormy weather."

It takes a moment for me to process what he's told me. I'm relieved that she's not his wife or lover. But it seems odd that Jarrod would rush off to console an adult sister when a storm is coming. "How old is Valerie?"

"She's twenty-eight."

"Isn't she old enough to deal with storms?" I hope I don't sound bitchy, but I really don't want Jarrod taking off with the heavy rain approaching.

"She could, if she were . . . like the rest of us." The sadness in his eyes tears at my heart.

"What . . . what's wrong with her?" I have a chilling moment when I recall what Charles said to Jarrod that night.

It was an accident, and we both know it. . . .

And I remember Jarrod's response. . . .

You destroyed her by leaving her when she needed you most, you bastard. . . .

Jarrod looks at the drops beating on the windowpanes. "It's a long story, and I need to get on the road." He looks back at me and then at Michaela. "Why don't you two come to New Orleans with me, and I'll tell you the whole thing on the way? Besides, I think it's time that you met Valerie."

We take my car, since Jarrod's is too small for the three of us. Before we leave, I hurriedly pack a small overnight bag for Michaela and me in case we get stranded in high water in New Orleans. Jarrod has said we can stay with him in that event.

I didn't argue. I'd do just about anything right now except let him out of his promised explanations. Charles. Valerie. Jarrod. Elizabeth and Rupert Colquitt. So many long-ago secrets.

Rain pelts savagely on the windshield as Jarrod steers the car carefully down the lane and onto the road to Tibonne. In the backseat, Michaela is quiet, but I notice she's clinging hard to the stuffed alligator Jarrod gave her. I have misgivings when I realize the ferocity of the storm. "Are you sure we should be doing this?" The rain is coming down in sheets, so heavy it's hard to see.

"I have to, Gabriella. I should have left sooner. If you want to change your mind . . ."

"No."

Jarrod proves to be an excellent driver in spite of the wind and rain. Still, my knuckles are clenched around the armrests and my shoulders are tense by the time we reach the outskirts of New Orleans. The noise from the rain and the road, along with Jarrod's need for intense concentration, have precluded the kind of conversation I'd hoped for.

The streets of New Orleans are running with water. Soon it will fill up the low-lying drainage areas and begin to back up, turning streets into rivers and yards into lakes. We splash through town, arriving at last in front of an elegant old Victorian house in a gentrified neighborhood. Jarrod pulls into the driveway and switches off the engine. I note several other cars parked toward the back of the house.

"Is this your house, Mr. Jarrod?" Michaela asks.

"No, sweetie, this is where Valerie lives."

He turns to me. "It's a group home," he tells me, "for victims of head injuries. The residents have all suffered blows to the head that have rendered them unable to function in the outside world."

I feel my face turn pale. "What happened to your sister, Jarrod? How was Charles involved?"

He clears his throat. "Charles was engaged to Valerie once. I made the mistake of introducing them. I was his tutor when he went to Tulane. He couldn't get into Harvard Law, but somehow made it into a good law school nonetheless. I imagine Colquitt money had some influence in the process. But he screwed around his first year and nearly flunked out. One of my professors recommended me to the Colquitts as a tutor, and they hired me to save his butt."

Good grief. Jarrod does have a long history with the Colquitt family.

"Charles never told me he was engaged to anyone before me," I remark.

"After the accident, Charles didn't want anything to do with Valerie. It was as if she'd never been a part of his life." His voice is edgy and bitter now.

"What accident? What happened, Jarrod?"

Jarrod adjusts his large frame in the car's small driver's seat. "Charles loved toys," he says. "His weekly allowance was more than I could earn in a year in my job as a teaching assistant. One day he brought home a shiny new motorcycle."

I can imagine what's coming, and an involuntary shiver crawls up my spine.

"Valerie and I still lived on the old home place, a small horse ranch north of here. Charles drove the motorcycle out to show us his latest plaything. I should have known something wasn't right the minute he got there. He was too excited, too animated. But he was often excited and animated, so I didn't think much about it. Valerie thought he was the most charming guy she'd ever met, and she was in love with him, so for her sake, I forgave Charles a lot of things."

He pauses as if gathering his emotions. "He took her for a ride, and . . . the bike swerved off the road and hit a tree. The police estimated he was doing over a hundred. Charles and Valerie were both thrown from the motorcycle before it hit the tree, or they'd both have been killed. Charles struck a fence that tore his leg open before he landed in a cotton field on the other side. Valerie wasn't so lucky. She landed on the pavement, headfirst. She was in a coma for months. . . ."

Tears are running down Jarrod's cheeks, and he doesn't try to stop them. I suspect he's been crying for Valerie a long time. I touch his arm and speak the only words I can find. "I'm so sorry."

Rain batters the car's roof above us. The three of us

sit quietly for a long time, then Jarrod says, "I'd better go in. Valerie freaks in storms."

"Can we all go?" I ask. "Unless it wouldn't be good for Valerie."

"It'd be okay for Valerie, but seeing the residents might upset Michaela. Some of them are in pretty bad shape."

"I want to go, Mr. Jarrod. I want to go meet your sister. Please?"

He looks at me. "What do you think?"

"I think Michaela has strengths that we underestimate," I say tentatively. "If what you told me earlier is true, about loving both of us, then let us love you as well."

The dwelling that Valerie and others like her call home is beautifully decorated and cheerful. As we step in out of the rain, we're greeted by a woman in a trim pants suit with a name badge on the jacket pocket: Gwendolyn Smith.

"Hi, Gwen," Jarrod greets her with a hug. "How's Valerie holding up in this storm?"

"Not too good. I'm glad you've come."

Jarrod introduces Michaela and me. "Gwen's one of the staff of caregivers here that makes this place so special," he tells us. "Valerie has lived here for many years, and Gwen's been taking care of her just about as long, haven't you?"

"Going on ten years," she says. "Valerie's one of my favorites."

"Where is she?" Michaela asks. "I want to meet her."

I see Gwen catch Jarrod's eye. She raises her brow.

"Let me go in and see how she's doing first," he says to Michaela. "Storms frighten her, and she sometimes gets real upset."

"Okay," Michaela says, "but I'm going to wait right here with my 'gator so I'll be ready when she is."

CHAPTER
Fifty

MICHAELA AND I SETTLE ONTO A COMFORTABLE SOFA in the large living area. I'm deeply troubled by what Jarrod told me about Valerie's accident. I have more questions now than ever before.

There are others in the room with us, but they seem to take no notice of us. One man, who is well-dressed and who looks as normal as anybody on the street, sits in a rocking chair and moves it steadily back and forth without breaking the rapid rhythm. His eyes are closed. I wonder if his spirit is still in his body, and if I could reach it with my gift, but I decide not to intrude on his private world.

Another has more obvious difficulties. He's in a wheel chair near a table, watching the Weather Channel on TV. Without meaning to, I tune in briefly to his state of mind and find nothing. Apparently, he's just attracted to the bright colors on the screen. I sense he was once a brilliant man, and a deep sadness wells within me.

"Mama, can I talk to him?" Michaela asks, nodding toward the man in the rocking chair.

"I . . . I don't know if you should bother him, *chérie*. He looks like he's asleep."

"Oh, he's not asleep. He's been thinking to me."

Michaela continues to surprise me with the strength of her powers at such a young age. "Like my grandnana was thinking to you that day in the enchanted garden?"

"Uh-huh. Only he's not a spirit. He's still alive."

Alive, and trapped incommunicado in that shell of a body, I think sadly. But Michaela doesn't seem sad about his condition. Without waiting for further permission, she goes to the man and puts her hand on his arm. She doesn't say anything out loud, and he doesn't stop rocking, but there is unspoken communication between them. Occasionally he nods his head.

Jarrod returns from Valerie's room in about thirty minutes. "She's in pretty bad shape," he tells me, his expression grim. "She's been crying. I got her to calm down, but her face is all red and puffy. Do you think we ought to let Michaela see her like this? I mean, we could wait—"

I shake my head. "Look," I say, and nod to where Michaela is "talking" to the man in the rocker. "She's not afraid of him just because he's different."

I don't know what state Valerie is in, but I have a feeling that Michaela will warm to her as she has to this injury victim.

"Okay," Jarrod says with resignation. "We'll give it a try."

Jarrod enters Valerie's room first. "There're some people here to see you, Valerie. Would you like to say hello?"

There is a muffled reply that I can't understand, but which sounds distinctly like Valerie doesn't want company. I expect Jarrod to turn us back, but Michaela pushes past him before we can stop her.

We watch as she approaches a thin figure huddled against the head of her bed, covers pulled up to her chin. Valerie's auburn hair is cut short in an attractive style, and her face, like Jarrod's, is beautiful. Only the lost look in her eyes betrays her injury.

"Valerie, I'm here," Michaela announces. "I'm going to take you home with me, and we'll be together for always."

She proclaims this as if she and Valerie have had some long-standing agreement for this arrangement. I don't know whether to smile or cry.

Jarrod goes to Valerie's bedside and kneels beside Michaela. "That's very sweet of you to ask Valerie to come home with you, Michaela, but, you see, she's been hurt, and she needs the people here to care for her."

Michaela's lip juts out. "I can take care of her. Why can't she come and live with us? Shadow Haven's really big."

This is a little more than I bargained for when I agreed to meet Valerie. Before I can decide how to react to Michaela's unexpected but passionate invitation, Valerie stirs.

"Come here," she says and pats the covers beside her, indicating for Michaela to climb onto the bed. Her words are heavy and slurred but intelligible. Michaela doesn't wait for permission, but scrambles to sit next to Valerie.

I exchange glances with Jarrod. Obviously, he doesn't know what to think about this either. I take his hand, and we watch Valerie and Michaela. I know, or can guess, what is going on. Jarrod, I'm certain, is clueless that Michaela is in Valerie's head, chatting away.

"She says she wants to go home with me," Michaela declares in a few moments. "She says she won't be afraid of the rain if she can be with me at Shadow Haven."

Valerie jerks her head up and looks at Jarrod. "Home. I want to go home." I could be mistaken, but it seems as if I see hope brighten her lackluster eyes.

Jarrod's face is growing red, and I can tell we've made a colossal mistake in allowing Michaela to come in here. "You are home," Jarrod tells his sister. "This is your home, Valerie. It's safe, and there are people here who can take care of you."

"Not home," she struggles to speak. "Too much rain here."

"She means it's lonely for her here," Michaela interprets. "She cries a lot. That's the rain she's talking about."

Jarrod frowns and tilts his head slightly. "Is that true, Valerie? Are you lonely here?"

Valerie's eyes fill with tears, and she nods.

"See?" Michaela pipes up. "She shouldn't be lonely. Not when she could have a family."

Michaela's imagination is spinning way too fast. "I think we'd better go, Michaela," I say in a low voice. "We're causing trouble." I can imagine Jarrod has done all he could to see that his sister has received the best care possible, and he doesn't need my six-year-old waltzing in and stirring things up.

"But Mama, how can you leave her here all by herself?" Michaela pleads. "It's raining outside, and Valerie's afraid of the storms."

Oh, dear God in heaven, what am I going to do with this child? She means so well. She is acting with a loving heart. And yet, she's about to cause a crisis that could be harmful to Valerie, and possibly to Jarrod as well. I haven't heard the full story of what happened the day of the accident, but I did hear a hint of guilt when Jarrod said, "I should have known. . . ." Does Jarrod think it's his fault that Valerie is here now?

"Take me home, Jerry," Valerie pleads. "I want to go home."

Jarrod covers his face with his hand and rubs at his temples. I can feel my heart beating heavily. Both Valerie and Michaela are looking at him hopefully.

"All right," he says after a while. "I'll arrange it with Gwen for you to come with us tonight. But tomorrow, or as soon as the storm's over, you'll have to come back to your home."

Jarrod lives in a two-story redbrick town house in a lushly landscaped neighborhood near the heart of New Orleans. The detached garage is at the back of the property, reached by a long, narrow brick driveway, but Jarrod stops when we get to the back door. "Wait here," he shouts, opening the door to the din of the pouring rain.

He shuts the car door, opens the back door to his house and dashes inside. Moments later he returns with an umbrella, and one by one, he helps each of us inside. He brings Valerie in last, carrying her gently in his arms. She and Michaela have been sitting in the backseat, their hands clasped tightly together. Whatever's going on, there's definitely already a bond linking those two.

Jarrod's home is distinctly masculine, decorated professionally and yet furnished comfortably. He carries Valerie into the living room and settles her on the couch. Michaela scoots up right next to her, and Jarrod covers them both with a velour throw. "Okay now, Valerie?"

The young woman gives him a radiant smile. "Home now."

Jarrod turns on the television to the Discovery Channel, and both Michaela and Valerie turn their attention to the program. Jarrod takes my hand and leads me toward the kitchen at the back of the town house. "I'm going to put the car away," he says, and is out the door before I can offer to do the soggy chore.

I take the opportunity to check out the refrigerator, expecting to find it bachelor bare, but I'm surprised to see it's fairly well-stocked. There's orange juice, milk, bread, butter, a number of jams and jellies, some apples, carrots, tomatoes, and a head of lettuce. The freezer yields some packages of hamburger meat, a couple of steaks, and a pork tenderloin.

I guess I was right. Jarrod must be handy in the kitchen. At least we won't go hungry or have to go out again in this storm. I hear him stomp his feet as he comes in the door. I take out the hamburger meat, anticipating creating something for a late lunch. It's been a while since the beignets.

"Gabriella?" he calls.

"In the kitchen."

He's dripping wet when he pads sock-footed into the room. "Hand me a towel, will you? Second drawer." He points to one of the cabinets.

When he's dry, relatively speaking, he turns to me. "I don't know what to say about Valerie's behavior," he says apologetically. "She's never been like this before. I'm worried about her."

I go to him and put my arms around his waist. "Michaela was out of line, and I didn't know how to stop her."

Jarrod is quiet, and we stand close together, holding each other, listening to the storm rage outside. "What if she really is lonely, Gabriella?"

CHAPTER

Fifty-one

"I CAN'T BEAR IT IF THAT'S TRUE," HE WHISPERS INTO my hair. "She's never said anything like that before."

"You know, just because she has difficulty expressing herself doesn't mean she doesn't have emotions. She seems fairly self-sufficient. Has she had a lot of therapy?"

"You can't imagine. It started when she finally came out of the coma. She emerged fairly coherent and seemingly not as injured as we'd thought. So the doctor got her into therapy right away. She had amnesia as far as the accident was concerned. Couldn't remember a thing about what happened, although she knew me, and she knew our parents. Then one day, she remembered Charles."

My chest tightens, but I remain silent. Jarrod seems ready to talk about that past he's kept to himself for so long.

"She asked, 'Where's Charles?' It would have made us all cheer that her memory was returning, except Charles was nowhere to be found. When his leg had sufficiently healed that he could travel, he returned to Boston. He never saw or spoke to Valerie after that."

"His toy was broken," I murmur, knowing I speak the truth. It was Charles's style to throw away what no longer served him.

"I guess that was it. After Valerie remembered Charles, she waited and waited for him to come to her, but finally she gave up. It was the worst turn she'd taken in her recovery. In fact, she almost went comatose again. I think she'd lost the will to live. I swear, Gabriella, if I'd been anywhere near him, I'd probably have killed him."

"I know how you must have felt."

"He didn't want to have anything to do with Valerie, but I wasn't going to let him off the hook for what had happened. See, I'd figured out what was wrong with him that day, but it was too late. They'd already taken off when I realized he was high on something. I went after them in my car, but I didn't know where to look for them." He grows silent, then says, "Gabriella, I know this is going to sound crazy, but I knew when they crashed. I felt it. I heard her scream, and I knew she was hurt."

So Jarrod is psychically sensitive, at least to a degree. "It doesn't sound crazy at all. There are lots of stories about people feeling the pain of others, or knowing when a loved one has died. It must have been horrible for you."

"It was, and is. Every time I look at her, I think, if

only I'd prevented her from getting on that bike." Jarrod is crying again now, a gentle giant in my arms.

"It's not your fault." I try to soothe him. "It was her decision to go with Charles."

"She never saw his faults. She had no idea he was stoned. When the police came to the house to report the accident, I told them to check Charles for drugs, and sure enough, he was loaded with amphetamines."

Although I'd never known Charles to take drugs, it wasn't beyond the realm of possibilities, especially when he was younger. As much as I wanted to know all this, the truth is a heavy load. No wonder Jarrod had been reluctant to share the story.

I draw away from him slightly. "I know it's early, but it's already been a long day. Do you have any wine in the house? I think I could use a drink."

"I'm sorry, Gabriella. I'm not a very good host." He goes to a small refrigerator that proves to be a wine cooler. "Red or white?"

"Red on a rainy day."

He takes out a bottle, examines the label, and retrieves a corkscrew from a nearby drawer. "I didn't mean to blubber on about this. It happened more than ten years ago. But I can't stand the thought that Valerie is unhappy in any way. I've fought hard to provide her with the finest care money can buy." He pours the wine into two glasses and hands me one.

"This is where the Colquitts come in, isn't it?" I'm beginning to see the picture. "Did you sue Charles?"

"I wanted to. I wanted to hang his sorry ass from the courthouse steeple. But I had to be practical. Valerie's medical bills were astronomical, and neither my parents nor I were wealthy. In fact, they sold their farm to try to pay the bills, and I think it finally broke their spirit. My dad died first, and Mom followed in just a few months. Thank God that Valerie never seemed aware that they were no longer around."

"Oh, Jarrod. I'm so sorry."

"Yeah, me too." His words are bitter and filled with anguish. "One day, not long after Mom passed away, I made a discreet phone call to Elizabeth Colquitt. I'd met her during one of their brief visits to Tulane. I never liked her, and often I looked the other way when Charles pulled his shenanigans, because I knew the pressure he was under from those people. But that day, Elizabeth and I had a quiet little talk. I told her that if she and Rupert didn't offer to help Valerie financially, I would go to the press with the police reports they'd somehow managed to suppress, the ones that revealed that Charles had been under the influence of drugs."

Somehow, what he's telling me doesn't surprise me, although it's a bit underhanded. He, in essence, blackmailed the Colquitts. As he was threatening to do again, to save Michaela.

I've played hardball with the Colquitts before. . . .
It's the kind of thing that might stop them. . . .

"So, did they? Help Valerie, I mean?"

"It took some doing, but with a little finesse and a

lot of nerve, I got what I wanted. I had them set up a trust fund for her so that she'd never want for anything in her life. How do you think we afford that group home? It's not your typical long-term care place. People like Gwen Smith don't come cheap. But I've always thought it was worth it, all the legal battles and threats and nasty underhanded dealings they indulged in, because I believed that in the long run, their money could make Valerie as comfortable and happy as her condition allowed. She deserved that, and Charles should pay. Since he copped out, I went to the source of the devils that drove him, his parents."

"I guess that's why they called you to help them take Michaela from me. They figured you owed them."

"That's exactly what they thought. And when I didn't do their bidding, they threatened to close the trust. It wasn't an irrevocable trust, my mistake, but it was the only way they'd even talk about a trust for Valerie.

"At any rate, that's why I was searching so frantically for some dirt on Charles. It worked before, and I had every reason to believe it'd work again. Blackmail is a nasty business, but exposure of the dirty deeds of her only son was the one thing Elizabeth Colquitt couldn't bear. It's ironic that Charles himself showed up to provide exactly what we needed."

I'm still shaken by Charles's reappearance, and I don't particularly want to talk about him, so I shift the subject. "Want me to make some lunch?" I ask, holding up the frozen hamburger meat.

"That would be great."

"Hamburgers or spaghetti?"

We decide on spaghetti, as there are no buns for burgers, and I slip the meat into the microwave to thaw. Jarrod checks on the girls and reports that Michaela is sound asleep in Valerie's arms. Valerie is watching TV.

"Guess there's no hurry on lunch, unless you're hungry," Jarrod says. "Why don't we go sit in the den and finish our wine first?"

The den is cozy, and Jarrod lights the gas logs in the fireplace, dispelling some of the gloom. He settles next to me on a love seat and puts his arms around me. While bustling in the kitchen with lunch preparations, I had an idea, and it's been buzzing around in my head. I'm not sure it's a good idea, but then again, it might be brilliant.

"Jarrod, I've been thinking about what Michaela said, about Shadow Haven being a big place, and about Valerie being with family."

I feel him stiffen slightly, and I hesitate. But I feel a nudge, a familiar jab, and I know I can't stop now. Grandnana's with me on this one.

"Why not let Valerie come and live with us there? I could have Willie hurry up and make the second floor livable for Michaela and me. I'll give her my room on the first floor, where it will be easier for her to get around."

He is silent for so long, I think I've made a terrible mistake in offering this, although it feels really right in my heart.

"That's noble, Gabriella. But Valerie needs full-time supervision."

"So, take the money you're spending now for the group home and hire a professional live-in nurse. She can have the room Michaela's using now. And I'm not being noble. Michaela's right about this. Valerie should never have to feel lonely or alone. Not when there're people who love her."

He studies me for a long moment. "Do you love Valerie? You just met her."

I don't even have to think about that. "I do love her, Jarrod. And obviously so does Michaela. Love's funny that way. You don't have to know somebody a long time to love them."

"I know," he says. "Technically, I've known you for eight years, but I've really only gotten to know you these last few weeks. But . . . I love you, Gabriella."

My throat tightens. "I love you, too, Jarrod."

He kisses me, and his lips are warm and tender. Those sensual sensations that have visited me from time to time, ever since I saw Jarrod the night of my ritual in the enchanted garden, ripple through me again.

"I have another idea," I murmur, feeling bold and willing to take a risk. "Why don't we become a family? A real family for Michaela and Valerie?"

"Is that a proposal?" he asks, moving his head away

only far enough to look into my eyes. I see a twinkle there, and a grin on his handsome mouth.

"Uh-huh," I whisper, drawing his lips to mine again.

"I thought the guy got to do the asking." This between kisses.

"Not necessarily," I grin. "Not if the girl is a Deveaux."

Six months later

SHADOW HAVEN HAS NOT BEEN JUST RENOVATED, IT'S been reinvented. Yes, there are new walls and windows and floors, plumbing and lighting and furnishings, all that—but the important change is that laughter and life have replaced the desolate silence that greeted me the day I returned.

Valerie is never lonesome now, and she's no longer afraid of the rain. Michaela loves hanging out with her, and we managed to convince Gwen Smith to move to Shadow Haven as a private duty nurse. It turns out Gwen was lonely too, unmarried, no children, growing old taking care of others she could love and who would love her. She's part of our family now.

Jarrod and I were married shortly after the police DNA tests proved without a doubt that the man who died on Marie's island was Charles Colquitt. Only then was I sure I was free at last.

Jarrod has moved his office from New Orleans to one of the bedrooms on the upper floor at Shadow Haven and does most of his business by phone and fax, although he has to make frequent trips into the city. I've learned that what Ira Peabody said about him, that he was a "do-gooder," is true.

Jarrod specializes in representing underdogs, victims of neglect and abuse, or manipulation by those stronger than they. He's not an ambulance chaser, but he deplores accidents that are due to gross negligence or caused by the misuse of drugs or alcohol, as was the case with Valerie's accident. I've also learned that he takes all cases *pro bono*, without pay, until there is a settlement. They say he's worked miracles, using negotiation rather than the courtroom to arrive at agreements that are fair to both parties.

His most recent miracle came in a plain white envelope delivered to me at Shadow Haven by none other than Ira Peabody himself. It seems that the Colquitts have some semblance of conscience after all. When they learned all that Charles had done, they found it in their heart to write a letter of apology—well, almost. The letter read:

Dear Mr. Peabody,

Please inform Gabriella Deveaux that we have no intention of pursuing custody of our grand-daughter. Recent events have opened our eyes to certain circumstances of which we were unaware, and we believe that our son, Charles, was in error in including that codicil in his will.

Also, please let Ms. Deveaux know that there
will be no challenge to her guardianship of
Michaela, and that she will retain full rights
over her daughter's inheritance until such time
as the child attains the age of twenty-one.

Sincerely,
Rupert Colquitt

The "certain circumstances" he referred to included not only Charles's faking his death, but also the discovery that their son had been a criminal most of his life. It began with petty theft: shoplifting as a young teen. They knew about this, of course, but had used their influence to cover up Charles's activities and keep him out of juvenile courts.

They didn't know, however, that Charles had sold drugs in college, which brought him into contact with a drug ring in New Orleans. It was then he first met Gustavo Torres, who has, by the way, recovered and is locked away in a maximum security prison. He told the authorities many things, but apparently the powers that be thought him still dangerous enough to serve a lengthy sentence.

The most shocking of the revelations made by Torres had to do with Shadow Haven. He swears that it was Charles who let the drug ring use my ancestral home as a staging area for their drug shipments. When Conrad Armand had his stroke, Charles found it a ripe opportunity to ingratiate himself with Torres's mob-linked boss. They used the small airstrip to bring in the drugs from South America. They were stored for a time at Shadow Haven, until Gustavo Torres could move them through the bayou to a remote landing, where the mules from New Orleans finished the distribution.

No wonder Torres didn't die in the swamp. He knew it like the back of his hand.

And Marie Françoise knew that all along. She attended our small wedding, which was held in the enchanted garden, and before the ceremony, she came to me with an explanation of why she failed to warn me that Torres was still alive. But she offered no apology.

She claimed she'd been told by the spirits that she was to allow Torres to escape, and not to warn me, because I needed that final challenge to fully empower me once and for all. I'm not sure I totally believe her. I don't like to think the spirits are that hard-nosed. But it did work. I've never questioned my powers since, and never will again. I just hope I never have to summon that much juice again, nor face such unutterable evil.

I have learned more than I ever wished to know about Charles's clandestine activities, and I can clearly see that I wasn't the only one he was able to manipulate. He was apparently a master at camouflage, truly the quintessential *loup-garou*. He lived a double life. A wealthy, successful businessman, and a gutter-level criminal. There's just one question remaining in the minds of all who knew him, and I suppose it will never be answered.

Why?

I'm in my studio this afternoon, drawn here inexplicably by a feeling that I must work on a certain stone that I bought months ago when I thought carving a memorial for Charles might help Michaela. I have since recommenced my work, taking only a few clients, but enough to restore my confidence in my gift. I still haven't had the courage to tell Jarrod about the Deveaux powers, although Michaela has inadvertently dropped enough hints about her own gifts, he must have some suspicions. He's never disdained or made fun of her, though, and he's never come to me asking if Michaela's crazy.

The stone in front of me is white marble, veined with dark green and black streaks, and it calls to me like a siren. I take a stance in front of it, tools in hand, and open myself to its summons. I close my eyes, and a misty fog fills my mind, swirling like Spanish moss in a storm. I see no image, but I hear a voice, faint but clear, calling my name.

I'm overcome with sadness, an ache for the pitiful being who is calling me. The spirit remains amorphous, hovering just beyond my recognition, but I receive its message, its directive for the stone, just as clearly as I once received Grandnana's instructions for her angel.

Hours pass as I work in a semi-trance, opening the

marble, drawing from it the impression that is being related to me in an unspoken communication. When at last I near the conclusion of the first phase of the sculpting, the spirit abruptly and ever so briefly shows itself. It's Charles, with a look so sad I can almost forgive him his monstrous deceit. His message is luminous; I see it more than hear it.

"Thank you for setting me free."

Suddenly, I come fully awake, jarred roughly back into the physical world by some force that wants me to have nothing to do with Charles, even in spirit. I gaze at the stone to see what has come from it, and I weep with pity for the spirit of Charles Colquitt. He's had me carve a pair of hands opening to release an ascending dove.

Without needing any explanation, I know what it represents, and why Charles did what he did in life. Even why he faked his death and tried to start over with a new identity in the Caymans.

He wanted to be free of the Colquitt heritage. Where my own legacy was one of love and acceptance, his was a loveless pursuit of money and power. He'd always been controlled by his parents, and his criminal career had been his way of fighting back. It doesn't make it right, but I can understand it now. I may never fully forgive him, especially for endangering the life of our daughter, but I can at last put closure on our disastrous relationship.

"Good-bye, Charles," I whisper, then turn and leave the room.

* * *

The moon is full and glimmers through the trees on a cold December night. Bundled in sweaters and windbreakers, Jarrod and I go out for a breath of fresh air after dinner. From outside, I can see lights on the huge Christmas tree sparkling in the main parlor, where Gwen plays checkers with Michaela while Valerie looks on.

I think back to last Christmas, a miserable event, when Charles gave me the torc. I could never have dreamed that it was cursed, or where its evil would lead me. Even after its cleansing I wanted no part of it. I've given it to a museum.

I tuck my hand into Jarrod's. "Let's go to the enchanted garden."

Grandnana's spirit is alive and well, as far as spirits go, in the cemetery, and I feel her the strongest when I stand beneath the angel's wings. Tonight is Christmas Eve, and I want her to know I'm thinking about her, even though with Jarrod here I won't be able to go into the full mental state where we're able to converse across the veil.

When we go through the iron gate, Jarrod looks up at the angel. "Can I ask you something, Gabriella?"

I grow uneasy. "Sure. What?"

"Have you ever gotten the feeling that Shadow Haven is haunted?"

Uh-oh. "What makes you ask that?"

He scratches his head. "Well, this is going to sound kind of crazy, but from time to time, I think I see a figure, or the shadow of a figure, floating through the house. I think it's a woman, and I get the idea that she's wearing some kind of outlandish purple dress."

"Would it bother you if the place was haunted?"

He laughs nervously. "Well, no, as long as she's a benevolent ghost. I've . . . just never thought I'd believe in ghosts. But I swear I've seen this one."

I recall the Outcome card that turned up in Nicola's reading. "The Fool." The one who takes a risk because he trusts all will be well. It's time for me to play this last card in my reading. I draw in a deep breath and step off the cliff into the abyss.

"Shadow Haven is definitely haunted. The spirit you've seen is my grandnana," I tell him. "I can't see her, but Michaela can. I talk to her, though. It's . . . a gift possessed by all the Deveaux women, the ability to commune with the dead. We're not witches, we just have strong psychic powers. You asked me once if there was any one incident that convinced Charles I was mad. I didn't exactly answer you truthfully, and I may regret telling you this now. But the Deveaux power is my truth, and my legacy, and I'll never deny it to anyone again. I told Charles about my gift because it's how I know what to carve for my clients. I speak to their dead loved ones to learn the essence of their being. But when I told Charles, he came unglued on the spot, called me a crazy bitch, and slapped me across the face. Although our marriage had been unhappy for a long time, this was the beginning of the end for us."

I look up at Jarrod. "Do you think I'm crazy?"

He looks a little dazed, but then he begins to smile. "I'm the one who's seen your grandmother's spirit. Who am I to say what's crazy?"

He takes me in his arms and kisses me thoroughly. From somewhere not too far away, I hear the sound of laughter. Deep-throated, gravelly laughter. Jarrod raises his his head, listening.

"Do you hear that?"

I look up at the angel, and laughter bubbles up in me as well. "Merry Christmas, Grandnana."

Passionate about reading?
Don't miss any of these unforgettable
romances from Pocket Books.

RUN NO MORE
Catherine Mulvany
How do you outrun your past
when your future's just as deadly?

ALWAYS
Jude Deveraux
An evil from the past…A hope from the future…
A love that will last forver.

OUT OF THE STORM
JoAnn Ross
There is no shelter from the storms of passion.

OPEN SEASON
Linda Howard
She's hunting for a mate—
but now someone is hunting her.

CROWN JEWEL
Fern Michaels
A true, passionate love is the greatest treasure of all.

NO WAY OUT
Andrea Kane
When a woman's deepest fears and strongest desires
clash, a child's life hangs in the balance.

Wherever books are sold.

LOVE IS IN THE AIR WITH THESE UNFORGETTABLE ROMANCES FROM POCKET BOOKS

ROXANNE ST. CLAIRE — FRENCH TWIST

In the land of romance, love is everywhere…but so is danger.

DORIEN KELLY — HOT NIGHTS IN BALLYMUIR

A passionate Irishman might be the answer to an American woman's dreams.

LORRAINE HEATH — SMOOTH TALKIN' STRANGER

Was it one night of uncontrollable chemistry or the beginnings of the love of a lifetime?

JANET CHAPMAN — THE SEDUCTIVE IMPOSTOR

He makes her want to risk everything—but can she trust him?

CAROL GRACE — AN ACCIDENTAL GREEK WEDDING

Sparks are flying—only it's not between the bride and groom!

JULIE KENNER — THE SPY WHO LOVES ME

He's Double-Oh-No. But she's about to change that…

SUSAN SIZEMORE — I THIRST FOR YOU

A beautiful mortal becomes embraced by darkness and passion when a vampire desires her for all time.

POCKET BOOKS
A Division of Simon & Schuster
A VIACOM COMPANY

POCKET STAR BOOKS
A Division of Simon & Schuster
A VIACOM COMPANY

www.simonsayslove.com • Wherever books are sold.

10413